VIKING
Published by the Penguin Group
Penguin Group (USA) Inc., 345 Hudson Street, New York, New York 10014, U.S.A.
Penguin Group (Canada), 90 Eglinton Avenue East, Suite 700,
Toronto, Ontario, Canada M4P 2Y3 (a division of Pearson Penguin Canada Inc.)
Penguin Books Ltd, 80 Strand, London WC2R 0RL, England
Penguin Ireland, 25 St Stephen's Green, Dublin 2, Ireland (a division of Penguin Books Ltd)
Penguin Group (Australia), 250 Camberwell Road, Camberwell, Victoria 3124, Australia
(a division of Pearson Australia Group Pty Ltd)
Penguin Books India Pvt Ltd, 11 Community Centre, Panchsheel Park,
New Delhi–110 017, India
Penguin Group (NZ), 67 Apollo Drive, Rosedale, Auckland 0632, New Zealand
(a division of Pearson New Zealand Ltd.)
Penguin Books (South Africa) (Pty) Ltd, 24 Sturdee Avenue, Rosebank,
Johannesburg 2196, South Africa

Penguin Books Ltd, Registered Offices: 80 Strand, London WC2R 0RL, England

First published in the United States of America by Viking,
an imprint of Penguin Group (USA) Inc., 2013

10 9 8 7 6 5 4 3 2 1

LIBRARY OF CONGRESS CATALOGING-IN-PUBLICATION DATA
Pierson, D. C.
Crap kingdom / by DC Pierson.
p. cm.
Summary: Tenth-grader Tom Parking's dream of being swept away to a fantasy land where he
becomes a hero nearly comes true when he finds himself the Chosen One of a nameless world,
the most annoying, least "cool" place in the universe.
ISBN 978-0-670-01432-3 (hardcover)
[1. Fantasy. 2. Heroes—Fiction.] I. Title.
PZ7.P6162Cr 2013
[Fic]—dc23
2012015578

Printed in the USA
Set in Golden Cockerel ITC Std   Book design by Jim Hoover

Crap Kingdom

DC PIERSON

VIKING

An Imprint of Penguin Group (USA) Inc.

To Matthew.
You know the rooms I was thinking about.

"Who can ever know what will be discovered? Eddie Carbone had never expected to have a destiny."

—Arthur Miller, *A View from the Bridge*

part one

1

THE PROBLEM WAS, his life wasn't bad enough.

Tom liked books and movies where a seemingly un-special kid was having the absolute worst night of his or her life, a life that was already terrible overall, and some-one appeared and whisked that kid away to a world where they were THE ONE, the hero, and all the things that made them awkward and misunderstood on Earth were the ex-act things that made them the only one who could save this other world from disaster.

Welcome, Chosen One, the people or elves or aliens of this new, endangered world would say. *Your coming was fore-told to us.*

Lying diagonally across his bed at seven thirty on a

Wednesday evening, Tom got the distinct feeling that his coming was foretold to no one, that his name was written in exactly zero magical books, that nowhere in any universe was a mystical elder waking from a trance, accidentally knocking an orb to the floor and shattering it in his haste to bustle down a hallway, kick open a door, and gasp to a bunch of other mystical elders, "Tom Parking just ate dinner!"

He *had* just eaten dinner. That kind of told you everything you needed to know about him and why his life would never be bad enough to warrant his being snatched away to other worlds. It would've been better if he'd been sent to bed without supper. But he didn't even ever have "supper." He had "dinner." How many kids who ever turned out to be Chosen Ones ever had "dinner"? None, that's how many.

He was full and sort of sleepy and he was lying on his bed, but he probably wouldn't actually officially "go to bed" until one or two in the morning. He would probably eat something at least once before then, more out of boredom than hunger. And all this on the night he felt was the worst night he'd had in a while. If, on a really bad night in your life, you still ate a full dinner, finished your homework, and stayed up to watch *The Daily Show*, there was no way your life was bad enough for you to ever get plucked out of it and told you were a hero in some distant realm. This thought bummed Tom out even more than his mom telling him that after the fall play was over, he had to quit drama club, which was the thing that made his night so bad in the first place.

"If you want to do after-school stuff, you have to do your schoolwork," she had said at the dinner table. "No grades, no drama club. That's just all there is to it."

He couldn't argue with her. She was a good mom. That was also a problem. Kids in movies and stories who ended up being the Chosen Ones had parents who were dead, or at the very least, awful. If they were alive, they spent that life locking you, their child, in closets. Tom's mom was single, but she was trying her best and pretty much pulling it off. Tom's dad wasn't dead or awful. He was just in California.

His mom wasn't telling him he couldn't do plays anymore because it was "all rubbish" and she wanted to crush his artistic ambitions or rob him of joy. She was telling him he couldn't do plays anymore because his grades were bad, which was a totally reasonable thing for a good mom to do. At dinner she'd repeated what she'd said so many times before, which was that his life was happening in the present tense, and he needed to realize that unlike in middle school, every single high school grade counted toward something in the future. Then she'd said the bottom line was he'd better study his butt off or no more plays, period. Tom wondered if he'd ever actually "studied" anything. You did your homework and you took tests, right? In between all that, were you supposed to just open up your textbook and look at it even if you weren't directly instructed to do so? How would you know when to stop? Tom was smart. He'd always been smart. So his grades weren't so good right now. Surely they'd get better at some point, right? Why couldn't she understand that this failure to ever do his homework was in no way a reflection of his character? Just because he almost always forgot when assignments were due didn't mean he couldn't have done them if he'd remembered. It was nice of her to buy him a planner, but in order for it to work, he'd have to remember to write things down in it. And the not-remembering was his whole problem.

Why did she have to care so much? Couldn't she be just a little more neglectful? Couldn't the food she made be just a little colder or blander? Why didn't she ever snatch it away from him and fling it against the wall for no reason? She cared so much about him having the opportunity to go to a good college and find a satisfying career, but what about his opportunity to ride a winged beast at the head of a rag-tag force of fantasy creatures battling tyranny in a faraway land?

It was Wednesday night. Tom had a Wednesday-night kind of life.

He turned his head and looked at his reflection in the mirrored door of his closet. Neither man nor beast nor shadow creature was going to pass through the mirror and spirit him away. The mirror was just a mirror and he was just a tenth grader and there was nothing remarkable about him in this world and that meant he'd probably never get to find out if there were any other ones.

2

BUT IF SOMEONE were going to whisk Tom out of his mundane life and take him to another world, they could not have picked a worse time to do it than Thursday night around ten PM, the night after Tom's mom had told him he couldn't do plays anymore if he didn't bring his grades up. On Thursday night around ten PM, Tom had just finished acting in the first of three performances of the Arrowview Drama Department's fall play, and Lindsy Kopec was touching his arm.

"That was amazing," she said. "I mean, do you realize? That was amazing."

She was talking about a moment they had apparently shared onstage. He wasn't completely sure what moment she was talking about. It was all kind of a blur to him.

Lindsy had clearly experienced some sublime thrill, some *WE-ARE-ACTORS!* thing, while Tom had mostly been trying to stand where he was supposed to stand when he was supposed to be standing there and not forget any words and be as loud as possible. It wasn't even like they kissed at any point during the play. They were playing cousins, in fact, in one of those big, old-fashioned comedies their drama teacher Tobe liked because there were a lot of parts so a lot of kids could be cast and a lot of parents wouldn't be upset, and the only swear words were innocent ones no one uses anymore, like *Phooey!* Tom knew this supposed moment of brilliance had happened during this one little semi-serious exchange between their two characters, when they were alone and the stage was lit by only a candelabra Lindsy held, and Lindsy's character was telling Tom's character that she was worried they might not receive their full share of their grandmother's fortune. In that scene, Tom had apparently done something that Lindsy said "seriously sent shivers up my spine" and that "honestly, actors work their whole lives to achieve." He could not remember what this thing was. It didn't matter, though. What was important was that he had done something that had resulted in Lindsy Kopec touching his arm. Grabbing it, even.

People were coursing all around them in the lobby.

Tom's mom wasn't there because she planned on coming to the Saturday night show, and he hoped Lindsy's parents weren't there, either. He wanted this moment to last as long as possible. With Lindsy gripping his arm, looking into his eyes like they contained a million stories and truths instead of just dull gray irises, all the homework in the world seemed doable. He saw himself sitting up straight in class. After his homework was done, he would stare at his textbooks until his eyes bled. His butt would be fully studied off. He'd bring in dioramas to go with every assignment, even when the teacher hadn't asked for any dioramas. He would do anything if it landed him back here. Maybe next time they would play people who weren't related to each other. The next play was going to be *A View from the Bridge*. There had to be kissing in that, right? Where did people kiss if not on bridges?

"Tom," she said, "*Thomas*. YOU are an actor."

"Lindsy," Tom said, not knowing what he was going to say next, but just trying to match what Lindsy had said as much as possible without actually saying his own name. "*Lindsy.*" Lindsy had said his full name, Thomas. He wasn't sure if Lindsy was short for anything, but he wasn't going to venture a guess.

Lindsy Kopec was a model. Like, an actual model. She didn't talk about it a lot, the way Tom suspected anyone else would if they were a model, and the fact that she didn't talk about it a lot made it that much more plausible that she actually did it. Tom could not believe that someone like Lindsy shared a zip code with someone like him. She seemed like someone who was on her way somewhere else and was just gracing the world that contained shabby things like Tom's school and Tom's suburb with her presence for some unexplained reason. Maybe she was some kind of teen spy, and a rogue Russian missile scientist had stashed nuclear launch codes inside a dusty book in the school library. It would explain why she spent so much time there. She claimed it was because she wanted to be fluent in French by the time she graduated so she could study in Paris, but Tom wasn't buying it.

"Lindsy," Tom said a third time. He still hadn't thought of a follow-up.

"Yes?" Lindsy said.

"Well . . ." Tom said. He took a swig from a water bottle he was holding, as though he was about to launch into a brilliant monologue and needed to be properly hydrated. Ideally the monologue would be about Lindsy's greatness, his own greatness, and how they should probably celebrate their mutual greatnesses by making out. But Tom knew he could never say something like that, and he was hoping the swig would give him extra time to think of something he actually would say that would have the same result.

Then Tom felt increased pressure on his arm, like Lindsy had grown five extra fingers to further express her enthusiasm for him as an actor, and as a man. Tom knew it was probably just someone else's hand. *And that's fine*, he thought. Better that Lindsy Kopec see that his arm was in high demand for squeezing, that she was just one of his many fans and well-wishers. Tom broke Lindsy's gaze and turned to see who this other person was.

It was his dad. Tom hadn't seen his dad in a really long time.

He had no idea what to do or say. With Lindsy two feet from his face telling him how great he was, he had been feeling elated, and a positive sort of nervous, all of which was very rare for him to feel. Seeing his dad again, he felt something entirely different. It was his third big feeling in twenty-four hours, an extremely high number considering he would have described himself as someone who usually had maybe four feelings a month, on average.

"Got a second?" his dad said.

Tom and his dad floated away from Lindsy and the circulating parents and kids.

"What are you doing here?" Tom said, and immediately anticipated his dad responding with something like "That's all the thanks I get?" or "Good to see you, too."

Instead his dad said, "I came to see your play!"

"Right," Tom said. "But I mean, like . . . what are you doing in town?" He knew this would piss his dad off, that he would say, *"I have every right to—"*

"I'm visiting town!" Tom's dad actually said, smiling in a way Tom had never seen him smile before, though granted, he hadn't seen him in a really long time. Maybe he'd mellowed or something. Maybe he was on antidepressants.

"Come with me!" his dad said.

"Okay," Tom said. "Dad . . . is everything okay?"

They were out of the lobby and halfway across the parking lot before Tom's dad responded. "Peachy," he said. It could have easily been the sarcastic thing Tom was waiting to hear, because no one says "peachy" unsarcastically. But it didn't sound sarcastic, unless Tom's dad had been in California developing a type of sarcasm so sarcastic it sounded fully, creepily sincere. "Get in!" he said, gesturing to a white minivan with rental-car plates.

Tom got in. His dad got in on the driver's side.

After he was buckled in, Tom wondered if he should be doing this. After all, people got kidnapped by their estranged fathers. But his dad didn't seem like the type. There hadn't been any kind of custody battle. Tom's dad had never sworn he'd get him back by any means necessary. He'd just gone to California, reducing their family population from three to two. Now Tom was wondering if he actually secretly wanted the kind of dad who would kidnap him. Then he wondered why the van wasn't moving.

Tom looked over at his dad. He was staring at the steering wheel like he'd seen a steering wheel exactly two times before, and even then, only on TV. Finally, he reached up and death-gripped either side of the wheel so his fists were exactly parallel, like he was milking a cow. Tom couldn't drive yet but he was reasonably certain that that was not how you were supposed to hold a steering wheel.

"Dad . . . you all right?" Tom said.

"Peachy!" Tom's dad said again, exactly as sincerely as he'd said it the first time. He turned the key in the ignition and reached both hands over to shift the van into reverse. Tom was pretty sure that on most modern vehicles you only needed to use one hand to shift gears. Something he knew for sure was that when you were backing the car up, you were supposed to look behind you and make sure you didn't hit anyone. So he was surprised when, while backing up, his dad continued staring straight ahead.

"DAD!"

Tom's dad slammed on the brakes. Lindsy Kopec's big, beautiful eyes were wide in the red glare of the brake lights. His dad had almost killed Lindsy and her parents, who were walking to their car. Tom waved to them with all the energy he wasn't using being completely embarrassed, so it was a very weak wave.

Without apologizing or acknowledging that he had done anything wrong, Tom's dad again reached both hands over and put the car into drive. Tom's mouth had gone completely dry in his moment of panic. He downed the last of his water and put the empty water bottle in the cup holder.

There was silence as they drove out of the parking lot, and no further near killings. Tom reached over and turned on the radio. Historically, it was his dad who would do this when the car got quiet. Whoever had rented the car last had the radio tuned to the local hip-hop station, unless his dad had it on that station, which didn't seem likely.

"Oh man," Tom said, attempting to lighten the mood, "your tastes sure have changed."

Tom's dad didn't laugh or say anything at all. Tom looked over to see what the deal was and saw that his father's face was melting.

Tom screamed.

"Sorry! Sorry!" his dad said. "It's wearing off! I could barely keep it going for that long!"

Tom kept screaming. His melting-faced dad kept driving. He reached up with one hand and wiped most of the face-melt off, revealing the non-melted face of an entirely different guy.

"I need to tell you something, and—" the entirely different guy said in Tom's dad's voice. "Hold on a second." He swallowed hard.

"I need to tell you something," he said in an entirely different voice, "and the thing I have to tell you, it's that there's this other world, right? And in it—*in it*"—the guy grimaced, choked, and went on—"in it, you're the Chosen One, so I need you to come with—I need you to *come with*—" and before finishing the sentence, he threw up on the windshield of the van. It came out in a spray that made Tom finally understand the phrase "projectile vomit." It was like a laser beam of vomit, Tom thought. The thought made him stop screaming.

"*Oh*, man. Ohhhhhh, man," the entirely different guy said. "You're never supposed to swallow a voice changer. That was really dumb of me." He reached down with both hands and activated the windshield wipers. They moaned as they scraped the windshield, doing nothing to the vomit spray, because the windshield wipers were on the outside, and the vomit was on the inside.

"That's dumb too," the driver said. "Those things should be on the inside."

Tom didn't know exactly what would happen next. He hoped the guy would say, "Check *this* out," and he'd reach over and hit a switch on the dashboard that Tom hadn't noticed before, and that switch would cause everything in the van to reveal its true, magical nature. The sliding passenger doors would fold out and become dragon's wings, the stereo would pour forth the chanting of a million wizards, and this magical supervan would rocket upward into the stratosphere toward a portal in the middle of a thundercloud.

But the guy with the melting face didn't hit any other switches after the one to activate the windshield wipers. Minutes after he'd turned them on, they were still scraping ineffectively over the dry exterior surface of the windshield.

Scrape.

Pause.

Scrape.

Pause.

Scrape.

A pause that Tom could've sworn was longer than all the other pauses.

Scrape.

Tom reached over and flicked off the wipers with just one hand.

"Thanks," the driver said. "There's lots of other stuff about the world, the world I'm from, that I think you'll be pretty excited about, but I think it's better if you actually see it. Then you'll believe me."

"I believe you," Tom said, hoping this would prompt the driver to say something dramatic like, "Would you believe … *this?*" and then he'd snap his fingers and transport them to an endless, swaying grove of fifty-foot-tall neon palm trees. He didn't. They just kept driving.

"What's your name?" Tom said.

"Gark," said the driver.

"Oh," Tom said. "It's, uhm, nice to meet you, Gark. I'm—"

"Oh, I know *your* name," Gark said. "I know it very well indeed."

Tom got excited. He just knew this would be the part where Gark told him that in this other world, his name rang out in the realms of legend and frightened the enemies Tom was destined to defeat. "Your name," Gark said, "is *Tim*."

"Tom," Tom said.

"*Tom*," Gark said, almost before Tom finished saying it, as though he could make Tom forget he'd ever said *Tim*. "Tom. *Tom*. Of course."

They stopped at a red light. The light turned green, and the van didn't move. Tom scanned the traffic light for any sign of secret magical properties. Maybe it had a fourth unknown color of light besides the standard red, green, and yellow, and if you drove through the intersection when this fourth color was illuminated, you would hit hyperspeed, and enter the land where Tim, or Tom, or whoever, was destined for destiny. But it was the same boring traffic light that had always hung over this intersection. They were just sitting there.

"I'm sorry, I think I've got the directions screwed up," Gark said. "Do you know how to get to Kmart from here?"

3

ONCE A YEAR, Tom's mom made him go through all his clothes and pick out things that no longer fit and box them all up so they could be given to charity. The last time they'd done this, after Tom had gathered up just about every T-shirt that he'd outgrown, a few shirts he used to wear in spite of them being way too big for him because he liked the anime characters that were depicted on the front, and a couple sweatshirts he'd received as Christmas gifts from an uncle who mistakenly thought he liked baseball, or more specifically, the Kansas City Royals, Tom's mom said, "Great, go put them in the washer." She told Tom to do this every year, but he'd never really thought about it before.

"Why?" Tom had asked. "They wash them at the place, right?"

In what Tom felt was a tremendous act of maturity, he had recently decided he would no longer wear a shirt that was too big for him just because he liked the artwork on it. It was an important personal milestone brought on by a mean girl in his history class calling his favorite shirt "a dress" one day. Now Tom was mostly wearing ironic shirts he and other drama kids had gotten from thrift stores. His newfound thrift-store expertise assured him that not only was everything washed before it was put on the rack, but it was washed in some special thrift-store-only solution that gave every piece of clothing the same smell, which was like cigarettes and a recently flooded church basement.

"That isn't the point," his mom said. "The point is to take the time to do it so we're not just giving these people our unwashed junk."

"But . . . *they* wash it."

"You still need to make the effort."

She gave him eight quarters, and he trudged down the stairs of their apartment complex to the laundry room in the sulkiest way possible. The sulking was going pretty well until his foot slid off the second-to-last step, and he had to stop sulking to keep himself from falling.

They ended up taking the clothes to a big metal drop box in the Kmart parking lot. The box had the logo of the charity painted on the side along with all kinds of rules about what kinds of clothes could and could not be donated. After they got out of the car, his mom tapped a long fingernail on the rule that said CLEAN CLOTHES ONLY PLEASE. Tom wanted to say, *Yeah, yeah, yeah,* but he'd gotten in trouble before for saying it in the tone he wanted to say it in. He tried to put his donations in the chute on the side of the box in the sulkiest way possible. He made sure not to trip on anything.

This was the same metal donation box Gark and Tom ended up parking in front of fifteen minutes after Gark had snatched Tom from the (possibly) loving gaze of Lindsy Kopec. Gark shifted the car into park with both hands and took the keys from the ignition.

"Why do you do everything with two hands?" Tom said.

"I'm unfamiliar with this apparatus," Gark said. "It's extremely different from our modes of transportation. Anyway, this is it!"

"What?" Tom said.

"The portal!" Gark said.

Tom looked at the empty parking lot. He looked at the glowing red Kmart sign. Nothing about this parking lot screamed *portal to another dimension.* Nothing about it screamed anything. It was a parking lot. If it spoke, it whispered, and the word it whispered was *boring*. But there was still the chance that Gark would utter a single mystical phrase, and a lightning bolt would shoot out of the cloudless sky, hit the pavement, and open a shining space-time rift right between them and the closest shopping-cart return stall.

Gark got out of the van, and Tom did the same. Then Gark said, "*Oh!*" and opened the driver's side door again. He leaned in and reemerged holding Tom's empty water bottle. He crushed the bottle lengthwise and shoved it in the waistband of his pants without offering any explanation. He shut the door again and walked toward Tom.

"Do you need to lock the doors?" Tom said.

"Yes," Gark said, and then did nothing to lock the doors. "C'mon! I've got so much to show you!" He ran right up to the donation box. He opened the rusty metal chute, and it gave off a yawning screech.

A blinding light did not shine out of the chute. No winged beast flew out to carry them away to wherever they were going. There was only the black rectangle of the open chute and Gark looking at Tom.

"Hop in!" Gark said.

In movies and books, Tom thought, portals were sometimes pretty inconspicuous. It seemed the more inconspicuous a portal was, the more magical the world on the other side. If that was true, the world on the other side of this donation box would be wall-to-wall wizards.

What the heck, Tom thought. He'd come this far. Even though the only magical thing he'd seen so far, the facemelting fiasco, was also the grossest and most disturbing thing he'd ever seen, it was still *magic.*

Tom took a running start at the chute. He wanted to remember this feeling for when he finally returned to this world and claimed Lindsy Kopec as his one true love: the feeling of not thinking and just doing something. Cutting the small talk and just asking her out to the movies. Just leaning over and kissing her in the moonlight after the movie while they waited for their parents to pick them up. He would do it all the way he did this. He took a dead run at a rusty metal clothing donation box, the chute held open by a guy he thought half an hour ago was his estranged dad, but who turned out to be an emissary from a fantastic universe where Tom was special, where Tom was needed, where Tom would prove the heroism he'd always suspected he had inside of him even though he had no good reason for suspecting it. He reached the box and dived.

He was sure he would land in another world. Instead he landed at the bottom of the donation box, and it really hurt because the box was metal and there were exactly no clothes in it.

Then Tom was sure he knew what was really going on. He had fallen prey to a serial killer whose MO was convincing people to climb into a metal donation box where they then suffocated. The guy had just killed his dad and worn his face like a mask. Tom had merely imagined his face melting away magically because he wanted his story to be true. It was selection bias, the theory Mrs. McEllary had talked about in her psychology elective, how sometimes wanting to see something a certain way will make you see it that way.

Tom thought, *A good serial killer name for this guy would be the Donator.*

Then he thought: *It's unfair that the victims of a serial killer don't get to come up with their killer's nickname. They know best, after all.*

Tom was mad at his adrenaline. It was supposed to kick in and allow him to fight back. But he didn't feel adrenalized: he felt scared and tired and above all, dumb. Maybe if he pretended he had become superstrong from an adrenaline rush, Tom thought, he might actually become superstrong from an adrenaline rush. He stood up. He banged his head on the metal ceiling. Okay, so he couldn't stand up. Still, he remembered where the chute was. He pushed with all his might in that direction. The chute slid open easily and cool air rushed in. Now all he had to do was climb out, physically overpower his would-be murderer, and make his daring escape. Or maybe his would-be murderer had left already and he wouldn't have to physically overpower him. That would be nice.

Then the Donator's face filled the rectangle of the open chute. He was back to finish the job.

"Here I come!" he said cheerfully.

The Donator leapt into the chute. His head hit Tom's head, causing that horrible head-on-head collision pain that always made Tom wonder how soccer players could stand to head-butt anyone when it clearly hurt them just as much as it hurt their target. Tom's best friend, Kyle, had played soccer throughout middle school. If Tom left this parking lot alive, he would have to remember to ask Kyle how they did it.

Again Tom landed on the floor of the box, this time on his back, this time with a full-grown human on top of him. The wind had been knocked out of him, and he couldn't get it back while he was being crushed by a person. He wondered if this was what it felt like when your lungs collapsed. He hoped the Donator would not be mad that Tom had damaged two of his precious organs before he'd had a chance to surgically remove them. If the Donator cut out people's organs, it would make the name twice as clever.

"Sorry!" the Donator said, and rolled off of Tom.

"Listen," Tom panted. The long-awaited adrenaline was giving him just enough diaphragm strength to beg for his life, which, if he was honest, was a way more Tom thing to do than making some last great physical effort. "I'm not gonna say that I've got like, rich parents or anything. We're not rich. But . . . but . . . anything we have . . . I mean . . . my mom would . . ."

"What are you talking about?" the Donator said.

"Just please don't kill me."

The Donator burst out laughing. "Kill you? You're the Chosen One! If I killed you everyone would hate me. Even more then they already do," the Donator said. "The portal's timed. Give it a couple of minutes."

"Okay," Tom said.

"Kind of creepy here in the dark, though, right?"

"Yeah."

"I think I have something for that."

The guy Tom thought of as the Donator snapped the fingers of his right hand, and it was like someone had switched on a light inside the donation box.

At first Tom wished this hadn't happened, because the only thing worse than being inside a dark metal box you could just assume was filled with grime and roaches and a crazy guy was being in a well-lit metal box where you could see the exact location of the grime and the roaches and the crazy guy. Then Tom saw where the light was coming from. It wasn't a flashlight or any kind of bulb. It was a flame, but not a flame given off by a lighter or a match. It was a purple flame rising from the palm of the crazy guy's right hand. It was unlike anything Tom had ever seen. It didn't burn like a normal flame. It poured upward from his box companion's hand. It was a tiny upside-down waterfall of purple light and mild heat. The man held it close to his face. He looked excited but not entirely confident in his mastery of it, like a kid holding a hamster.

"The Tame Flame," he said. "Not my people's native magic but still, pretty cool, right?"

Tom nodded. So, he thought, the guy actually was Gark. The most negative thing Tom could imagine—that he was about to be serial killed—turned out to be fake, and the most fantastic thing—that this guy was actually from some other universe—might actually be true.

"You guys have roaches too?" Gark said, noticing some of the box's amenities. "We have roaches where I'm from, so you won't miss them."

"That's good," Tom said.

"Shouldn't be long now," Gark said, "which is good because—c'mon, c'mon, don't be like that, hey ..."

The fire in Gark's hand was becoming more firelike, the orderly droplets of purple light becoming tongues and curls of standard fire. It grew wilder and crawled up Gark's arm. In its tame form it had burned silently. Now it popped and hissed, seeming to want to make up for all the time it had spent pretending not to be a dangerous fire.

"Don't worry," Gark said, "I can . . . Hey, flame! Hey! Let's—HEY! OW! OWWWWW!"

Gark started whipping his flaming right arm around what little space there was inside the box.

"Roll!" Tom said. "Roll on it!"

"Okay!" Gark said. He threw himself onto the floor of the box. Tom huddled as far away from the burning as possible while Gark rolled, banging repeatedly into the far side of the box, howling in pain.

The light went out. Tom could hear Gark panting as he finally lay still.

"Good idea," Gark said.

One second later, it was brighter than ever in the box, because every piece of Gark's clothing burst into flame.

Tom lunged toward Gark to try and help him beat down the fire, but he didn't land on Gark. He didn't land anywhere. He had been flying through the tiny space in the box and then, instantly, he was underwater.

It wasn't like he'd dived into a pool. It was like he'd just appeared, submerged, in the deep end. He was confused and panicked until he realized he was underwater, and then he was thrilled even though he still had no idea what was going on. The water felt glorious after being in a metal box that was insufferably hot even before it became filled with fire. It would put out Gark's full-body inferno. Best of all, it meant that they were through the portal, in another world. Tom hoped this entire world wasn't underwater, but hey, he was the Chosen One: he probably had gills.

4

TOM OPENED HIS eyes. They immediately started to burn. Then they really started to burn, and he really started to panic, and in his panic his mouth sprang open and foul-tasting liquid rushed in: soap. His mouth was full of soap. He hadn't gotten in trouble for swearing as a kid and even if he had, his parents weren't from the 1950s, so he'd never had a mouthful of soap. It was not the kind of new experience Tom was excited to have, and he wanted it to be over.

He saw Gark a few feet away, floundering in the soapy water, little charred bits of his clothing floating all around him. Gark saw Tom, gave him a double thumbs-up, and smiled, showing all his teeth. He seemed to immediately regret the decision to open his mouth.

Tom swam upward. There was intermittent light from

above, like they were underneath a layer of lily pads. As he got closer to the surface, he realized it wasn't lily pads or any other kind of aquatic plant. It was clothes.

Tom swam past acid-washed jeans and a training bra. He felt the weight of his own waterlogged clothes. He suddenly became aware of the stuff in his pockets. The contents of his wallet would be soaked, and—oh dear God—his phone.

At pool parties he'd seen kids move to throw another kid in the pool, only to have the first kid say he had his phone in his pocket, and then the attacking kids, sympathetic because they, too, had phones in their pockets, would wait patiently while he removed his phone, keys, and wallet and set them on some patio furniture, and then, finally ready to be pranked, he'd get picked up and hurled in, stiffly, all the surprise gone. It was the least fun fun had ever been. But now Tom understood. His phone would most certainly be dead. And though not a lot of people called or texted Tom besides his mom and Kyle, he liked knowing that everyone had the option.

Tom breached the surface and still couldn't see anything. Something had attached itself to his head, covering his eyes. He reached up and removed a pair of wet tighty-whiteys from his forehead. Then someone poured liquid soap in his face.

"*Gargh!*" Tom said.

"*Ahhhh!*" said the guy who had just poured soap in his face.

Tom immediately ducked back beneath the surface to wash the gross, waxy stuff out of his eyes. He resurfaced and saw the culprit: a man on a raft holding a bucket. Tom noticed another man on the raft. The other man noticed Tom.

"*Thief!*" he screamed, picking an oar up out of the water and rearing back, preparing to hit Tom's head like a golf ball on a tee. "*Clothes-thief!*"

Gark popped up next to Tom.

"Hold on!" Gark said. "That's the Chosen One! Official king's business!"

Tom thought, *These guys are gonna be so embarrassed when they realize they almost beheaded the Chosen One.*

"Oh, *that*," said the man holding the bucket.

The man holding the oar dropped his ready-to-kill stance and looked at his oar almost apologetically, like he felt guilty for promising it a head-whacking and then having to take it all back. He extended the oar to Tom.

"Here," he said, and sighed. He hoisted Tom aboard, and Gark came next.

"I'm hereby commandeering this soaping vessel in the name of the king," Gark said, "effective immediately! Bear us to port, where we may thence to the castle!"

The oarsman looked at his would-be-murdering oar as if to say, *Get a load of this guy.*

"Listen," the bucket man said, "we got a job to do here. You'll go in with us when we go in to refill, and that's it."

"Oh," Gark said. "Well, in the name of the king, I command you to . . . do that!"

At last, Tom could keep his eyes open for longer than three seconds without fantastic pain. He took in their surroundings. They were in the middle of a lake dotted with islands and archipelagos of wet clothing. The water's surface had the slick, rainbow-y look of bathwater. The oarsman steered toward a specific spot about fifteen feet away from where Tom and Gark had surfaced. The other man nodded for him to stop, and then poured out the last of the soap in his bucket. He tapped the bucket's bottom a few times to make sure he'd used all of it.

"There," he said, "*Now* we can go."

✳   ✳   ✳

Tom and Gark sat on one end of the raft and the two clothes-raft operators stood, simultaneously rowing and eyeing them. The one who'd been holding the bucket was wearing a Cincinnati Bengals jersey and leopard-print tights, and the man who'd tried to take Tom's head off was shirtless and wearing swim trunks that were clearly meant to be worn by a six-year-old boy. They had a pattern of sharks swimming across them, but the guy was much bigger than a six-year-old, so the sharks were all bent out of shape, too big in places and too small in others, like they'd been swimming in radioactive waters.

The raft passed through small canyons between tiny waterlogged hills of twisted fabric. Tom marveled at the landmasses of wet clothes. He thought, *What if this is somehow a way station for discarded clothing from all over Earth? What if it's cast-off garments from all over the universe?* He looked closely, hoping to see kimonos, or orange robes Tibetan monks might wear, or maybe, just maybe, alien fabrics of colors never before seen by human eyes.

He saw a pair of blue jeans, and the only thing alien about them was their enormous size. Mickey Mouse, wearing sunglasses, peered out at them from a T-shirt on the opposite wall of the canyon. They rowed into a larger bay.

Clotheslines were strung across it, with jackets, shirts, sweaters, pairs of pants, and every kind of undergarment hanging from them, drip-drying. The sun broke through this jungle canopy every so often, and it was like a sun shower as they floated underneath the perpetual dripping of a hundred thousand pieces of throwaway clothing.

Women wearing outfits as mismatched as the raft guys' stood on ladders placed precariously on the decks of larger rafts. They strung the clothes up, while more clothes were handed to them in baskets by men on rafts below. Tom watched as one of these women pulled a maroon rag out of a basket. It was twisted, the way guys would twist towels in locker rooms so they could whip each other. The only time Tom had seen this happen in real life was after freshman PE, and it was always halfhearted, like the guys involved didn't really want to do it but thought they were supposed because they were in a locker room and that's what you did, right? Maybe it happened more often, and with more enthusiasm, after actual competitive sporting events. Again, Tom would have to ask Kyle, his only real connection to the mysterious and sweaty world of athletics.

The woman untwisted the rag so she could hang it up, and as she did so, Tom realized that it was not a rag. It was, in fact, a T-shirt with ARROWVIEW printed in yellow on the front. Tom had been right to think of gym class. Here, however many million miles away, if the distance was even measurable in miles, was a woman hanging up a gym uniform from Tom's high school. The clothes that bubbled up from the bottom of the lake weren't from all over the universe or even all over the world. They seemed to be mostly from his town.

"Gark?" Tom said.

"Yes?"

"What happens to the clothes after you guys pull them out and dry them?"

"People buy them and wear them."

"Ah," Tom said.

"Or they used to, anyway," Gark said. "Everyone pretty much has their thing that they wear now, so unless that thing falls apart, they're set."

"What if your thing that you wear gets dirty, and you want something else to wear while you clean the first thing?"

"I don't understand," Gark said.

"Well . . ." Tom felt weird being the position of defending laundry.

"I guess we haven't picked up on a lot of the stuff about clothes yet," Gark said. "They're still a pretty new thing around here. You still get some old-timers who remember a time before this portal brought clothes in, and they like how it used to be, so they'll just be, y'know . . ."

"Naked?" Tom said.

"Yeah," Gark said.

"Good to know," Tom said.

Tom spotted a skinny kid wearing an extra-extra-large T-shirt commemorating a church bake sale, standing on a little island of denim, his body pretty well hidden by hanging laundry. He was stuffing pairs of briefs into the pockets of his gym shorts. The oarsman saw him, too. He drew the bloodthirstier of the two oars out of the water, reared back, and whacked the kid with it. There was a wet smack and the kid went flying. The oarsman laughed. He looked back at Tom. Tom forced a close-mouthed smile. He didn't want to display any knockout-able teeth.

"What do you call the thing that kid was grabbing?" Gark asked. "With, like, the stretchy stuff that goes around your waist?"

"Underwear?"

"Yeah," Gark said. "Kids love that stuff. I don't have much use for it myself."

"Also good to know," Tom said.

They reached a wooden dock. "Thanks for the lift," Gark said. "I'm Gark, by the way."

"I know," said the oarsman.

"Oh! And this," he said, becoming puffed up and grand, "is Tim."

"Tom." Tom said.

"*Tom*," said Gark. "Well, can't sit here all day chatting." Gark hopped up and off the raft in one swift motion and, after his right foot got caught on a loose dock plank, fell down and got back up in six awkward motions. He turned and extended a hand to help Tom up onto the dock.

"You okay?" Tom said.

Gark nodded, wiping blood away from his nose with his other hand.

"Our transport awaits!" Gark said as he led Tom down a crisscrossing series of docks and gangplanks toward dry land. He'd said their modes of transportation were very different from the rental van, and Tom was excited to see exactly how different. Would it be a cart pulled by a weird four-legged pack-beast? Maybe the transport would just be the beast itself, and when Gark whistled it would lower its head, allowing them to climb aboard.

Tom had never realized he had so many expectations

for fantasy worlds. Now that he was actually in one, he found that he had tons. One of the things he expected was a population of strange beings very unlike himself, whether they were reptile people or bird people or minotaurs in astronaut helmets. On the dock, though, he was surrounded by what appeared to be humans. No one had strange alien ridges on their noses or pointy elf ears, at least no one he'd seen so far.

Even in a world where everyone else was human as well, he expected to be stared at by strangers because of his out-of-place Earthly manner of dress. Yet as he and Gark walked through the crowd on the docks, no one stared at him, and it didn't seem like it was because they were worried that he might melt them with his gaze or that they would be executed for daring to make eye contact with the Chosen One Whose Coming Was Foretold. It seemed like the reason no one was staring was that they had the same number of eyes and teeth and limbs he did and they were wearing clothes like his, from Earthly stores in Earthly malls, so they were indifferent to him just as he would be to a stranger he passed on the street who wasn't attractive or famous or peeing their pants because they were crazy. A teenage girl with red hair and pretty green eyes passed them on their left and as she did so, Tom tried to catch her eye. It worked, but when she looked back at him she gave him a look he could've gotten from any girl in one of those Earthly malls. *Great*, he thought. *I've been in this world for ten minutes and already at least one person thinks I'm a creep.*

The dock became a path leading to the top of a hill. The sun was bright and hot, and there was only one of it, like on Earth, and it shone down from a sky that was blue, like on Earth, and these things were disappointing to Tom for reasons he couldn't quite explain. But it was nice to be drying off in the sunshine. They reached the top of the hill. On the other side of the hill was a parking lot.

It wasn't exactly like the parking lot in front of the Kmart, but the only differences were that the Kmart parking lot was paved and this one was just grass and dirt, and the Kmart parking lot had been mostly empty and this one was full.

It wasn't full of sleeping griffins, either.

It was full of cars.

5

GARK HAD CLAIMED the vehicles in his world were vastly different than the ones in Tom's world. It turned out he'd meant that the cars in his world were cars from Tom's world but with a lot of trash stuck to them.

They found Gark's car. Tom was not a car guy, but it looked to him like a windowless, mirrorless version of a 1980s sedan. Gark took Tom's empty water bottle from the waistband of his pants. He reached into the car's driver's seat, pulled out a half-used roll of black electrical tape, bent down, and taped the bottle to the left front tire of the car. The tire was covered entirely in flattened, weathered bottles of various shapes and sizes. In fact it was made of them, Tom realized as he looked closer. It was like a tank tread made of water bottles and weathered, gooey straps of electrical tape. Gark stared proudly at this fresh new bottle, like it somehow made the makeshift tire complete. Tom noticed that every tire on every vehicle in the parking lot was like this. Some of the tires were made of crushed soda cans. The ones on the car across from Gark's were made of grocery bags.

"Let's go!" Gark said. He reached through the space where the driver's side window would have been and pulled up on the tab to unlock the door, and then opened the door and climbed in. Tom did the same on his side. Gark had left the keys in the ignition.

Before starting the car, Gark leaned over and looked at a plastic cup that was fused into his dashboard cup holder. He noticed there were two inches of brownish liquid in the cup and said, "Perfect. I'm parched."

"How long has that been in there?" Tom asked.

"Not long," Gark said. "It's just rainwater that collected while I was gone." He put his hand through the space where the windshield would have been, demonstrating how the rain had reached the cup, and also how the one or two bugs in the water had gotten there as well. *No wonder he thought he could just throw up while driving,* Tom thought. *In this world, it would've ended up outside the car.*

Tom reached for his seat belt, only to discover that it had met the same fate as the tires, the mirrors, and the windshield. In its place were ten or so shoelaces hanging from one side of the passenger seat, each one spaced a few inches apart.

"You just tie those across you," Gark said.

"Okay," Tom said, reaching up to tie the top lace to the corresponding loop on the other side of his seat. He tried to lift his shoes up off the floor once he realized it was one big puddle of standing water.

Gark had accidentally tied two laces in the same loop. "Oops! Let me fix this, it'll just take a second."

Twenty minutes later, they were moving at last, crossing a grassy but otherwise featureless plain at a speed of maybe ten miles an hour. Tom looked over to see what their actual speed was but all of the needles on the dashboard panel that told you things like how fast you were going and how much fuel you had left weren't there.

"Where did you get these cars?" Tom asked.

"They're not cars," Gark said. "They're conveyances."

"They're cars," Tom said.

"The parts came from your world," Gark said, "but we combined them in our world, adding our own special touches." To emphasize this, he leaned forward and took a sip from a very long straw that led to the dashboard-fused rainwater cup. He coughed.

"Where do you guys get the gasoline?"

"Oh, that stuff?" Gark asked. "We don't have that here. That stuff is for cars. These are conveyances. They run on motion juice."

"Is that just what you call gasoline?"

"No! Motion juice we make ourselves. It doesn't have that annoying thing like gasoline where it runs all smooth. With motion juice—"

Bang! There was a small explosion behind Tom. He looked behind him out the no-window and saw a cone of fire pouring out of the gas tank.

"*. . . it does that so you know it's working,*" Gark yelled over the roar of the flames.

"*It's supposed to do that?*" Tom yelled.

"*Yep,*" Gark yelled, and smiled. "*Motion juice!*"

Tom looked back. The fire just kept coming out of the side of the car. Safety, he thought, was not a real concern here. He reached up and undid his top safety shoelace. "*Ooooh!*" Gark yelled. "*Rebel!*"

✳ ✳ ✳

They rounded a hill, and Gark's village came into view. On its outskirts there were a few "conveyances" like Gark's. Their still-burning vehicle drifted into a tight space between two other conveyances. It was so tight that Tom didn't know how they were going to get out. Then he watched Gark turn the engine off and throw his door open with gusto, causing the kind of metal-on-metal smacking sound that would have made Tom's mom pull a piece of paper and a pen out of her purse so Tom could start writing the other car's driver a note. Tom opened his door just as hard on his side. It banged the door next to him, hard. It was pretty fun.

The motion-juice fire had gone out, leaving a cloud of awful-smelling black smoke Tom had to wave away to breathe or see anything. Finally, he'd flapped his arms enough and got a good look at the village. It was mostly forts.

These were not the castle kind of forts. These were the kind of forts Tom would build in the living room when he was little and his parents were out for the night and there was a babysitter over, with a couple of kitchen chairs with a blanket strung over them to create a dark, private interior space. Sometimes he had even incorporated the couch, provided the babysitter was not asleep on it.

Here, in Gark's village, tarps often stood in for blankets,

and old doorless refrigerators or rusty smashed-open vending machines sometimes took the place of chairs. Some of the forts were made of actual blankets and chairs. The blankets were dirty and the chairs were beat up, and they had fully grown adults running in and out of them, conducting business, but that was really the only difference between them and the things Tom used to build and climb in to hide from imaginary enemies.

They walked into the village, dodging sleeping people in dirty thrift-store clothing and zigzagging between blankets strung over chairs placed back to back and a few feet apart.

"What is this place called?" Tom asked.

"Uhmm . . ." Gark said. "It's not really called anything."

"And what are you guys called?" Tom asked. "I mean, your people."

"Good question!" Gark said. "Nothing in particular."

Tom liked this idea a lot. He'd never thought about fantasy worlds as being on actual planets. He mostly thought of them as flat, two-dimensional maps stretched out on the first few pages of the book that detailed a hero's adventures within that world. Tom preferred to think that this village, humble as it was, and the lake, soapy as it was, were the whole of this world. If there was a singing grotto or a Forest of Undoing around as well, he wouldn't complain. But once you started naming things it indicated there were things beside the thing you were naming, because why would you name something if not to set it apart from something else, and once you started doing that, the world got a lot larger and less mystical and less innocent.

As they wove their way through the network of blanket forts, Gark was announcing Tom's arrival.

"Chosen One here!" Gark hollered. "Chosen One walking a sacred and predestined path to the castle of our sovereign!"

Tom was so excited by this mention of an actual king in a legitimate castle that he didn't notice as they passed a mangy toddler fighting an equally mangy dog for a scrap of gristle right in the middle of his sacred and predestined path, and when the dog gave up and let go, the toddler went flying backward into Tom's knees, causing Tom to fall forward into a generous-sized puddle of what he hoped was brown water.

"Oh!" Gark said, and ran to help Tom up. "Not to worry!" he shouted to everyone around them. "The Chosen One shall encounter many dangers on his journey, and he shall handle them all with equal—*oof!*—aplomb!"

Tom was back on his feet. He thought momentarily about wringing his shirt out, then decided to just accept the fact that in this world, he would always be wet.

Gark's pronouncements made a man sitting outside his fort look up from what he was doing, which was roasting gray meat on a gray TV satellite dish that had been repurposed as a grill. A little fire licked its underside. The meat rested in either the concave or the convex part of the dish, Tom couldn't remember which was the right word. The man looked Tom up and down and snorted.

Let him snort, Tom thought. There were lots of examples of a Chosen One being scrawny and not all that intimidating and sometimes even covered in mud. If anything, it was the norm. You didn't see a whole lot of Chosen Ones who looked like Chosen Ones, with muscles and long, dreamy hair. Mostly they were kids like Tom, nerdy and not all that special-seeming one way or the other. If people snorted at you, maybe that meant you were doing something right.

They were about thirty paces past the barbecuing guy when another man ran right across their path. The man was on fire.

It was the second man totally engulfed in flame that

Tom had seen in a span of two hours. Still, Tom yelped involuntarily. It wasn't something you got used to.

"Don't worry about him," Gark said.

"Did he screw up a spell, too?" Tom said.

"I wouldn't say, I mean, not to contradict you, but I wouldn't say I screwed up the spell, so much as the fire has a mind of its own," Gark said. "And, no. That's just a customer from The Johns."

"The Johns" created an image in Tom's mind of a business run by two guys named John whose main job was to set their customers on fire.

"The Johns?" Tom said.

"Yep," Gark said. "Our oldest drinking establishment."

They turned down the alley the flaming man had run from. The oldest drinking establishment in the kingdom was three portable toilet stalls all lashed together. The sheds had their front panels cut off, creating the effect of a little barn with one side open to the elements. Above the cut-open part, each individual shed had a brand name emblazoned on it in extruded green plastic: MOBI-JOHN.

"I know it looks like they're drinking their own pee," Gark said, "but they're not."

Gark was right: there were two patrons seated on the

toilets, fully clothed, with long straws like the one from Gark's conveyance running down into the toilet bowls.

"Then . . . what are they doing?" Tom said.

"Well," Gark said, smiling, "I know in your world, you use those things for, you know . . . and that's what you do. But what we do—" and here Gark seemed like he was a great chef telling Tom his secret ingredient—"is fill them with our native liquor, thinkdrink. The plastic and the drinker's body heat combine to keep the thinkdrink at a steady warm temperature. People love it. It has one disadvantage, though."

"What's that?" Tom said, suspecting that even though Gark had said very explicitly that it wasn't pee, he would now admit that it actually was.

"It's best served warm," Gark said, "but if it gets too warm, it starts a fire."

"Oh," said Tom. "But it gets you drunk?"

"Oh yeah," Gark said. "You start remembering all kinds of stuff."

Tom was confused. Admittedly, he'd never been drunk before. But he knew from TV and movies that a lot of people drank to forget. If you listened to five songs that mentioned going to a bar, usually four of them were talking specifically about going to the bar to drink and forget something or someone.

"Thinkdrink makes all your memories, but especially painful ones, clear and sharp," Gark said. "That way you can sit and think for hours about where you went wrong."

"Why would you want to do that?" Tom said.

"Because then you're thinking of the past," Gark said, "and the past is better than the present and they're both better than the future. At least, that's what everybody says. Anyway, I don't drink it much myself. Mostly my memories are happy so it only makes me think of happy stuff and I guess that isn't the point."

"Thanks!" someone behind them said. Tom turned and saw the previously on-fire guy walking out of a booth. He was now fully extinguished, though his sweater and plaid pajama pants were burned. He waved to the guy inside the booth, which contained a long Tupperware storage tub full of grayish water, a stool for the proprietor to sit on, and a sign reading JUMP IN HERE AND GET PUT OUT, FIVE MONEYCOINS. PAYABLE AFTER EXTINGUISHING. The dripping man passed Tom and Gark and went back into The Johns, resuming his place at the bar, or on the toilets, or whatever the proper term was here.

"It was like I was right back there," the old man said to

his old-man companion one toilet over, "the night she died."

"Yeesh," Tom said out loud.

Tom kept reminding himself that no matter how gross or dangerous his surroundings, at the end of this path they were walking, there was a king, and a prophecy with his name on it, and it was all inside an honest-to-goodness castle.

"This is it," Gark said a few minutes later.

They were standing in front of what appeared to be a small fiberglass castle from a miniature golf course. Built out from this tiny castle was an actual structure, the biggest Tom had seen in the kingdom. It was a patchwork of planks and boards composing a rough, uneven dome that was maybe the height of a two-story Earth building. It looked like someone had taken every set piece the Arrowview Drama Department had ever constructed and nailed them together, unpainted side out. The fiberglass mini-golf castle was just the entrance to the actual castle, and the actual castle was a wooden monstrosity that was the most sturdily built thing in the kingdom, yet also seemed like it could be knocked over by an extra-strong sneeze.

Maybe there will be swords inside, Tom thought. *There had better be swords inside.*

"THIS IS IT?"

The king of the nameless kingdom was talking about Tom.

The king was old and bearded, the way Tom thought of kings as being, but he was wearing an unzipped black goose-down jacket with nothing underneath it, so his stomach protruded, bare and covered in salt-and-pepper hair, and the knobs of his knees poked out of Hawaiian-print shorts. There were green shower sandals on his feet and a baseball cap where his crown should have been. Unless the cap was his crown, in which case, his crown had white letters on it that said BIKINI INSPECTOR.

"This is he!" Gark said.

"Him," the king said. "You mean to say 'this is him.'"

Tom knew "this is he" was actually correct, because his mom corrected him about that kind of thing a ton. He hesitated to correct a king, though, even if he was a king whose throne appeared to be a blue Igloo cooler, with its open top serving as the chair back and lots of towels and blankets inside to act as a seat. Also, the king had a British accent. Tom liked British accents a lot. They made anyone who had one sound smart no matter what they said. If the king had a British accent, he probably knew what he was talking about way more than Tom or even his mom did.

"He's awfully small," the king said.

Tom felt like it was probably time for him to pipe up and defend himself, but he didn't know what to say, exactly. A Chosen One wouldn't wait to have it all figured out, though. He'd just act.

"Your Highness," Tom said, "I won't let you down."

"I'm afraid you already have," the king said.

"How?" Tom said. "I don't even know what I'm supposed to do here."

"And that's exactly it," said the king. "A true Chosen One would not need to be told what to do, he would just do it."

"Come on," Gark said. "He hasn't even been here an hour. He hasn't even heard the prophecy!"

"In my opinion," the king said, "a Chosen One needing

to hear the prophecy that foretells his coming before he can do the thing he's come to do is a little like the sun needing to hear a poem about itself to be reminded how to shine. But go ahead, if you believe it will help."

"I'll go and grab it," Gark said, running out of the throne room, which was a big wooden cavern cluttered with criss-crossing beams and lit by torches. Tom didn't think it was a very good idea to keep torches in a room that was basically a big jumble of flammable wood, given the kingdom's overall fire safety record.

"You must understand it is nothing against you person-ally," the king said. "Gark is rather an abnormality here. He is perhaps our least intelligent citizen. He is also the one with the most positive attitude. Which is strange, because his father was one of our most respected citizens, and also one of our most negative."

"Why was he respected?" Tom asked. Tom had often been accused of being negative, and in his experience, it made people like you less, not more.

"Because negativity is one of our most valued qualities. Gark's father, Garko, was a masterfully depressing person."

Say something smart, Tom thought. *Something smart and Chosen One—like.*

"That's interesting," Tom said. "On Earth we think of happiness as kind of the goal."

"Oh, we do as well," the king said. "But our people are happier when their expectations are lower. The past was better than today, today is bad, and tomorrow will be worse. Viewed that way, anything that happens that is remotely good is very good. But you must also realize it's an accident. You might pursue a pattern of behavior that would cause more good things to happen, but with each triumph, you are getting your expectations out of sync with how the universe normally works. Eventually, you are going to fail, and when that failure happens, you will feel even worse than you had when you started. So why start?"

"Uhm," Tom said, "That's . . ."

"A quote. I was quoting Garko, rest his miserable soul. Garko, Garko, Garko," the king said, staring into the shadows, getting nostalgic. "Ah, there's a good example! Our names, you see. Gark's father was Garko. Garko, son of Garkon. Garkon, son of Garkona. And so on and so on. When it is time to name your offspring, you name them after their father if it is a boy, the mother if it's a girl, and drop a letter. One letter each generation. It reminds us that the past was better, that we are all our parents, but less."

"What if you have two boys or two girls?"

"Most people stop at one. I did. It's not an experience one seeks to replicate."

Tom was an only child. He imagined his dad telling his mom that Tom was an experience he did not seek to replicate.

"What happens when you run out of letters in your names?"

"For most, that is four generations from now, and we'll worry about it when it happens. If it happens at all. We did not expect to exist even this long."

Tom marveled at how depressing Garko must have been if the king considered Garko even more depressing than the king was.

"When we transitioned out of a life of mere survival, it was Garko the Great Cynicist who kept our expectations low. All this Chosen One nonsense is really for his sake. I do not believe he would have wished to see his son go through life as an optimistic person, so I am letting this all play out in hopes that it will be a spectacular failure, Gark will finally realize that idealistic endeavors are simply asking for trouble and become so disillusioned he'll choose to continue the legacy of his father. He actually found you and brought you back, which is impressive. If only he would apply his energies to some really productive brooding, he could easily be one of the greatest men in Nggghthththhh."

"I'm sorry, what did you say?"

"Nggghthththhh? The name of our kingdom."

"Gark said the kingdom didn't have a name."

"It doesn't," the king said. "But there are times where, grammatically, it makes sense to speak the name of the kingdom aloud. And since it does not have a name, it is traditional just to mumble unintelligibly for the length of the average kingdom name."

"Why not just name it?"

"No one would be able to agree on a name. We'd end up with something everyone hated."

"Can't you just make a proclamation?"

"That would be awfully arrogant. Can you imagine how mad people might get if I was just to go around proclaiming things?"

"I thought that's what kings were supposed to do."

"I suppose. But in our society, it is more the king's job to set a mood, to discourage outbursts of irrational ambition or exuberance. We've always had an army, but I've found that they're most effective just being at home, bored, chatting with their friends and neighbors, complaining about the state of things and imagining the horrible ways they might get worse. I suppose if I started doing rash things like issuing proclamations, I might have to tell them to take up arms and gather around me to protect me from an angry populace. As it stands now, no one is mad at me because they know I can't do anything and they trust me not to do anything even if I could because it's all futile."

"Oh," Tom said.

"Unless you have an idea for a brilliant kingdom name to which everyone will instantly agree?"

Tom was silent.

"No? Then we shall continue to be nameless. For if we name our kingdom," the king said, "we might develop an identity. A culture. A sense of ourselves. And what happens if those things are taken away? If we do not develop a sense of ourselves, we will not miss each other when we're gone. If our kingdom is destroyed—"

Tom was about to ask who would want to destroy them when Gark came clomping back in. "Here it is!" he yelled, waving a white piece of paper over his head. He paused and tried to catch his breath. "Do you want me to read it to him? You said '*Hear* the prophecy,' so . . ."

"*You* said 'hear the prophecy.' I was just repeating what you said," said the king. "Just give it to him and let him read it."

If he could read it for himself, Tom thought, that meant it wouldn't be in runes or pictographs. But when Gark handed it over, he realized it was even less impressive than that. It looked like it had been printed out on any computer and typed up using any word-processing program on Earth. It was formatted exactly like a paper Tom would turn in for school, double-spaced 12-point Times New Roman. It read:

The Chosen One must be retrieved from Earth.

He will bring down the Wall and restore the

   kingdom to glory.

His name is Tom Parking.

It was a cool enough prophecy, Tom thought. The problem was presentation. It was a white sheet of printer paper with three lines on it. If Tom had been told to write a prophecy on his home computer, he would have at least made sure the words were centered in the middle of the page. He didn't dare point these things out, though. Sure, it was a prophecy any kid could have made in any computer lab. But it was also a prophecy that named him as the Chosen One.

"Gark, where did you get this?" Tom asked.

"It was slipped in through my window at night," Gark said.

"I must confess," the king said, "there is one very small part of me that wants this prophecy to be right about you. So, Tom—"

"Come on," Gark said. "It's *Tim*, it's right here on the page."

"It is right here on the page," Tom said, "and it's Tom."

"Yes, Tom, what is it exactly will you do as Chosen One?"

"Uhm, I guess whatever the prophecy says?"

"I find the idea of a Chosen One reading his own prophecy like an instruction booklet distasteful. You've read the prophecy. What now?"

"Uhm, there's a lot of things in it that I'm unclear on...."

Gark perked up. "'The Wall' refers to—"

"Ah ah ah!" The king said. "Now we must interpret it for you as well?"

"Just help me out here!" Tom said. "Trust me, I'd love to actually *feel* like I was your Chosen One, and just come in here and know exactly what I was doing and start doing it, but I don't, and you said there's one part of you that wants me to succeed, so why not help me as much as you possibly can? I thought, like, maybe in your world I'd have special magical powers or something, but I clearly don't have any, and you guys aren't offering me any magical swords or any- thing like that, and I clearly need all the help I can get, so why not just tell me as much as you know and stop holding back?"

Tom was out of breath. He started trying to breathe through his mouth instead of his nose, as the throne room had the stale cantaloupe-y smell of old dog pee.

"As I said, Gark surprised me by retrieving you," the king said. "Thus, I haven't yet put enough thought into how we here in Ghhhhddkdffrr will deal with you. I must de- liberate with Gark, as you are his project. You are free to explore the castle. I know you Earth types enjoy that sort of thing. Garko once said that, in exploring, you will either be disappointed when what you find fails to meet your expec- tations, or disappointed when things are exactly what you expected because they do not exceed your expectations, or thrilled when things exceed your expectations, but those exceptional things will always turn out to be evil or danger- ous. I am reasonably certain our castle contains only things that fall within the first two categories."

He waved Tom away.

Tom wanted to say something else, to not let the king have the last word, but he didn't know what to say. He turned and walked out.

He should have corrected the king! That was it. When Gark said "this is he," and the king told him it was actually "this is him," Tom should have jumped in and defended Gark. The king would have been impressed by Tom's guts. It would have set a whole different tone. Why was he only now realizing this after it was too late?

Gark's and the king's voices faded, and so did the dog-pee cantaloupe smell. The planks and beams jutting out from the walls made the place feel like one enormous back-stage area for the weirdest show in history. Tom started to pretend that he was backstage, and that any second now he would round a corner and reach the real kingdom. This was the part no one in the audience was ever supposed to see. Any second now he'd step onstage, and he would be on a sunny hilltop with huge ivory towers in impossible geometric shapes off in the distance, and there would be dragons circling in the sky. He wanted a kingdom with just a few dragons. Even if the dragons had health problems.

Then he rounded the corner and saw the first thing

he'd seen since coming here that made him feel like he hadn't rolled bad dice in a role-playing game.

She was beautiful. She was sitting in a golden shaft of light with dust motes dancing in it. She was completely still, like she was sitting for a portrait. She was probably good at sitting still for portraits, because she would be highly in demand as a subject, because she was incredibly beautiful, and also because she was a princess. There were no two ways about it. When little girls said they wanted to be princesses, this is what they were talking about. As they grew up, their expectations could be modified by the slow realization that there was not a huge call for actual princesses in the modern world, but somewhere deep inside of them, in a place they would not admit existed to themselves or anyone else, an image lingered that looked exactly like the one in front of Tom: the princess, with the big pink cone of a princess hat, and the thin veil, and the long blonde hair and the big eyes containing wisdom and innocence and sparkling blue in equal amounts.

Likewise, any boy who'd ever clutched a wooden sword and whacked his friend with it and then argued with that friend about whether or not that friend was "dead," the argument going on longer than the game had, so long that they were both called in to dinner, that boy had felt that he was fighting for the honor of a princess very much like this one, and for the rest of his life, somewhere inside of him, the stakes of every struggle great or small would be measured against this vividly imagined bounty of princess love. He would always sort of be rescuing her.

By now the idea of the princess as a passive totem of prettiness had been revised and revised, and yes, Tom would admit, princesses could kick ass or wear short haircuts or do whatever they wanted, but somewhere, for everybody, there was still this princess. Not that she was actually out there. You knew that. But an un-erasable part of you still thought you might get to meet her if you slayed enough dragons.

Tom did not doubt for a second that she was a princess. Everything about her said "princess," and said it in a measured, assertive-yet-soft, regal tone. A princess tone. And then she turned and, in an actual princess tone, said: "Greetings. I am the princess."

"Hi," Tom said, "I'm Tom."

"Of course," she said. She had one of those accents that's incredibly distinguished but not quite from anywhere in particular. "I have heard much of your coming."

"You have?" Tom said.

"Yes. You are the Chosen One, are you not?"

"So they say," Tom said. In his head, it had seemed like the cool thing to say, but when he actually said it, he realized he had no idea what he meant by it.

"Come closer, Tom," she said. "I must tell you a secret."

"Uh, okay," Tom said. He took one step forward. He was nervous and he didn't want to overcompensate or undercompensate and he was pretty sure he smelled like the worst kind of garbage so he wanted to be far away so as not to offend her or creep her out but he also wanted to be so, so much closer.

"Closer," she said. Tom stepped closer. *This is definitely close enough*, he thought.

"Closer," she said again, this time a little more playful and a lot more authoritative, so Tom took several steps, and then an additional one for good measure, until her impossible face was the only thing on his mind's movie screen, and he felt like he'd stepped into some sort of princess-generated electrical field. *The last step was probably a mistake,* he thought. *That was one step too many and I've definitely messed it up.*

"Closer," she whispered.

He stepped even closer. Now his dirty white sneakers were touching the hem of her skirt. "That's better," she said. It was the greatest moment of Tom's life. Every moment this close to her was the greatest of his life.

"My father hates you!" she whispered.

"No!" Tom said, pretending to be shocked. He was still whispering.

"Yes!" She was still whispering too. A look of real dread came into her eyes. "I cannot believe I'm saying this, as he is mine own blood, but he is in league with foreign enemies and your coming here, just as the prophecy said you would, puts his plan to surrender our kingdom to those enemies in jeopardy!"

"Really?" he whispered. He did not have to pretend to be shocked this time, because he really was shocked.

"It's true! He seeks to undermine your confidence so that you will return home and not fulfill the prophecy! But you must stay here and do it! At all costs, at the risk of your own life and limb, you must stay here and do as was prophesied, or we shall all perish, or worse!"

This was great! Well, it wasn't great for this princess or for the king's endangered subjects, but it was great for Tom, because it explained everything. The kingdom was so unimpressive because the king was weakening it to make a takeover easier for the enemy, breaking the will of the people so they'd never fight back. It explained why the king was dismissive of Tom: he didn't want him to succeed. And it was great for Tom because a beautiful princess was six inches away from him, telling him he was their only hope, telling him she was his only ally, telling him her life was in his hands, and mauling him. Not in a painful way, just in a way where every time what she said got more dire she would move her hands somewhere on Tom's torso and squeeze, tightly, as if her life depended on it. Tom's first instinct was to touch her, just her hand or something, the way she was touching him, but he didn't want to be rude, so he spent all that energy throwing a little mental party, and at that party, every part of his personality was toasting him, saying, *YOU DID IT!*

"Promise me you shall stay and fulfill the prophecy." She seemed close to tears.

"I promise."

"*Promise me!*" She was squeezing his arm so hard now. Tom had no complaints.

"I promise, my liege!" *Liege* might have been a little bit too much. Was she his liege even if he wasn't from here? Or was he her liege, since he was the Chosen One? He probably shouldn't fling *lieges* around if he wasn't sure.

"Call me Pira," she said.

"I promise, Pira."

"Now—quickly—kiss me to seal the promise!"

Tom had had a "first kiss" already, technically. There was so much first kissing between the ages of eleven and fifteen that one had even trickled down to him. But when the princess asked him to kiss her he felt like he'd never kissed anyone. This, like everything when it came to princesses, was different.

"Are you sure?"

"Yes!"

He began to lean his head in. Her eyes closed.

A dimple just next to her bottom lip appeared for a half second. He never would have noticed it if he'd had his eyes closed like you were supposed to when you kissed someone, and it reminded him that he should close his eyes, and he was about to close them when he saw it again: the dimple. Not a smiling dimple, which was typically on a person's cheek. It was the kind of dimple you got when you were supposed to be paying serious attention in class but someone farted and you were trying really hard not to—

"BWA-HA-HA-HA-HAAAAAAA!"

Her shrieking laugh doubled her over. The head Tom had been one second away from kissing was now planted firmly in her skirts as she cackled.

"Sorry! Sorry! I couldn't keep—I couldn't keep it going. Ohmigod! Ohmigod. You should have seen your face. Seriously? Seriously." The voice now coming from Pira was totally different. "Did you like that, though? 'You must fulfill the prophecy!'" She switched back into her regal princess voice for a second. "My like, princess voice? Pretty good, huh? I was like, about to crack up the *whole* time! You seriously bought it, didn't you? It's okay! I was like, superconvincing! Not to be all, like, self-absorbed or anything."

Tom backed away from her. She was still pretty, and her eyes were still striking, but there was something about them that was now, well, crazy.

"So you're not the princess."

"Oh no, no, no, no, I totally am, but *seriously*"—she filled each hand with skirt ruffles and brought them to her sides—"who would wear *this*?" Then she resumed cracking herself up.

"Is your name even Pira?"

"Oh yeah! I'm *Princess Pira*," she said like a haughty

courtier, tucking her head into her neck to give herself a double chin. "No seriously, I am, it's just like, the whole 'princess' thing is so"—and she mimed throwing up.

"So there's no conspiracy between your father and—"

"I don't think so, *God,* how bad would I feel if there actually was? Can you imagine? No, I was just, like, entertaining myself, I guess."

Tom had wanted so badly to believe her. He had been very happy in a world where there was a reason why the king hated him, and he was still recovering from the whiplash of being pulled right back out of it.

"Hey, cheer up, okay? Hey! This'll be fun, wait here."

She jumped up and ran out of the room, so fast that the stool she'd been sitting on wobbled from leg to leg before it finally stopped. Tom sat down on it. He told himself not to be surprised if it turned out to be a hundred snakes pretending to be a stool. Nothing here was what it seemed: it was worse.

"*Bang bang!* Gotcha, cowpoke!" Tom turned and saw Pira, standing in the doorway, dressed as a cowboy, pointing toy revolvers at him. At least, he hoped they were toys. She was wearing a fake mustache. It was long, curly, and brown. She had transformed convincingly from classic princess to classic cowboy in about six seconds.

"Hilarious, right? I've got like tons of costumes. My dad ordered the clothes guys to bring me anything cool that they find."

"How do you know what cowboys are?"

"*Everyone* knows what cowboys are. Don't be crazy."

"Well then what are they?"

"Guys who look like this and say what I just said!"

It was hard to argue with that.

He sat on the stool as she paraded before him in legitimately impressive Viking and pirate costumes. They both had mustaches. When she came out dressed as a race-car driver complete with a gold-visored helmet, Tom was relieved to finally see a costume without a mustache. Then she lifted the visor on the helmet. *Oh, there it is,* Tom thought: *mustache.*

Finally she came out wearing a puffy multicolored jacket and neon-orange warm-up pants, and no mustache.

"What is this one supposed to be?" Tom said.

"This is just what I wear," she said.

Tom sighed aloud. He couldn't help it. He knew it was unreasonable and probably sexist to expect a princess to dress the way Pira was dressed when he first laid eyes on her, and he could imagine his mom yelling at him, telling him that princesses could be whatever they wanted, even race-car drivers with mustaches, and he knew she would have been right. But he'd wanted her to actually be the way she seemed. For a moment, it was so like how he'd wanted it to be.

"What's the matter?" she asked. "When you came in you were all," and she pantomimed eagerness and excitement, "and now you're all," and she pantomimed depression by half closing one eye and letting her tongue loll out of her mouth like she'd just sustained a head injury.

"I dunno."

"Come on. What is it? Am I freaking you out? I'm not freaking you out, am I? I'm freaking you out. Oh God."

She started to squeeze the front pockets of her track jacket as hard as she'd squeezed Tom's arms back when she was the capital-P "princess." She stared down at the ground.

"No, no, it's not that! Seriously, it's not. Your costumes are amazing."

"They're *hilarious*," she corrected him, sounding close to tears.

"They're hilarious, right, that's what I meant."

"What is it then?"

"I don't know how to say it without, uhm. Offending you."

"It's fine. I want to know. *Tellll meee*," she said, hopping around like a six-year-old who has to pee.

"Okay, well, your dad, right? He does hate me, you were right about that."

"He does? That's too bad, but it's not a surprise. He's kind of like that. Hates everything. It's sort of his job. I wouldn't take it personally."

"I'm trying not to, but it seems like the only person who likes me here is Gark, and your dad says no one respects him."

"That's pretty right, yeah. About no one respects Gark."

"I mean, I don't get it. Gark's just happy, right?"

"Right, but like my dad would say, he's happy in an *opt-o-mistic* way," she said, over-enunciating "optimistic" and pronouncing it like it had an *O* in it, which led Tom to believe it was a word she didn't use very much. "It means he's looking forward to things, trying to make them better, instead of being happy in a settled way, where you're just, like, 'eh, this is what I have, could be a lot worse and it probably will be a lot worse so I guess it's fine for now.' I'm happy too, I mean, I laugh a lot, but my dad says it's normal for kids my age to experiment with laughter and that as long as it's, like, laughing at stuff, it's healthy, because it's, like, a healthy cynicism. That's why he's okay with my costumes. It keeps me busy and I only like 'em 'cause they're stupid and ridiculous. If I just started, like, jumping around going *TRA-LA-la* for no reason, just 'cause I was happy, that's when he would be worried and tell me to knock it off, which is fine, 'cause I'd never do that anyway, eww."

"It's just . . . I never expected to be the Chosen One of anywhere, so it's cool for that reason, but if I'm the Chosen One of a place like this, what does that say about me?"

"What do you mean, a place like this?"

"I just mean—I just mean—" Tom said, stumbling.

"You mean it sucks?"

"You guys say that here too?"

"Of course we do, we *live* here! Of course it sucks! No one here would ever argue with you about that. Wanna make friends here? Just go into any place out there, any house or whatever, and say, this kingdom sucks, your house sucks, you suck. And that person'd be like, 'Yeah, it does, doesn't it? You suck, too! Wanna stay for dinner?'"

"Well, if you all agree it sucks and you're all just fine with it, what does it say about me that I'm your Chosen One?

Does that mean I'm supposed to change everything? Because it doesn't seem like any of you want things to change and I wouldn't know where to start."

"Wow," Pira said, "you're pretty negative."

"Thanks a lot."

"No, I mean it!"

"I know you do!"

"No, I mean it as a compliment! I honestly don't see why my dad doesn't like you. You guys are like, a lot alike."

"Okay, fine, but 'negative' wouldn't be considered a compliment where I come from."

"Maybe it's good that you're here then. Maybe this is like, where you belong. I mean, you just found out there's this whole other place than the place you're from, and in it, you're like, special, you're like, a hero, and all you can think about is how much you don't like everything. I'd say that makes you pretty negative. For real. Like, Gark's-dad-level negative. I would seriously not be surprised if my dad hired you to give me lessons."

She was totally right and Tom knew it. He felt like a completely ungrateful piece of crap. There were probably tons of kids all over the world who would trade places with him in a second. A lot of them wouldn't even need for the other place they'd discovered to be through a fold in the fabric of reality. They'd never left the town they were born in, they'd never been one state over, they'd never been on a plane. If they were from a hot place they'd be grateful just to get to go to a place where it snowed, and if they were from a place where it snowed, they'd be grateful for a place with a beach. Here he was in the midst of this other universe no one on Earth had any idea existed and all he could think of was how it was mostly made of junk from Earth and how much that sucked.

So: he wouldn't do it. If his task was to be the most miserable person among the most miserable people, he wouldn't do his task. He would do something else. He would find the beauty in this world. He would fulfill the prophecy in his own way and be his own kind of hero. He would do it for Pira, even if she didn't understand why he was doing it and would have thought he was perfectly heroic just for making fun of stuff, which is pretty much all he did back home.

Suddenly the king and Gark burst in. Or rather, the king entered normally and Gark burst in. It seemed like it was maybe the only way he was capable of entering a room.

"We've got it! We've got it," Gark said. "We have reached,"

he said, drawing himself up in an attempt to look important, "a *compromise*."

"Yes," the king said, "that is what you might call it, if a
compromise was an agreement between two parties where
one of the parties holds all the power but is merely making
concessions to the other party so the other party will stop
annoying him."

"Here it is!" Gark said. "Here is our compromise plan
for how you may remain here and be our Chosen One and
fulfill the prophecy that foretold your coming."

"Though it is my desire to see you fail spectacularly for
reasons I explained to you in private," the king said, "it is
also my concern that any attempt at heroics on your part
might inspire certain segments of the populace, and this
would be a very bad thing, as heroics have been tried before
in the service of the kingdom of Chhhhdddrrrdd, and they
were a heartbreaking failure. In fact, it is what inspired my
policy of reduced expectations, and I do not wish to see that
work undone. That is why, if you are to be our Chosen One,
you will do so in a limited capacity, in a preexisting role
here in the kingdom. I am prepared to offer you the title of
Executive Assistant to the Undersecretary in Charge of the
Royal Rat-Snottery."

"Rat-Snottery?"

"There are these big rats we get in the fields around Grrrhhetphtpp," Pira chimed in, "but they like, have this condition where their noses get so filled up with snot they die before they're big enough to eat."

"Precisely," said the king. "So it is the task of the Rat-Snottery to clear said snot from their noses and bottle it. It is quite versatile. Used for a variety of things."

"It's actually not so bad with the technology they have now," Gark said. "You don't even have to do it with your mouth anymore."

7

"YOU SHOULD REALLY check out the Rat-Snottery," Gark said. "I'll take you by there. Come on."

And then they were out in the street, or whatever they called the endless tangle of dodgy spaces between countless blanket forts and lean-tos and half structures. Tom was speechless. His "destiny" was a job. His mom was already pestering him to get a job in the real world. And he'd been dreading it and avoiding it, but he might have embraced it and gotten a job at Kmart if he knew that waiting on the other side of a portal in a clothes Dumpster in the parking lot was a gateway to a world in which he was a hero. He didn't think he'd feel the same way if he knew that, waiting on the other side, was just another job, especially a job as assistant to the guy in charge of rat-snot.

As they walked, he tried to distract himself by looking at the garbage around him. He stepped over a cereal box with a soccer player's picture on it. He didn't recognize the player or the brand of cereal. *Is this British garbage?* He looked up from the cereal box and he saw something magnificent, something that must have been garbage from a special effects studio.

Standing just outside of the nameless kingdom, its eyes staring straight into Tom's when he looked up, was a replica of a fantastic creature. It was a sort of a dragon-dog, just a little bigger than any dog he'd ever seen. Its skin was a rich purple marbled with blue, and its dark green eyes were a thousand miles deep. He wondered what movie it had been in, or what art exhibit, or whether it had simply been in some lunatic sculptor's basement for years, the guy going down every day to work on it just a little bit. It had been worth all that time, he thought.

Then it blinked.

It was alive. Tom ran toward it. He felt he had to. There was something in its big green eyes that said, *Get here as fast as possible.*

He'd been trailing behind Gark, who was talking so fast trying to sell him on the Rat-Snottery that he didn't notice his Chosen One slipping away. Tom covered the patch of dirt between him and the edge of town in seconds and ran out to the beast. It was so still except for the blinking. It didn't have fur or feathers or scales, but skin like liquid glass holding in a churning sea of purple and blue. There was a storm system inside of it, with little rivulets of blue electricity that would become visible every so often, like if the veins on your arm were constantly shifting beneath your skin and were also made of lightning.

Magic, Tom thought.

The beast flared its nostrils and reared up on its haunches, exposing a belly criss-crossed by the same blue streaks as the rest of its body, with one long yellow interior stripe running down its center. Standing on two legs, it was easily twice as tall as Tom. Tom was aware that he should probably be scared, but he couldn't find fear anywhere inside of him. He just felt awed and calm. Then it started to fall forward, and its front paws landed on Tom's shoulders, and the force would have driven him straight into the ground were it not for what seemed like some graceful weight distribution on the part of the beast. Its mouth was big enough to bite his head off, but he still couldn't find any fear, any survival instinct. He was filled with a totally un-Tom-like certainty that everything was going to be okay. He looked into the twin translucent planets of the thing's eyes and all of the sudden, he was somewhere else.

He was high above an unbroken layer of cloud that stretched on forever in every direction, and he was falling, or rather not falling, but gliding down, fast as anything, and he saw something small breaking the cloud layer the way a boat cuts the water. Through the V-shaped break in the clouds, Tom could see a crystal kingdom on a jagged mountaintop, a thing of insane precision and daring and beauty. The sun glinted off the cloud-parting spire that crowned the kingdom, and Tom was fully enveloped in the glare.

Then he was down there, circling a network of structures cut out of diamond, connected by sky tunnels, built into the side of a hellish and inhospitable mountain. He saw strong men in crystal armor filled with colored cloud, gorgeous girls in long dresses that were half vapor. They lived in homes that were like bubbles, their transparent walls filling with a rainbow of swirling gases when they needed some privacy. Smoke and flame of every color shot through the city's heart. A void howled at the center of it all, and a huge orb of glass like a miniature gaseous planet hovered just outside of this void. He saw ten thousand crystal-clad soldiers marching in a bowl-shaped parade ground. As he descended toward the ten thousand soldiers, he realized these weren't just images flashing before his eyes, he was a part of this: the soldiers began looking upward and hailing him. A hero's welcome. A Chosen One's welcome.

"Tom! Tom!" Could it be the men greeting him? No, it was a single voice, coming from very far away, struggling to be heard over the fierce wind that blew out of the void. The voice grew louder.

"TOM!"

It was Gark.

Tom remembered where he actually was just in time for something to hit him in his side, sending him rolling out of the creature's grasp. Gark had tackled him, and they'd both fallen into a human heap. There was a roar that sounded like it came from six huge metal lungs, and Gark was knocked off of Tom by the beast. It stood over Tom on all fours, claiming him, and its internal lightning ricocheted up to its once-peaceful green eyes and set them on fire. The eyes met Tom's and he was immediately in the fire and then breaking through it, and then he was back above the kingdom.

The cloud cover was draining away in every direction, and for the first time Tom could see that the mountainside kingdom of diamonds was surrounded by vast plains of permanent war, and he was everywhere at once, watching slave armies being driven against one another like opposing tides by diamond-armored men dictating their movements from the orb hovering over the battlefields. He saw the valley parade ground converted into an arena for gladiatorial combat, the stands full of bloodthirsty fans, and one combatant was a centaur-like thing driven mad by starvation, and the other combatant was Tom.

Then he was back in the nameless kingdom and it was on fire and all the citizens were being driven out, single file. Among them were the king and Pira and Gark. And then Tom saw Gark in real life, and he was relieved to see he had not been captured. Partially he was relieved because he sort of liked Gark, but also he was relieved because Gark had snatched him out from under the dragon-dog and was pulling him back toward the kingdom, which was not actually on fire.

The creature unleashed another metallic six-lunged roar.

Gark yelled, "*Slowwave truepants!*" Tom thought: *That's a weird response.*

They ran a few more steps, then Gark yelled, *"Close!"* He stopped running and let Tom go. Why was he stopping? He was just standing there, and the creature was running straight at them. Gark was definitely a goner. The dragon-dog leapt, but then crumpled in midair just inches from Gark's face. It fell to the ground, like it had collided with a window. The mixture of gases beneath its skin roiled as the thing stared Gark down with pure hatred, and its internal lightning began to congeal in little pools of energy on its skin, gathering and meeting and growing until the thing barked and sent the concentrated electricity at Gark like a dragon's fire-breath, but made of blue light. It was impressive, but it danced away harmlessly over the surface of the invisible barrier that had protected them. The monster turned and slunk away over the featureless surface of the land beyond the nameless kingdom. Gark turned to Tom.

"Whoa! Sorry about that."

Tom just stared at him. Gark offered him a hand, and dusted him off once he was standing upright.

"So, now you've met an Elgg."

"That's an Elgg?" Tom was still trying to catch his breath.

"Yup. It's an emissary of the Ghelm. They're the people we share this world with. Or . . . I dunno if 'share' is the best way to say it. They'd enslave us and burn our whole village if it weren't for the Wall. We can cross it going out, but nothing can come in. And if we cross it going out like you just did and we want to get back in we have to bring it down for a second and put it back up."

"I thought you guys said you didn't have magic."

"We do! It's just that our native magic's something different entirely. You want to see an example?"

"Sure." He waited for Gark to give an example. Gark just stood there.

"Ew, who farted?" Gark said.

Tom smelled it too. "Not me!" he said, which was the truth.

"Neither did I," Gark said. "In fact, no one farted. But the spell makes you think someone did. That's *our* magic."

"Oh. Great."

"The Ghelm send those things over here, hoping to catch one of our citizens outside the Wall. They'd take them back and torture them and try to find out how to bring it down. There's a couple of words, and everyone knows them, but no one would ever tell. Ever."

"Maybe what I'm supposed to do is like ... defeat them?"

"Sure! Maybe you'll work so hard in the Rat-Snottery

we'll accumulate tons of rat-snot and they'll be really intim-
idated and surrender?"

Tom realized Gark was not being sarcastic.

"Speaking of which, they close soon! We'd better hurry
so you can check out your office."

"I'll check it out next time."

"What do you mean?"

"It's late at night in my world. I should probably be
heading back."

"Oh . . . okay," Gark said. "Let's go find my conveyance."

There was a diaper hanging on a stick poking up out of the
sea of old clothes. Gark told Tom that all he had to do was
hold his breath and hold on to the stick and go ten or so feet
down and before he knew it, that little part of the universe
would swoosh around like a revolving door and deposit
him back in his own world. The sun was on its way to setting and the water was cooling off. The oarsmen who had
agreed to take Tom and Gark out to this spot lit a torch as
Tom climbed into the water.

"So," Gark said, "I'll be back tomorrow and then we'll
get started?"

"Give me a few days, okay?" Tom said.

"I really think you should've taken a look at the Rat-Snottery," Gark said. "They're doing some great things these days with nostril wideners."

"It's just . . . I have to think about it," Tom said.

"Think about what?" Gark said.

"All of this," Tom said. "It's a lot, is all. So, I'll see you in a few days?"

"Uhm . . . okay," Gark said. "Are you mad at me?"

"What?" Tom said. "No! No. I mean . . . the pretending-to-be-my-dad thing. That was . . . weird. If you could not do that again, that'd be good."

"Yeah," Gark said. "Yeah . . . that was dumb."

"It's okay," Tom said. "Well . . . bye."

"Bye," Gark said, the way you said it when someone was leaving much sooner than you'd expected them to.

Tom grabbed the pole and went down hand-over-hand into the water. Despite the burning, he opened his eyes and watched the dark hulk of the bottom of the raft outlined in the dying daylight and the glow of the oarsmen's torch as it rowed away from him. The boat had disappeared and his lungs were starting to burn as much as his eyes when the revolving door turned and spat him and a whole lot of soapy water back into the donation box.

The box's chute screeched as he pushed it open. He climbed out. It was still nighttime. He took his phone out to check the time but he remembered his phone was very likely broken from having been underwater. The screen was dark. He held down the power button. The screen flashed bright white before going dark again, this time for good.

Tom started walking home, a boy in saturated clothing walking alone through a darkened subdivision. He didn't love the idea of almost drowning twice every time he wanted to make a trip to his nameless kingdom. At least he'd know better than to bring electronics next time.

He reached the apartment building. Tired as he was, he took the stairs two at a time so he could be home that much sooner. From the open balcony hallway of the second floor he could see the sun just starting to rise in the distance. He tried to put his key in the door as quietly as possible.

There was someone sitting in the recliner in their living room. It was his mom. She was asleep in a bathrobe. Quiet as he'd tried to be, her eyes sprang open as soon as he stepped off the welcome mat.

"Where were you?"

His life in this world was about to get worse.

8

"DUDE?"

It was lunch period on Friday, the day after the first night of the fall play. Tom and his best friend, Kyle, were sitting at their usual table in the lunchroom, or rather, their usual corner of the cooler, older drama kids' usual table. Last year they'd been, at best, tolerated after they staked out the very end of the table. Even though they'd gotten to talk to and be funny in front of a lot of the older kids during the fall play, they still sat in the corner. No need to push their luck.

Tom had his head resting on the metal bar behind him that corralled the line of kids waiting to get food and had been staring straight ahead for five minutes, his untouched chili cheese burrito cooling in front of him, when Kyle took it upon himself to say something.

"You okay, dude?"

"Huh? Yeah, yeah," Tom said. "Just tired."

"I sent you a text in second period."

"My phone's broken."

"Yeah? That sucks! What happened?"

Tom thought long and hard about his answer. When he'd come home last night, or really very early this morning, he'd told his mom that he hadn't answered her calls because his phone was broken. His story was that some juniors and seniors had gone over to somebody's house after the show and he'd gone along and before he could even call her, he'd gotten thrown in the pool, and he was really sorry, and then he couldn't get a ride back from anyone until much later, and he knew that he should've borrowed someone else's phone and called her but he didn't think, and again, he was really really sorry. She'd called Kyle, and Kyle hadn't known where he'd ended up. He was home asleep when she called. Tom had told his mom that Kyle had left before the people went to the party. Then he'd taken back the word *party*. It wasn't a party. It was just some people hanging out at somebody's house, and there wasn't any drinking there, and no, nobody was doing drugs.

Tom was shocked by how easily all this had rolled out of his mouth. He was even more shocked when his mom believed it. But of course she believed it, it was way more plausible than saying, *I was semi-kidnapped by a guy who was impersonating Dad and then taken to another world.* But he'd still lied to his mom, and he never lied to his mom. He hated to think about the world of lies he'd have to construct if he wanted to justify returning to the nameless kingdom every day. What concerned him wasn't that she'd eventually catch on, what concerned him was that she would keep believing him and believing him and the awful knot he had in his chest would keep growing. She was mad and he was in trouble, but she still trusted him, and today was the first day since he was five and he'd lied about hiding cookies under the couch that he'd ever been unworthy of that trust.

He didn't want to start lying to Kyle, too, so he said: "Doesn't matter. Something dumb. Hey, sorry about my mom calling you."

"It's cool. Where did you end up?"

Tom just shook his head.

Kyle smiled. "Niiiiice."

"No," Tom said, "it wasn't like that."

Kyle knew Tom had been putting all his romantic efforts toward Lindsy Kopec. Tom's romantic efforts included talking to Lindsy whenever she talked to him first, trying to make her laugh in these conversations, and furiously analyzing her every word and movement afterward. Kyle was sworn to secrecy about Tom's feelings, and he was also under strict orders to keep a watchful eye on her interactions with other guys, Tom's romantic rivals, and report back nonstop for the comparing of notes. So Kyle had to know that Tom wouldn't have just randomly hooked up with some other girl. Kyle also had to know that if Tom had actually gotten anywhere with Lindsy Kopec, he would not have been silent for most of lunch with his head slumped against a metal bar, he would have been standing at the cafeteria cash register buying sodas and chips and snack cakes for everyone who came through the line, never mind the cost, high fives all around.

So he could tell Kyle it wasn't a girl, but he couldn't tell Kyle what it actually was. He wasn't sure he knew himself. He didn't even know what to call it. He wasn't going to tell anyone, so that saved him from speaking its name aloud. But he still had to think about it. And he couldn't just make a random noise in his head every time he thought about it, the way they did when they were referring to it: "Gghurrrghhpfp" or "Wrrrrrrrrrrrrt" or whatever. He'd asked his brain to come up with a temporary name for the kingdom so he could use it while thinking about whether or not he wanted to go back there. His brain had answered:

CRAP KINGDOM.

It fit. He knew, and frequently used, words way stronger than "crap," but it wasn't like this nameless kingdom was so offensive that a stronger word would even apply. It was bad, but no effort had gone into its badness. It was just plain *crap*. It would have to try harder if it wanted any other swear-word name.

He didn't like that he thought of it that way. Every time he thought of it as Crap Kingdom, it seemed crappier. It was like the time an elementary school friend of Tom's had gotten tagged with the name "Stinky," and though Tom had never thought of him that way, the more other kids called him that the more Tom started to notice, *Hey, you know what? He is kind of stinky.* And Tom was never sure if it was just that he'd heard him called that so many times that his mind suddenly tricked him into thinking this kid who had once been his friend really was stinky, and it didn't really matter, because if you kept hanging out with Stinky you might get tagged with a mean name yourself. "Stinky 2" or something.

Tom had always felt awful about that and he hoped he was now mature enough not to let a nickname for a thing come to stand in for the thing itself. He was almost an adult. He couldn't wait to be an adult, in fact, and adults took things as they came. They realized that everything wasn't always going to be exactly how you wanted it, even fantasy worlds. After all, it was still a magical universe that was a secret to everybody but him. Wasn't that enough?

CRAP KINGDOM, his mind answered. *CRAP KINGDOM*.

"Do you need to talk about anything?" Kyle said.

It was a weirdly mature question coming from Kyle, and Tom felt bad for making their friendship, which consisted mostly of penis jokes and quoting *The Venture Bros.*, so momentarily serious.

"No," Tom said. "I'm okay."

After eating just about nothing at lunch, Tom went to his fifth-period class, American History, and continued staring into space, thinking and worrying. He wasn't missing much by not paying attention, because his teacher, Mr. Marshall, had turned what was supposed to be a lecture on

Patrick Henry into a slide show of pictures of himself and famous basketball players he'd had the pleasure of teaching summer youth sports workshops with. The lights were off, which made it even more jarring when the door opened and the room flooded with light, and standing in the doorway was a police officer.

Mr. Marshall paused in the middle of a story about one of his famous basketball buddy's hilarious golf cart antics and nodded to the police officer. The cop nodded at Mr. Marshall, then looked out at the class.

"Tom Parking?"

Tom's stomach, not weighed down by any lunch, jumped all the way into his chest.

It was the middle of the period, so there weren't a ton of kids around to stare at Tom as he and the police officer made their way down the hall. But the kids they did pass, all of them swinging oversized cardboard hall passes in one hand, stared at Tom and his police escort hard enough to make up for it.

Tom wondered what he was accused of. Was it illegal to climb into clothing donation boxes in the Kmart parking lot? Maybe it was one of those wacky laws they printed on kids' menus at buffet restaurants, strange stuff from cowboy days that was still on the books, like, did you know it's illegal to hitch your horse up outside of a post office? Did you know it's illegal to climb into a clothing donation box with a man who's about to accidentally set himself on fire once his magic spell goes haywire?

They entered the front office. Secretaries stared at Tom with a mix of fascination and disgust. Principal Scott stood outside of his office, dwarfed by a tall man in a suit standing across from him. The principal looked excited to be in a situation that required him to be serious. The man in the suit was rattling off a list of words that Tom might have thought were exciting if they weren't being said about him.

"...arson, car theft, possession with intent to distribute. The kid's a one-man crime factory, moving on a Federal level." The serious-looking man seemed to be purposely speaking loud enough for everyone in the office to hear.

There must be some kind of mix-up, Tom thought. Then he realized that's what guilty people always said. No matter what happened, he needed to remember not to say "There must be some kind of mix-up."

"Mr. Parking," the principal said.

"Mr. Parking," the serious-looking man said. "I'm Agent Taylor. Principal Scott, is there an office we can utilize?"

"Of course," the principal said. "Right this way."

The principal stared at Tom with that same mix of disgust and fascination as he led them down a little hallway to a conference room lined with posters about the importance of good nutrition and exercise and character, all of them featuring either ducks, apples, muscular people rowing boats, or the White House.

"You may want to wait outside," Agent Taylor said to the school police officer. "Frankly, we have no idea what this child is capable of."

The agent opened the conference room door and nodded for Tom to go inside. The school police officer looped his thumbs in his belt and gave Tom a good final dose of staring.

Tom walked in. He heard the door shut.

"Have a seat," Agent Taylor said.

Tom sat. Agent Taylor walked slowly up to the table. He leaned on forward on it. He looked at Tom and smiled.

"Fun, right?"

Tom was silent.

"It's me!"

"I ... don't ..."

"Gark!" Agent Taylor said.

"Oh," Tom said. So he wasn't about to go up the river for crimes he did not commit. Tom realized he could relax.

Then he realized he could not relax.

"*What?*" Tom said.

"Yeah, just coming to see if you'd given any thought to our offer!" Agent Taylor who was Gark said. "Hope you don't mind if I keep this face on. Figure I'm gonna have to walk out of here, and I wouldn't want to embarrass you."

"You wouldn't want to embarrass me?" Tom yelled. "That's why you took me out of class and told everybody in school that I'm some kind of criminal mastermind?"

"You're lucky that sarcasm is our main form of communication, or I don't think I would know you weren't being serious right now," Gark said. He lowered his head like a moping child, which was a really strange thing to see a movie-star-handsome FBI agent do. "You didn't like me pretending to be your dad, right?"

"Right."

"So I figured why not do something that would justify you being gone from school for a long time, which you probably will be when you're spending more and more time as our Chosen One," Gark said. "Plus, I thought you'd think it was cool. I thought you guys thought criminal masterminds were cool."

"It's a cool thing to read about, not a cool thing to be," Tom said. "I still have to live here. I can't just disappear. And even if I could just disappear, I don't think I'd disappear just so I could come with you and eat rat-snot!"

"You don't *have* to eat it," Gark said. "I was very clear about that! They have these tongs now—"

"That's not the point. The point is ... my phone broke. I got in trouble. I had to lie to my mom. And if stuff like this is gonna keep happening, I don't know if I want to go back."

Now Gark was silent.

Tom hadn't wanted to decide anything until he'd at least had a full night's sleep, but Gark's coming here now had forced him to pull out a rough draft of his thoughts on the subject and pass them off as the final project.

"How about this," Gark said. "I'm sorry. I'm sorry I pretended to be your dad. I'm sorry I pretended to be this." He gestured to his face. "Just ... think it over a little more. And when you come to a decision, just write it down and drop it in the box. I'll warn the guys on the lake to be on the lookout for it. They'll do me a favor. They love me."

"Okay," Tom said.

Tom got up. Gark opened the door for him.

"Everything go all right?" the school cop said to Gark who he thought was Agent Taylor.

"Yes, it did," Gark said.

Tom looked at Gark.

"Oh, by the way," Gark said, addressing the principal and all the staring secretaries. "There's been a huge misunderstanding. This boy is innocent of all charges. It was . . . another boy."

"Oh," the principal said. "Well, I'm glad that's sorted out."

"I'm just gonna head back to class," Tom said. He looked at Gark one last time. Gark looked back at him.

"Well," said Gark as Agent Taylor. "See you later, Tom."

Tom didn't say anything. He half smiled at Gark. He wasn't good at smiling even when he was happy, so he was definitely struggling now.

"Agent Taylor," said one of the secretaries. "Could you please move your van? It's blocking the school buses."

Tom got called down to another office after school: Tobe's.

Tobe was the head of the Drama Department. He directed all the plays and taught all the drama classes, including a class in which older students could direct their own one-act play, so at any time he was overseeing four or five little productions and one big one, in addition to student-run forays into video and comedy and dance. He talked constantly about needing "a life of his own outside of school" and not being able to have it because of all these projects, but then he would turn around and start another new project. Tom and thirty or so other kids loved him for it. He was bald and had a silly-looking mustache, gave no indication of ever having been young, and they would have followed him right into hell.

On the way down, Tom imagined that the conversation would center around Tom's brilliant performance in last night's show, and perhaps the very obvious sparks between him and Lindsy Kopec. Tobe wasn't generous with praise of any kind, and he certainly had never asked Tom about his love life, but for some reason, that was the image that formed in Tom's mind of what was going to happen. When he imagined it, a high five was involved. It was natural that he would be called in to Tobe's office for something good after being called to the principal's office for something bad. Tom felt that the stuff that happened in the Drama Department after school balanced out any unfortunate stuff that happened to him during the school day. It healed his wounds.

Whatever it was, he was going to enjoy it.

"I can't be in the show at all?"

"The school policy on extracurricular activities dictates that a student who misses any portion of the school day for a disciplinary reason can't participate in any activities the following afternoon or evening."

"Okay, but I didn't do anything. The guy told Principal Scott I didn't do anything."

"I understand that."

"You don't believe me?"

"I believe you. But the policy is the policy. I get an e-mail sent to me at the end of every day that tells me who's cleared to participate. You weren't on that list."

"But there wasn't any disciplinary . . . anything, because it was a mistake! It was totally random."

"I understand, Tom. But I'm not supposed to concern myself with that. I'm supposed to concern myself with the e-mail."

"That's so unfair!"

"Yes."

"You won't even call the principal? He'll tell you—"

"Tom, I don't think you did anything wrong. It isn't fair, but this is the policy. I'm sorry. Kyle's the swing, he'll fill in tonight and tomorrow."

"Wait, tomorrow night too?"

"Disciplinary issues from a Friday carry over to the weekend. Again, policy. It's not how I would have it, but it's how it is, and I can't make exceptions. We get to do a lot of very neat, very creative stuff here, and the only reason I'm allowed that freedom is because I stick to their rules."

Tobe's office was awkwardly placed, in a room that was really just a hallway between the auditorium and the drama room and the makeup room and the scene shop. For a moment, Tom could not remember which of the many doors lining Tobe's office he needed to leave through. He knew he needed to leave, though. He thought he might cry, and he didn't want to cry at all, but he definitely didn't want to cry in front of Tobe.

Tobe never would have gotten the e-mail if Gark hadn't appeared in the guise of an FBI agent. Last night Gark had robbed Tom of his moment with Lindsy, and today he had robbed him of the chance to try to re-create that moment after the two remaining performances.

Tom remembered what door he needed to go out of. He started to back up, but something tripped him and he fell backward into the door, hitting the bar that triggered the latch. The door swung open and he fell all the way out into the hallway.

"Oh! Jeez. I'm sorry." Tobe ran out to help Tom up.

Tom looked down to see what had tripped him: it was pink and furry and lying on the floor in a heap. A pink bunny suit, complete with a big furry bunny mascot head sitting on top of it.

"Sorry," Tobe said, "I let some kids use it for a skit in class this morning. They were supposed to hang it up when they were done with it. Are you okay?"

Tom was standing now. "Yeah," he said, "I'm fine."

Now he'd lied to Tobe too.

Tom never knew if something good was going to happen, but he was good at predicting bad things. Not big ones, just little things. As he got on his bike after school, he knew that he would ride home and fall asleep and wake up just when he would have been stepping onstage had he not been banned from the play. He wouldn't set an alarm or anything. It would just happen.

He woke up at 8:04 PM. He experienced the momentary disorientation of waking up when it's dark outside after falling asleep in the afternoon, and then he remembered where he was and who he was and what he'd predicted to himself that day after school, after talking with Tobe.

He heard his mom's keys jangling in the front door. She was just getting home from work. He predicted more bad things. She would wonder what he was still doing home: didn't he have the play tonight? He would tell her what happened. He wouldn't lie, exactly. He would exclude the parts about the FBI agent who was actually Gark but he would tell her that he'd been called down to the principal's office but it had turned out to be a misunderstanding and his name had been cleared. Regardless, she would say something like *"What* is going on with you?" in reference to their talk earlier that week and the phone breaking and the staying out late and then this, missing the play because of disciplinary action. And she would tell him no more plays, no more anything, until he got focused.

He turned out to be right about everything she would feel and say, except he hadn't predicted that, after the whole discussion was over, she would tell him to order a pizza. But that was a good thing, and he was only good at predicting bad things.

* * *

Tom spent the weekend in his room, thinking and sleeping.

He woke up early on Monday morning. He went into his mom's bedroom and sat on the side of her bed. He was never awake before she was, unless he'd stayed up all night trying to finish some essay for school that he'd put off until the last minute, but on this particular day, he'd actually gotten a good night's sleep.

"Mom?"

She rolled over and opened her eyes.

"Hey, I was thinking. . . . I've been thinking about everything you were saying about my life is happening in the present tense and I have to balance school and after-school stuff, so if I come home right after school and just study and work really hard and bring my grades up, I mean, I can bring you progress reports from my teachers and everything. . . . Auditions for the next show are in three weeks. If I work really hard until then, and I mean, not just until then but in general, but from now on, can I audition? Would that be okay? All the stuff that's happened this week, I'm never going to let it happen again."

She took a deep breath. The covers rose and fell.

"Let's see how you do," she said.

* * *

Tom shut her bedroom door quietly and went into the kitchen. He knew there was still a slice of pizza in the fridge. He'd been rationing them out all weekend instead of just eating all the leftovers on Saturday morning the way he usually would've. This, he felt, was a sign of his newfound maturity.

After breakfast, Tom took a notebook from his backpack. He wrote the word *NO* on a piece of notebook paper in big, unmistakable letters with a Sharpie. He ripped it out, folded it up, and stood for a second. Then he crumpled it up and threw it in the trash can under the sink. He bent over the counter and on another sheet of notebook paper wrote *NO* in smaller letters, in pencil. He ripped it out, folded it up, then got a Ziploc bag out of the top left drawer next to the sink and put the folded paper into it. He zipped up the bag and put it in his pocket.

He put his backpack on and went down the stairs and got on his bike and rode to the Kmart parking lot. He stopped his bike next to the clothing donation box and put the kickstand down. He walked to the box. The little door creaked as he opened it. He held it open with one hand and took out the plastic bag with the paper in it and brought it up to the little door, putting it just inside, still holding on to it with two fingers. He paused. Then he moved his two fingers apart and the little bag with the folded piece of paper in it slid down and Tom heard it hit the bottom of the rusty box that would every so often become the portal to another world. He released the handle and the door closed: *Wham*. He walked back to his bike, got on, and rode to school.

part two

9

FOR THE NEXT three weeks, Tom was boring. He came home every day right after school, missing drama meetings and hangouts with Kyle. He did all his homework. Then when the homework that was due the next day was done, he worked on projects and essays that weren't even due for weeks. It was insane. And most insane of all, after the homework and essays and projects were done, he'd just plain *study*. Pop quizzes would be announced in class and everyone would groan but for once, Tom didn't join them. Was this what being prepared was like? It kind of felt like being a superhero. A very boring superhero whose power was taking pop quizzes, but a superhero nonetheless.

At home, when the work was done, he'd watch TV. But

only once the work was done. Then he would have a brief, blissful, satisfied few minutes of watching whatever was on before his eyes started to get heavy and he went to bed. Back when he was the procrastinating type, he could watch stuff for hours, knowing he should go to bed but never feeling tired. Now there were actually periods of time where he didn't have anything he should be doing other than watching TV, but the work involved in getting all that other stuff done made him too tired to actually watch for very long. He was so proud of himself. He wanted to shoot a video of himself turning the TV off at 11:15 and rolling over and going to sleep, and send it to the American Maturity Council.

He'd wake up at 7:30 and actually go out to the kitchen and eat breakfast, and every time he did it he wanted to run to the window, open it, and scream "Look at me! I'm awake before eight AM without anyone having to wake me up! My *mom* isn't even awake yet!" One morning he woke up at 7:29, a full minute before his alarm was supposed to go off. No loud noise or nightmare woke him up, either. His eyes just sprang open with a whole sixty seconds to go before the alarm would buzz. It was eerie. He went out to the kitchen to get a grapefruit, the most mature of breakfast foods.

Every Friday he'd get a progress report from his teachers. On the Friday of his third week of responsible grown-up living, he had two Bs, two B-pluses, two As, and one A-plus.

That night, he heard his mom's keys in the door again at 8:04. He brought the progress report out to her. She looked it over. She smiled. They hugged. She told him to order a pizza.

On Monday after school, Tom sat in the third row of the auditorium waiting for *A View from the Bridge* auditions to begin, feeling like he'd never had more of a right to be anywhere in his entire life.

He put his foot up on the red metal back of the chair in front of him and started bouncing his leg absentmindedly. He saw Lindsy sitting with some of her friends in the front row. He slid down into what he imagined was a cool, devil-may-care pose. Any Lindsys who happened to look back and see him would think, *Oh my, that rebel has no regard for polite society's rules about posture.* Lindsy turned to say hi to her friend Margot. Then she spotted Tom. She smiled and waved. He saluted. She turned back and continued talking with Margot. He immediately felt dumb. Why did he salute? All he needed to do was wave back and smile. That was all that was required. There was no need to try to score points with an interesting variation on the standard smile-and-wave. Then his absentmindedly bouncing leg drove its knee into his mouth. It really hurt.

He looked around to see if anyone had noticed him kneeing himself in the face. They hadn't. He shook it off and looked down at the photocopied script pages they were supposed to read for the audition. Normally, instead of really going over the lines, he'd be sitting back here goofing off with Kyle, but Kyle wasn't there.

"What parts are you gonna audition for?" Tom had asked Kyle earlier that day in the lunchroom. "I was thinking I would—"

"I don't think I'm gonna try out," Kyle had said. Kyle always said "try out" instead of "audition" like it was a baseball team and not a play, just like he said "practice" instead of "rehearsal."

"Seriously? Why?"

Kyle shrugged. "Just some time off."

Tom couldn't remember which one of them had first expressed an interest in doing drama. He didn't remember it being a conscious decision. It was more like they'd been drawn down to the Performing Arts wing by a mysterious voice that whispered: *Hey. You get to stay after school and fool around pretending to be other people and it's actually encouraged. There will be fake guns. There will be fake swords. There will be real girls.*

And there had been all three, though Kyle was the only one who'd kissed any of the girls in an offstage context. Tom wasn't bothered by it. He'd been focusing on Lindsy. In the meantime, there had been tons of chances to do British accents and get attention from crowds and older, funnier kids, so that tided Tom over in the absence of girl activity. He wasn't concerned. He really wasn't.

Even though he definitely wasn't concerned and definitely wasn't jealous, sitting in the auditorium waiting for the auditions to start, Tom was maybe just a little bit glad that Kyle wasn't there. For one thing, it made it easier to prepare, and he was all about preparation now, all about focus.

There were other reasons, too. It wasn't that he was jealous of Kyle, or that he thought Lindsy liked Kyle, or ever would. It was something much less specific.

At the end of freshman year, Tom and Kyle had had tiny chorus parts in the musical. They didn't have all that much to do, which was sort of a gift actually, because it meant they had a chance to sit back and hang out with the older theater kids they'd been admiring all year. One afternoon, they were lingering up against the cinder-block wall at the back of the stage with two older girls, Jessica and Ella, while the choreographer Tobe had brought in especially for the production was running twelve other kids through some dance involving a lot of multicolored silk. Tom and Kyle and the girls were talking at full volume because the choreographer's boom box drowned them out. It was fun.

Then Kyle and Ella went off to get snacks from the snack machine. Tom had given Kyle four quarters and instructions to bring back one of those big Kit Kats and then he was left alone with the other older girl, Jessica. She was looking off after Kyle and her friend as they left and then the choreographer hit the pause button on the boom box and the music stopped and the dancers' silks started drifting down to the ground.

Jessica said, "Your friend Kyle is very handsome."

She didn't say it in a way that indicated she liked Kyle. Supposedly she had a boyfriend who was already in college. She just said it matter-of-factly, like it was something Tom ought to be aware of. It bothered him anyway.

It wasn't that he was jealous. It was just that he didn't need cooler older girls telling him his best friend was handsome like it was something all the adults had gotten together and decided. He and Kyle were supposed to be nerds. They'd had a lot of practice at it ever since sixth grade when Kyle had finally hung up his soccer cleats. They'd finally found this place, the Drama Department, where a nerd was maybe not such a bad thing to be. They could now go about getting girlfriends the way they were supposed to, by having girls realize their nerdy exteriors actually concealed untapped reserves of sensitivity and talent and smartness. No one was supposed to cheat by being just plain old-fashioned hand-some. That wasn't part of the plan. Granted, Tom had never really said the plan aloud, or even really admitted to himself that there was a plan. He just assumed that it was assumed.

So while he would miss his friend, he was also grateful not to have Kyle's supposed matter-of-fact it's-just-out-there-and-people-notice-it handsomeness around. He'd worked really hard to be here. He needed to get a part and perform brilliantly so that he could re-create that magic moment with Lindsy Kopec and then hopefully take things one step further, all while keeping his grades up. He couldn't do all that if he also had to worry about everyone thinking Kyle was so great just because he was good-looking or whatever. Noticing Tom was great would be a lot more rewarding for people because Tom's greatness was inside. It wasn't just a face or a haircut.

Tobe walked down the aisle between the stage and the front row of seats.

"Let's get started," he said.

10

IT WAS THE third name down on the cast list:

ALFIERI—TOM PARKING

Tom was ecstatic.

It wasn't the part he'd wanted, necessarily. There was the male romantic lead, Rodolpho, and Tom hadn't read the whole play yet, but he knew that Rodolpho got to be extremely cool and Italian around the female lead, Catherine, a role Lindsy Kopec had been a shoo-in for. Tom didn't know how to do an Italian accent, but how hard could it be? He'd worked hard at everything these past three weeks. An accent would be no sweat.

Lindsy had gotten Catherine, but Rodolpho had gone to some senior. But Tom's character, Alfieri, narrated the play, so he had a lot of big speeches. Would he rather have a girl fall in love with him for acting suave and romantic, which almost seemed like taking the easy way out, or would he want a girl to fall in love with him for his ability to handle long speeches bursting with big words? The second one, absolutely. There was much more to Lindsy than just her looks, and Tom's performance as Alfieri the narrator would speak to the sophisticated side of her. And if she wasn't into long, well-written, well-delivered speeches, he probably didn't want her anyway. Actually, he probably still wanted her. Once he had her, he was pretty sure he could make her come around on the well-written speech stuff.

He practically galloped into the drama room to get his script from Tobe.

Tom flung his backpack so hard across his bedroom that it smacked the wall before falling onto his bed. Then he flung himself onto the bed equally hard. He unzipped his bag and took out the script. He wondered if he should read the play first or just go through and highlight all his lines. He knew the right answer: he should read the play. But he also wanted to know how many lines he had right away. He decided he'd go through really fast and highlight his lines and then go back through and actually read the thing, and then he'd do his other homework, because as he kept reminding himself, he had to keep up his recent level of excellent academic performance if he wanted to actually be in the play. No problem. He flipped past the five-page introduction by the author, which he told himself he would also read later.

The first line of the play was his, and it was one and three quarters of a page long. Even better, it mentioned Al Capone. *See what happens when you work hard,* he told himself. *You get to say two-page-long monologues about Al Capone in front of Lindsy Kopec.* Well, it wasn't about Al Capone exactly; he was just mentioned. But still.

His yellow highlighter was flying across the page. Marker fumes filled the air. It was the glorious smell of Tobe trusting him to pull this off. He skimmed his lines as he went. This was heavy-duty grown-up drama. He was going to blow the guy playing Rodolfo off the stage with the sheer force of his talent and extreme maturity. He finished highlighting his first speech and took a second to admire the continent of neon-yellow he'd just created. Then he turned the page and skimmed down the side of the next one for his character's name. Nothing. Same thing on the next page, and the next. Not a big deal. He was the narrator, he dropped in and out, he set the scene. He was outside of the story looking in. It was fine—he'd already had the mother of all lines on the very first page. Rodolfo hadn't even had a single line yet.

Then he hit page 30 and there he was again: Alfieri. The role made famous by a young Tom Parking. Again he skimmed the line as he highlighted it. He stopped after two sentences and put the marker down.

The two sentences he'd highlighted read:

```
Who can ever know what will be dis-
covered? Eddie Carbone had never ex-
pected to have a destiny.
```

He read it one more time. This time, even though he knew what the real words were, his mind insisted on hearing it this way instead: *Who can ever know what will be discovered? Tom Parking had never expected to have a destiny.*

He'd made a massive mistake.

*   *   *

Tom couldn't say he hadn't thought about Crap Kingdom at all since dropping the note into the clothing donation box. He had thought about it the way anyone would think about a mystical world they'd just learned existed on the other side of the Kmart parking lot. But his feelings on the subject hadn't really had time to change. He'd been upset about getting in trouble, sad about lying to his mom, and mad about missing the last two nights of the show, and he had immediately channeled those feelings into three weeks of schoolwork and nothing else.

Also, he'd never really said no to anything before. He had spent his life asking to be a part of things and having someone else say no—groups of friends, plays, girls. It was the first time anyone had ever put him in the position to decide his own fate. He had to admit there was something cool about being offered something, especially something that in theory he'd always dreamed of but never thought possible, and then being able to say, "You know what? Not for me." It was a weird sort of power. He felt powerful.

Any time he thought about it, he figured he'd traded a miserable life in a fantastical universe for a decent one in the real world. It was like a more efficient *Wizard of Oz* where Dorothy had landed, taken one look around, said, "I get it, thanks," and then woke up in her bed in Kansas having learned never to look farther than her own backyard without ever having to be kidnapped by flying monkeys.

Now, though, staring down at these words, Tom wondered if he'd made the wrong decision. He had never expected to have a destiny. He'd thought almost exactly that a few weeks ago, the night before Gark came and told him he did have one. You didn't get more than one destiny, did you? When it was gone, it was gone, and he'd sent his away without a second thought and devoted himself entirely to academics. Last year he'd heard this girl Julie saying she wasn't going to audition for the fall play because she was going to take some time off to focus on her studies. Tom thought she was being ridiculous. Now he realized he'd given up an entire universe to focus on his studies.

There had been a thousand reasons, and they'd all been good ones. He didn't want to work in the Rat-Snottery. He hadn't gotten any magical powers. He didn't want to have to lie to his mom a bunch. Existing in this world and in that one simultaneously had seemed impossible. But isn't that exactly what Chosen Ones were supposed to do: impossible things? That night when his mom first told him he needed to focus, really studying had seemed impossible, yet he'd just done nothing but study for weeks on end. He put his mind to it and he actually accomplished it. Who's to say he couldn't have done that in Crap Kingdom? He should have barged in there and said, *Quit it with all this our-kingdom's-name-is-a-random-noise stuff. This kingdom's name is Tom-Town and there will BE. NO. ARGUMENTS.*

Tom stood up and started pacing around his room. It was a tough room to pace around because his new hard-work regimen had not extended to organizing his room and there were dirty clothes everywhere. They made him think of the waterlogged landmasses of laundry in the lake that was the gateway to the nameless kingdom. Sure, it was gross. The whole place was gross. Tom's room was gross, too. If he was honest, Tom was often gross himself. So who was he to judge them?

What if Gark finding him was the only cool thing that ever happened in his entire life? A lot of people got As on their report card and got into good colleges. A lot of people did high school drama. Not a lot of people were mentioned by first and last name in a prophecy in another world. Who can ever know what will be discovered? Tom hadn't stuck around to find out.

He couldn't go back, could he? No. He'd built something here. Something he'd worked really hard for. His home was here. His life was here. His mom was here. Lindsy Kopec was here. He wished he could call Kyle, but his phone was still broken. Not that he'd have confessed everything to him. He just needed to talk to somebody.

He sat back down on his bed and tried highlighting lines to distract himself. It wasn't as much fun as it had been a minute before. All he kept thinking was that this was the stuff he was going to do instead of being a hero. He tried reading more closely. At the end of the play, it turned out that the main character Eddie's destiny involved getting killed in a street fight. *See,* Tom thought, *you don't want to get killed, do you?*

It didn't help, though. Maybe you got killed. Maybe you were a hero. Maybe both. But what could possibly be worse than not finding out and wondering forever?

11

THE NEXT DAY at lunch, Tom couldn't find Kyle. He wasn't sitting in their usual spot. Tom had been looking forward to talking to him all morning. Without his phone, he just had to hope he ran into people. When they weren't where he expected them to be, he didn't know what to do.

"Hey Tom," Jessica, the girl with the college boyfriend, said when Tom sat down at the drama table across from Kyle's empty space. "Congrats!"

"Thanks," Tom said. "Have you guys seen Kyle?"

"He's over there," Jessica said, pointing across the lunchroom to a table by a big window that was totally vacant except for Kyle, who was sitting with his back to them.

"Does he even still like us?" said her friend Ella, twirling one of her pink pigtails around her finger.

"Sure," Tom said.

"Does he *like* like us?" Ella said in a fake husky-sexy voice. She and Jessica cracked up.

Normally this would have bothered Tom, but he was too distracted to worry about who wanted to date Kyle. He needed someone to talk to about destiny. He left his tray of food and his backpack and walked over to Kyle's table.

"What up, Kilroy?" he said to Kyle's back.

Kilroy was Tom's nickname for Kyle. It was also his actual last name. Tom and Kyle had been friends since fourth grade, and sometime in sixth grade, Tom had gotten really into the idea of calling each other by each other's last names. He saw it in movies a lot, especially movies about private schools where everyone wore ties and blazers to class. Tom started attempting to call Kyle "Kilroy" and Kyle, in turn, started to call Tom "Parking." Kilroy sounded pretty normal and natural and even kind of cool, as Tom had intended, but Parking was awkward, so before the end of eighth grade, Kyle stopped calling Tom that and Tom gave up calling Kyle "Kilroy" not long after. It would still slip out again every now and again, a reminder of a shared and dorky history.

"I'm Kyle," Kyle said.

"Oh," Tom said. "Right. Why are you sitting over here?" Tom sat down across from Kyle.

"I'm looking out the window," Kyle said.

"All right," Tom said. There was something weird and far away about the way Kyle was acting. "Are you okay, man?"

"Yes," Kyle said. "I'm very well. I'm very happy to be here."

"That's . . . good," Tom said. "Can I ask you something?"

"Yes," Kyle said.

"Okay, well, and this is all just like, hypothetical. But let's say you get a chance to go somewhere. And you're really excited about it, but you go to the place, and it sucks, and you never want to go back. But then once you're not there anymore, it's all you can think about. Like you feel like . . . it's your destiny."

He expected Kyle to say *Is this about Lindsy?* But Kyle didn't, which was yet more proof that something was going on with him.

"Appreciate the place you're in," Kyle said, still spacey. "Appreciate the sky and the birds and the sun."

Tom nodded. This was actually good advice.

"Appreciate being in a body," Kyle said.

Tom nodded, though this advice was much weirder.

"Now . . ." Kyle said. "Please?" With a small hand gesture, he indicated that Tom should scoot over, because he was blocking the window.

"Okay, sorry." Tom scooted down the bench of the lunch table. Kyle resumed staring out the window. He reached down, grabbed a French fry, brought it to his mouth, and started chewing. He chewed and chewed. He looked down at nothing in particular, as if he'd been moved by a great emotion. Then he looked up at Tom.

"These are delicious," Kyle said. "Would you like one?"

What was wrong with Kyle?

Tom had been pretty much out of Kyle's life for three weeks, phoneless and tucked away in his study cave. Maybe he'd missed Kyle's slow transition into whatever he was now. Maybe he could've prevented whatever it was that had happened. He couldn't help but feel like whatever was going on, it was about him. He wasn't supposed to be here, he was supposed to be through that portal doing whatever he was meant to do, and because he wasn't, existence was flying apart.

* * *

Rehearsals for *View* didn't start until the next day. Tom had the afternoon free. If he was going to go back, today after school would be the only time for a while where he wouldn't miss rehearsal or be missed by his mom.

Once he knew his destiny was secure in that other world, he thought, he'd be able to concentrate in this one.

Tom had been in the donation box for he didn't know how long when he realized he didn't know how frequently or infrequently the portal opened. What if it was once a week, or once a year? His phone was at home, broken, and he didn't have a watch to tell time with. He had no idea how long he'd been inside the box, though it felt like forever. What if he went crazy here in the box, from the heat and subsequent dehydration? This led to another, greater worry: what if he'd always been crazy? He wasn't going to go insane in the box: he was in the box because he'd always been insane. It explained everything. The weird visitor from the weird world, the weird world itself, the way Kyle was acting today—none of it was real. He wondered how much of the past few weeks had been paranoid delusion. Did he still get to play Alfieri?

He should get up. He should get out. He should get his bike from the Kmart bike rack and go home.

He stood up as much as he was able to in the cramped space.

Then the floor disappeared.

12

TOM SWAM UP and up and breached the surface in a nameless kingdom where it was nighttime. A blank blue craterless moon lit up the lake of clothes. Tom swam toward the nearest waterlogged clothes pile and pulled himself up with great difficulty. He walked around the little island of clothes and saw another one that was within leaping distance. He backed up, took several soggy running steps toward the edge, and jumped. In this way, jumping from island to island of socks and shoes and underwear and dresses and T-shirts and rags, he made his way out of the open lake toward the bay of ladders and baskets, all of them abandoned now, moonlit and creepy. He reached the dock and jumped on to it from the final clothes island. He hadn't tripped or fallen once in the entire journey and felt extremely proud of himself.

"Nice try!" someone yelled. "Take it all off, clothes-thief!" At the land end of the dock, a guard stood up and started waving an oar around like he was going to clobber somebody. In this kingdom, an oar's function as a boat pro-peller seemed less important than its function as a people clobberer.

"Hey, I'm just—I'm—I'm the Chosen One!" It just came out. The clothes-raft operators they'd encountered that first day hadn't seemed really into the idea of a Chosen One and he didn't expect this one to be any different, but it was worth a shot.

The man stopped in his tracks.

"Chosen One? I thought you were already here."

"I was," Tom said, "and then I left. But now I'm back. For good." Tom didn't know why he said "for good." He had to be back in his world in time for dinner. But it seemed like something a Chosen One would say.

"Oh," the man said. "Well, in that case, right this way."

He wasn't even being sarcastic.

"If you could not tell the king about this, I'd really ap-preciate it," the man said as he escorted Tom toward a con-veyance. "He said he's changed his mind about Chosen Ones in general and we're now supposed to treat you with the utmost respect and things. So . . . I apologize."

Tom was so glad to hear that the king had reconsidered, and so glad he'd come back to find that out. "Don't worry about it," he said, feeling extremely generous toward all mankind on both sides of the portal. "It could happen to anyone."

Tom bid the night watchmen farewell at the edge of town, then stumbled through the sleeping town toward the castle. When he reached it, he could see flickering light leaking through the planks and portholes. Good, somebody was awake. Tom strode right in. He was the Chosen One, and he was back for good. Well, for good minus daily trips home for dinner and homework and sleep.

He walked into the throne room. Gark and the king were sitting at a table with a third person who had his back to Tom. Tom felt like he'd seen that back earlier that day, on Earth. In the lunchroom. In fact, he'd said "What up, Kilroy" to it.

Kyle turned and saw Tom.

"Tom?"

Tom just stood there.

"Hello, Tom," the king said. He smiled. "I'd like you to meet our new Chosen One."

13

"HEY," KYLE SAID. "What are you doing here?"

Tom had wanted to ask Kyle what Kyle was doing here. Now he didn't know what to say.

"Yes, Tom, please explain why you've chosen to grace us with your presence once again."

"You guys know each other?" Kyle said.

"Unfortunately, yes," the king said.

"What? Really?" Kyle turned to Tom. "Dude, you never told me you knew about this place."

"You never told me you were here, either," Tom said. "What's going on?"

Both Tom and Kyle turned toward the king.

"Kyle, I apologize for the confusion," the king said. He

closed his eyes and began rubbing them with his fingertips the way Tom's mom did when she had a migraine. "Some time before we met you, Tom was incorrectly named as the Chosen One. Thankfully we soon received a corrected prophecy with your name in it."

"There was another prophecy?" Tom said. "How does that work?"

Someone nudged him. Tom turned. It was Gark.

"That's Gark," Kyle said, "Gark, meet—"

"I know!" Tom said.

Gark handed Tom a piece of paper without looking into Tom's eyes. Tom looked at it. It had the same alignment of words on the page as his prophecy, same font, same size type, same everything. It said:

The Chosen One must be retrieved from Earth.

He will bring down the Wall and restore the

kingdom to glory.

His name is Kyle Kilroy.

"This is exactly the same as my prophecy," Tom said.

"With one noticeable difference," the king said.

"Dude, why didn't you tell me?" Kyle said. He didn't sound upset exactly. Just confused.

"I don't know . . . magical kingdoms and stuff . . . you're not supposed to talk about it right? And anyway, it all happened so fast . . . I mean, Gark came and I came here and saw everything and then I went home and got in trouble and decided, I'm not going to do this if all it means is it ruins my life back home and all that happens is I get to work in a rat-snot place."

"Rat-Snottery!" the king corrected him.

"What's that?" Kyle asked.

"Wait," Tom said, "he doesn't have to work in the Rat-Snottery?"

"That was your task," the king said, "an assignment based upon what I felt your capabilities were."

"What's Kyle's task?"

"Redesigning our entire society," the king said.

"What?" Tom said. "I thought you liked things the way they were!"

"We did. Until Kyle."

"What . . . and I say this with, you know, Kyle's my best friend back in our world, but, what makes Kyle so special?"

"I have a tiny spark of optimism within me that I keep

alive strictly so I may familiarize myself with the mind-set of those who might fall victim to optimism, and properly dismantle their hopeful outlook for their own good. Despite my best efforts to resist, Kyle fanned this spark of optimism into a flame with his great wisdom."

"What wisdom?"

"What was it, Kyle, that you said upon that first auspicious meeting?"

"Uhm," Kyle said, seeming embarrassed: "Think positive?"

"*Yes!* That was it. 'Think positive!' Brilliant in its simplicity . . ."

"That's it?" Tom said. "That's basically like saying, 'cheer up.'"

"He said that as well!" the king said.

"You guys have been depressed for generations, and that's all it took? 'Cheer up'?"

"Words to that effect had crossed our minds before," the king said, "but it is not what Kyle says, it is the way he says it."

"I guess I said it cooler before," Kyle said.

"That's really all you want out of your Chosen One?"

"Now that we have it, and we like it, we know that it is what we wanted, yes."

"If somebody had just told me that was all you wanted—"

"How could we tell you? We did not know we wanted it."

"If I'd just known—"

"You said no."

"You kept intruding into my world and bothering me in a way that was totally ruining my life! Did you ever bother Kyle that way?"

"We didn't have to. He said yes right away."

"Before or after he got to redesign your entire kingdom?"

Kyle shrugged. "It all happened pretty fast," he said.

"You don't get to just switch Chosen Ones," Tom said, "especially not based on a prophecy that's been printed out by someone who just learned how to use a computer! Do you guys know what computers are? Or printers? Prophecies come on stone tablets and scrolls, not printer paper!"

"You do realize that by calling into question the validity of the prophecy which names Kyle as our Chosen One, you are calling into question the validity of the prophecy that named you the Chosen One."

"Well, fine, but you said that you never believed any of this prophecy stuff to begin with, it was just something to keep Gark busy."

"Oh," Gark said. His eyes never met Tom's.

"Sorry, Gark," Tom said. "You shouldn't have had to find out this way."

Gark shook his head, shrugged, and kept looking away.

"It was," the king said. "And then I met someone with the characteristics of a true Chosen One. Now I believe that our mission to restore this kingdom to glory is very real. Prophecies do not concern me. My old friend J, the greatest citizen this kingdom has ever known, greater even than Kyle, did not need to have his greatness foretold in any prophecy in order to do what he did. My question is, why have you returned here, to this place you thought so little of?"

"I don't know," Tom said, "I thought I might have missed something."

"You have," the king said.

"Guys!" Kyle said. "Can I—this is all, like, a lot. Can I talk with Tom for a minute?"

"Of course," the king said. "Gark and I will retire to our beds. I would never presume to tell you what to do, Kyle, but you have worked very hard tonight and I recommend you find yourself in bed soon as well."

"I will," Kyle said. "Come on, Tom."

"I'm not mad at *you*," Tom said to Kyle. They were standing in front of the castle a few minutes later. The sun was starting to creep up over the horizon, its light reflected in filth puddles in the alleys of Crap Kingdom.

"Dude, I'm so glad to hear that, because seriously—"

"Hello, Kyle!" shouted a passerby in a cowboy hat and six T-shirts.

"Good morning, Clar. How's the new lean-to comin', man?"

"Going . . . *good*, Kyle!"

"Great!" Kyle shouted back.

The man stopped in his tracks, clearly confused.

"Great's even better then good!" Kyle explained.

"Ah!" said the man, and moved on down the street. "Greaaat . . ." he said, trying it out as he walked.

"Anyway," Kyle said, "seriously, I had no idea about any of this. You being the Chosen One before me, I mean. They never told me anything about it, and if they had—"

"Hi, Kyle!"

"Sorry, one second." Kyle turned to speak to a middle-aged woman who was wearing striped pajama pants and an orange crossing-guard vest. "Vina! What's up?"

"I was just trying to remember what it was you said when you stopped by our house the other day . . . 'Today could be better than . . .' What was it?"

"Tomorrow could be better than today," said Kyle.

"Right!" she said, "Sounds so simple when you say it . . ." and wandered away.

"Do you know everyone here?" Tom said.

"I've been spending a ton of time here," Kyle said. "Anyway, sorry, but dude, if I would've known, I would've at least told you. I mean, I'm mad at the king for not telling me about any of this. We gotta work something out though, seriously, because I know you would love this place if you really, like, I know it's not much to look at but I just feel like there's really so much potential here, for—"

"Kyle?"

Tom and Kyle turned to see, standing at the end of the alley in front of the castle, a girl about their age dressed in bubble wrap. It was wound around her body so many times that you couldn't see anything, and there was so much of it that it was sort of bulky and ridiculous. But she was still a girl dressed in only bubble wrap. "My friends and I were wondering if you would come by later and tell us what things are," she said.

"Sure," Kyle said, "Later. Remember that thing I gave you?"

"Yeah," the girl said, smiling.

"When the thing on that thing points at the 'three,' I'll be there."

"Okay, see you then," the girl said, and disappeared among the men carrying random rolls of fabric, and women pushing hazardous-material containers on hand trucks.

"You didn't tell her whether it was the big hand or the little hand," Tom said.

"It's one of those fancy watches that only has an hour hand," Kyle said.

"Ah," Tom said. "What did she mean by . . ."

"I just tell them about their trash and stuff, like, what it is on Earth. Because they kind of don't know what everything's used for, but I guess you couldn't expect them to."

"I should be getting back to the portal," Tom said. "It's probably getting pretty close to dinnertime on Earth."

"Okay," Kyle said. "No problem."

Tom turned and started trudging down the alley.

"*Tom!*" Kyle yelled after him. Tom turned back.

"Stay still," Kyle said. He smiled, and suddenly, they were standing on two banks of denim and wet cotton on the lake of clothes.

"What." Tom said. "Just. Happened."

Kyle smiled bigger. "Awesome, right?"

Kyle has magical powers, he thought. *MAGICAL POWERS.* Why hadn't he gotten magical powers?

"Yeah," Tom said. "Awesome." He was very upset and confused, and he wanted to be home as quickly as possible. "Okay," he said. "I better go. You coming?"

"Me? Oh, no. I don't go through here anymore."

"What do you mean?"

"I could tell you, but it's going to be so much cooler for you to see it for yourself. And I've been wanting to try it out with someone else anyway. What are you doing after school tomorrow?"

"I have rehearsal."

"Well, right after school. It won't take long. And you're gonna love it. I swear."

"Okay, tomorrow after school. Oh, speaking of school, how come you were so weird today at lunch?"

"Uh, that wasn't—" Kyle started to say, and then stopped himself. "Never mind. You'll see tomorrow."

The thing that made Tom the most upset, more upset than he was about the new prophecy or the magical powers or anything, was the look on Kyle's face when he said *you'll see tomorrow*. He wasn't being smug or mean. He was just excited. Tom wanted to be that excited. Instead he walked out to the water, felt it finally get too deep for him to stand in, and started swimming. He swam out toward the diaper that marked the portal's mouth.

"Hey, I'm really sorry about all this, man," Kyle yelled after him. "It's all so crazy, right?"

"Yeah," Tom said. "It is."

14

KYLE WAS A JOCK. He never hadn't been.

Tom met Kyle in fourth grade. Kyle had spent his elementary school years in all these sports leagues Tom knew about but never realized everyone took so seriously. Kyle's parents had put him in soccer leagues and hockey leagues, and rather than complain about it, the way Tom would have, he'd actually seemed to enjoy it. Kyle would say, "I can't come over and watch *Lost*, I have soccer practice that night," and Tom would say, "That sucks," and Kyle wouldn't immediately agree. It was like watching a good TV show and running around a field getting all sweaty were the same thing to him.

And it was in this world of people who enjoyed

running and sweating that Kyle had picked up these positive clichés. Tom was sure of it. The "think positives" and the "give a hundred and ten percents." Only in the boneheaded world of youth sports could these phrases hold any water. While Tom had always thought of Kyle as a reformed jock, as having traded in the post-practice juice boxes of his youth for the mature black hoodies and graphic novels of adulthood, he now realized, as Kyle repeated all the platitudes the king thought were so genius but apparently wouldn't have been if Tom had said them, the jock had been in there waiting for the right time to pop out and stab their friendship in the back, or kick it in the back with cleats on, or whatever.

Kyle was the new Chosen One, and he had magical powers. This was all Tom could think about as he lay in bed, staring up at the ceiling. Tom would have done everything differently if he'd been given magical powers. He would have even considered that job in the Rat-Snottery if he'd been allowed to clean out the rat's noses with jets of magical flame. Maybe Kyle hadn't even been given the powers, maybe he'd just had them when he'd crossed over. That was almost worse. It meant that Kyle was just better. It meant Tom had no cause to be upset. There was no injustice, there was no one to blame. Kyle was just more qualified for the position Tom had been dreaming of his entire life.

"Come on," Kyle said when Tom met him in the courtyard outside the Performing Arts wing the next day after school like they'd agreed. They trudged around the side of the auditorium to a gravel depression in the ground that was mostly shrouded from view by bushes.

"This is going to be quick, right? I have rehearsal in like, twenty minutes." Tom no longer had any way of telling time since he didn't have a phone, so he just estimated how long it had been since the last bell of the day.

"Don't worry about it," Kyle said.

"I'm just saying, I don't have time to go all the way to Kmart," Tom said.

"No Kmart," Kyle said. He held out his hand. "Grab it."

"What are we doing here, again?"

"Just trust me." Kyle grabbed Tom's right hand in his left and then stood shoulder-to-shoulder with him. "How it works is, we fall backward. I've never done it while trying to bring someone else but it's supposed to work. Like when you were a kid, did you ever try to fall backward just to see if you could do it? Your body won't let you. But if you're with me, at the moment when your body would normally catch you, you'll go. On the count of three," Kyle said. "One . . . two . . . *three!*"

Kyle fell backward, and Tom tried to as well. The moment came, the moment where normally his brain would say "nope" and one of his legs would involuntarily shoot back to catch him, but it didn't happen. He fell for real.

Something ripped open behind him, like he'd fallen through an extra-thick sheet of construction paper, and he was in blackness for a second, still falling backward, his right hand still in Kyle's left, and he could tell by the momentum of his body that he should be hitting the ground, but there was no ground. They didn't fall straight down, either. They kept swinging on the same trajectory, all the way around, as though their feet were attached to a bar and they could only swing around it, and they swung past where the ground should've been again and came all the way up and when they once again reached a standing position they ripped through another sheet of thick time-and-space construction paper and they were somewhere else entirely.

They were still standing. The momentum of the fall, or the spin, or whatever it was, made them stumble forward a few paces.

"Awesome, right?" Kyle said.

Tom looked around. They were standing at the bottom of what looked like a crater. Kyle began to run up the dirt incline toward the crater's rim. "Come on!"

Kyle was looking up over the rim when Tom caught up with him. "Aw, crap," Kyle said. Tom looked up over the edge. On the horizon was Crap Kingdom, a collection of shacks and forts behind a shimmering, curved wall of light. Between them and the kingdom was an expanse of brush, and between them and the brush were a whole pack of the dragon-dogs Gark had called Elggs. The closest one turned its head toward Tom and Kyle. It blinked, its green eyelid coming from the bottom of its eye, and then pulling up from the bottom again like a window shade. It barked its six-lunged bark. All of its brothers looked over and saw the boys.

The wave started from the back. A single rippling band of light passed over, or under, the creatures' skins, like eight TVs all programmed to show different parts of the same image, and when it reached the one closest to Tom and Kyle, passing over the final Elgg's body until it finally winked out at the tip of its nose, they charged.

Tom backed away as fast as he could while trying not to trip. Kyle stood fast.

"*Kyle!*" Tom yelled.

Tom saw the dragon-dogs at the head of the pack leap right at his friend's neck, their sleek faces split in two by wide pink mouths lined with hundreds of jagged teeth. They were feet from Kyle's face, then inches, then *KROOOOOSSSSSSSSSSSHHHH*: they were blown backward by a ball of light that came from Kyle and flew out in every direction. Tom winced when he was about to be hit by it, but right before it got to him, a hole in the shape of his silhouette appeared in the ball's surface and it passed harmlessly around him.

Kyle turned to him. "We gotta go now." He put one sneaker on the rim. "Stay ahead of me, okay?"

Tom ran up and hopped over the edge. He found himself looking out over the sandy, scrubby plain, a seemingly infinite expanse of land that looked like the not-so-good part of the beach you had to walk over before you got to the actual beach. On the horizon, the Wall encircling the kingdom looked like it was made of the same light that Kyle had just emitted except it was static, thick on the ground and then dissipating as it sloped off toward its domed peak in the gray sky.

"Run straight!" Kyle said.

Tom did. In his peripheral vision, he saw a flash of purple from behind a stand of brush on his left. Then there was a blue light behind a decaying sand dune. The Elggs were getting up and giving chase.

Tom wished he'd paid more attention in PE. Then he realized there was really nothing in PE that he could've paid attention to that would make him better at running. Being good at running was just a matter of running every day no matter what, and that was exactly why he wasn't good at it.

He looked back over his shoulder. The Elggs were gaining on them. Then he noticed Kyle's footsteps in the sand. As soon as his foot left an imprint, the imprint started to glow with the same light as Kyle's energy ball, the same light that made up the Wall ahead of them that seemed farther away the more they had to run. Footprint-shaped columns of light grew from them. Every few seconds Kyle's neck was in serious danger once again, and then the attacking Elgg would be snapped back as the columns of light whipped around like solid vines and ensnared its back legs. Tom looked forward again. The Wall drew closer, but not close enough. Not close enough at all.

The path they were running had worked its way between two rows of dunes, a little canyon. The sounds of the pursuing Elggs had faded. Ahead of them, the Wall became more and more translucent, the way mist does when you get closer to it and the things inside the mist become clearer.

Then the view was blocked when something came streaking across the canyon. It looked a lightning bolt with a protective casing, a protective casing with arms and legs and teeth. It was an Elgg that had somehow evaded Kyle's energy tendrils. It leapt in from one side, bounced off the opposite dune, and came to a rest in front of them before they could even slow down.

Kyle shoved Tom aside. He hit a dune just in time to see Kyle barreling ahead, gathering a head of magical light like the glowing heat-shield of a spacecraft upon reentry. This thunderhead of magic hit the Elgg, knocking it off its feet and then driving it forward as Kyle kept running. It tumbled end over end, its innards a whirlwind of sparks, its face angry and panicked and bewildered and, in its helplessness, kind of cute.

"Behind me!" Kyle barked.

They kept running, the Elgg bouncing ahead of them against the canyon walls and Kyle's energy shield, constantly scratching to try to regain its footing, and failing. Columns of light were still growing from Kyle's footsteps, and the longer Tom ran behind him, the closer they came to whipping him off his feet.

"Kyle??!" Tom yelled.

Kyle looked back and saw the vines of energy snapping at Tom's heels.

"Right, sorry," Kyle said. The vines began to shrink and fade until only normal, size-11 sneaker prints were left in the sand.

The dunes on either side of them grew smaller until they tapered off at last, and the boys were running through the open field that bordered Crap Kingdom. With nothing to bounce off of, the confused and probably nauseated Elgg fell off to their left.

Tom could feel something else whipping at his ankles, something much smaller than Kyle's footprint-generated energy vines. He looked down: his right shoe had come untied. Ugh. Well, they were almost there, and the Wall was almost entirely invisible now. Besides, Tom knew he could handle the untied shoelace. He'd basically spent his entire life with one shoelace untied. It seemed like he'd either learned the wrong way to tie his shoes all those years ago or he'd learned the exact right way to tie your shoes if you wanted at least one of your shoes to come untied every day at the worst possible moment. Anyway, they were almost there. It seemed like the Elggs were off their scent, finally. Plus he was getting into kind of a groove with the running thing. He was actually pretty good at it, he thought, for someone who—

The second he started feeling cool and competent, he tripped and fell facedown in the sand. He heard Kyle's footsteps ahead of him, growing fainter, and then he heard a high-pitched squeaking. He looked up to see a creature staring at him. It was like a mouse, if someone took a mouse's eyes and placed them all the way down on either side of its neck, so its head was just a place for a nose and whiskers and ears, and if it wanted to look at you, like this one was looking at Tom, it had to move its body back and forth rapidly, hoping to catch a three-dimensional glimpse of you with both eyes at once, and failing, and squeaking all the while. This must have been one of the indigenous snot-filled rats. Tom wondered if it was laughing at him. It had no right to laugh, he thought. Not when it couldn't even grow to full size without another species blowing its nose for it.

Then, above the squeak, and above Kyle's receding footsteps, there were louder footsteps, behind Tom. The Elgg that Kyle had battered all the way through the canyon must have conquered its nausea. Tom looked up and to his left and saw it bounding off dunes, headed right for him.

Tom struggled to his feet, but something deep and primal inside him told him he would not make it up in time, and if even if he did, he would not run fast enough. His hand jutted out and grabbed the indigenous weird-eyed rat thing. He flung it side-armed at the approaching monster. He missed, and it flew off to the right. The Elgg's head turned that way, though, and the beast made a detour to wherever the rat thing had landed.

Tom stood up and started galloping, trying to keep his feet as far apart as possible so he wouldn't trip again on his still-untied shoelace. He heard a panicked final squeak and a chomping noise. He leapt off a sand embankment. Kyle glanced behind him and saw Tom was there. He seemed unaware of the whole shoelace/rodent-toss fiasco. Tom looked back just in time to see the Elgg leaping off the embankment after them. Apparently it was still hungry.

"*Slowwave truepants!*" Kyle yelled. He spun around, stopped, waited for Tom to reach him, and yelled, "*Close!*" Just inches away from them, the Elgg bounced off the Wall, hard. It had spent the whole afternoon bouncing off things that hadn't been there a second ago, and it was pissed. It scrabbled to its feet, its green eyelid bands scrolling rapidly over its eyes, and it sneezed, or scoffed, or something, ejecting blue fire and rodent blood all over the transparent Wall right in front of Tom and Kyle's faces. Then it turned and wandered away.

"*Woo!* That was fun. Good job, man," Kyle said. He wasn't out of breath or anything.

"Thank you," Tom said. "How do you know how to do all this stuff?"

"Oh, man, I wanted to show you but it's actually back where we just came from . . . Oh well, I guess I could just teleport us."

"You can teleport us back there?"

"I think so, yeah. We'd have to step outside the Wall. You can't teleport through it. But we'd just have to take, like, two steps out and close it again."

"So why didn't you teleport us here?"

"'Cause that was more fun, wasn't it?"

"More *fun*? Dude, we *almost died!*"

"I knew I could handle it! And if anything else happened, I could handle that, too!"

Tom was mad at Kyle for endangering their lives, but he was more mad at him for being certain that he hadn't endangered their lives, that any danger they'd been in was well within his powers to manage. Tom suspected that Kyle was probably right. After all, the guy could emit expanding balls of energy. His footprints came to life and attacked his enemies if he wanted them to.

"All right," Tom said. "All right, fine. But I should probably head back now, so if we're going to teleport anywhere, it should probably be the portal—"

"Dude, the portal sucks. Forget about the portal."

"Okay, well then, this new way you have of getting here, can I use it to go back now? Rehearsal's probably started already, and—"

"Don't worry about it," Kyle said. "That's what's so cool about it. Remember when I was weird in the lunchroom? That's because . . ." Kyle looked around as though someone might be listening, though there was nothing but a pile of scrap metal on one side of them and the invisible Wall and an endless field of brush on the other. "That's because *it wasn't me.*"

"What?"

"It's called soul-swap. It's this other way of getting between our world and this one. Your body stays on Earth. You and me right here, we're just, like, duplicates, basically.

But like, our 'us,' whatever makes us who we are, is here too. That's why we're seeing this, what's going on here, instead of whatever's going on in our bodies on Earth. You know how when you take that portal outside of Kmart, your body leaves here and goes there? In a soul-swap, it doesn't. It stays on Earth and it gets kind of . . . piloted, I guess . . . by a random soul from a place that's kind of like, between here and there."

"You mean limbo?"

"The thing with a stick? No."

"No, limbo, the place between life and the afterlife. You've seriously never heard of limbo before?"

"No, I guess not. Besides, it's not a place between here and the afterlife, it's a place between Earth and Ffffffttth-hhp."

"Are you gonna start doing that too?"

"It's fun to do the nonsense words. Come on, try it: Pfff-ttccccckkk . . . *Fffttzzzzthrp* . . ."

"Those both sounded like farts. So, this soul—"

"Well, not a soul, exactly, but that's the closest word . . . I mean, it did belong to someone else at one point . . . but anyway, it comes to Earth and it gets in your body while your soul or your you-ness is being projected here. And when you go back, you get back in your body and it goes back into samba."

"Limbo."

"Dude, I was making a joke. Stop being so serious."

"Well, now I definitely want to go back. Some random soul is, like, piloting me around during rehearsal? I'm going to get kicked out of the show!"

"It's fine, okay? You'd be surprised how—"

"I don't think you've ever met yourself when you were like that, man, you were *so* weird."

"But every soul's different. Maybe yours is cool. Besides, I didn't even get to show you the—"

"Please! I wanna go back!"

"Okay," Kyle said. "Fine."

Tom realized he'd hurt Kyle's feelings. "See you tomorrow?" he said.

"Sure," Kyle said.

"Are you mad at me?" Tom asked.

"No," Kyle said. "I mean, I'm about to push you . . . but it's not an anger thing. It's just how you go back."

"Uhm," Tom said, "Okay."

"Ready?"

"Yeah."

Kyle faced Tom and put both hands up, palms out.

"Bye," he said. Then he shoved Tom, hard.

Tom fell back before he knew what was happening. Once again, just as his eyes met the sky, he felt his body tear through a construction-paper barrier between realities, and the gray sky of Crap Kingdom was gone and he was swinging backward through a void, and then up again.

There was another rip, and Tom had the bizarre sensation of crashing back into his own head, into his own body, standing upright in the real world as he knew it. The force of it caused him to take a single involuntary step backward.

Lights shone in his eyes. He was standing onstage. The other cast members of *A View from the Bridge* were in street clothes all around him, sitting on black orchestra chairs and rehearsal furniture, holding scripts. Several of the girls and a few of the guys had tears in their eyes. Somewhere, one person was clapping.

Tom turned out and squinted. Tobe was sitting in the third row. Were there tears in Tobe's eyes too? They were definitely sparkling an unusual amount.

"Tom," Tobe said. "That . . . was *brilliant*."

15

"SO YOUR GUY'S a badass?"

"I guess! I didn't even have the script in my hand. Or, he didn't even have the script in his hand. However you say that."

Tom had been looking forward to talking to Kyle ever since he'd returned to his body and found the entire cast of *A View from the Bridge* and its hard-to-please director caught up in the performance he was giving, or the performance this other soul was giving in his body. He couldn't text Kyle to ask if he was here or in the nameless kingdom, so he waited for lunch and was disappointed when he walked out with a tray full of food and saw Kyle sitting by himself in the corner again. But Kyle turned and waved him over. He was just sitting by himself so he and Tom would have a chance to talk privately. The only reason he was here, he'd said, was to talk to Tom about the whole experience of having someone else in his body, living his life. He'd wished he'd had someone to talk to about it the first time he'd done it. Tom was more than happy to talk about it. He was more than happy in general. Tobe had called him "brilliant."

Tobe never said anything was brilliant. Tobe had problems with Shakespeare. For Tobe to tell him, not even after an opening night performance but during a rehearsal, that he had done brilliantly, *that* was brilliant.

His body was so innately talented that any old soul from any universe could hop in it, steer it around for an afternoon, and the result would be *brilliant*. Tom wondered what would happen this afternoon at rehearsal if he was just himself. Would he remember what he'd done to garner that kind of reaction? When he got onstage, would it all just come flooding back to him? He hoped it would. Seeing everyone's faces after Tom had finished his final speech had been the first good thing to come out of Tom's association with Crap Kingdom, and it hadn't even happened there. And he hadn't even seen Lindsy after rehearsal. He wanted to talk to her. Maybe, in the course of complimenting him, she'd tell him exactly what he'd done so he could replicate it. Maybe she'd drag him into a bathroom and make out with him. "Come back today! Hell, let's go back now," Kyle said. "See what your guy gets up to."

"It's always the same guy?"

"Always. They attach themselves to you."

"How do you know all this stuff?"

"That's what I wanted to show you yesterday. So come today and we'll do it."

"I shouldn't. Rehearsal again."

"Dude, that's the whole point, is that you can be there *and* here."

"No, but I mean, me, I need to be there. I want to be there today."

"Suit yourself. I'll stick around in case you change your mind."

"Did you just get this text?"

Tom looked up from his book. He was sitting in the back of his sixth-period class. Bridget, a girl Tom's age who was also in Drama Department, had turned all the way around in her chair and was talking to Tom from the row of desks in front of him. She had recently dyed her hair pink, though she insisted it was not because Ella, an older girl everybody liked, had pink hair. She'd developed the idea independently a long time ago but just hadn't gotten permission from her mom until recently. It was a coincidence, she'd insisted to anyone who would listen and even some people who wouldn't.

"No," Tom said. "Phone's broken."

"How did *that* happen?"

Tom decided it would be a bad idea to say, *It was drowned in a watery world-spanning portal that has recently been made obsolete by my best friend's mastery of the soul-swap spell.* Instead, he shrugged.

"Oh," Bridget said. "Well, check it out."

She handed him her phone.

The text message said: REHEARSAL CANCELED 4 THIS AFTERNOON—TOBE.

Tobe had acknowledged that it was probably hypocritical of him to text his student actors, since students weren't supposed to text during school hours, but it was practical and efficient and if they were going to text anyway, which everybody did, they might as well all be grown-ups about it. He insisted this didn't violate his otherwise strict adherence to school rules because there was no rule that explicitly stated that he couldn't text his kids. Tom had always loved that Tobe didn't realize his name would come up on kids' phones once they'd programmed his number in, so he didn't need to sign his texts "TOBE."

"Okay," Tom said. "Thanks."

"Get a new phone!" Bridget said, as though it were something he'd just decided he didn't want to do. She turned back around.

Tom was disappointed that there wouldn't be rehearsal, but he was also a little relieved, because he hadn't memorized his lines for the first ten pages, which they were supposed to be running off book for the first time that afternoon. The first ten pages contained his monstrous introductory monologue and he'd had every intention of learning it when he got home last night, but instead he'd just lain on his bed re-creating his masterful performance in his mind, even though he hadn't actually been there for it.

Tom thought about borrowing Bridget's phone and texting Tobe back to ask him what pages they'd be doing when rehearsal resumed. But he was already near enough to the Performing Arts wing to just stop by between classes, and he tried to stop by whenever he could. There were certain people you just wanted to be around, and Tobe was one of them. There was always a chance you could make him laugh or something. Also, Tom hadn't seen Tobe since the end of yesterday's rehearsal, and he thought maybe Tobe would drop some hint about what Tom had done yesterday that had moved kids to actual tears.

Posters from old Drama Department performances lined the walls of the drama room, and they'd always sparked Tom's imagination. He'd think of how lucky previous generations of kids had been to get to do certain plays. Then when the time came for a poster to go up for a play he'd actually been in, it kind of diminished the whole thing. The ones he had actually been there for didn't seem as cool for whatever reason. He didn't know why things he was involved in were automatically less exciting to him than things he didn't get to be a part of.

Kids were filtering in for Tobe's next class. Tobe was sitting at his desk at the front of the room. Tom walked up and Tobe looked up from his computer.

"Hey," Tom said. "I saw about rehearsal."

Tom wanted Tobe to say something like, "Speaking of

rehearsal—yesterday was no rehearsal, Tom—you were *performing!*" Tom wasn't sure why he always wrote compliments for himself and put them in other people's mouths in his imagination. Tobe was silent.

"Are we doing the first ten pages tomorrow instead, or the next ten?"

Tobe sighed. "Maybe neither. Look, you don't know this... I mean, of course you don't know it, because I haven't told it to you yet, but once I tell you, you don't know it, okay?"

"Of course not," Tom said quietly. *A secret!* He was scared, because someone who seemed invincible to him sounded genuinely worried, and he was excited, because that person was about to take him into his confidence.

"The school doesn't want me to do *View.*"

"What? Why?"

"The immigrant thing."

Tom still hadn't read the whole play, but at one point he knew that the main character, Eddie, came to see his character, the lawyer, about some illegal immigrants who were staying in his house.

"Are people protesting?" Tom got images of angry parents ringing the auditorium, holding up signs and shouting slogans on opening night. It was actually pretty exciting.

"No, but Principal Scott's worried that people might protest, which is worse. If someone were actually protesting, we could do something to make them happy, or just say we're ignoring them and going ahead anyway. But this anxiety's almost worse because there doesn't have to be anyone actually there protesting."

"So we're not doing it?"

"I don't know. I have to go talk to him this afternoon. Plead my case."

Before Tom knew what he was saying or why he was saying it, he said, "Do you want me to come?"

Tobe half smiled, which was about as much as Tobe ever smiled, which was one of the reasons it was nice to make him laugh when you could. "No," he said, "I think I'll be okay. But thank you for offering."

Tom did not know why he had chosen to be bold just then. He always heard about people being impulsive, seizing the moment, but how did those people know which moments they were supposed to seize? He always looked for opportunities to be impulsive, but he was always impulsive at the wrong times. He left knowing he was going to spend all afternoon thinking about how dumb he was. Or maybe he didn't have to sit around all afternoon thinking about it.

Tom hung out by his locker after the last period of the day let out. Kyle's locker was right next to his. Eventually Kyle appeared out of the weather patterns of kids gossiping or roughhousing.

"Rehearsal got canceled," Tom said. "I can go to 'the place' now if you want."

"You mean Krrgmmmppmmmp?" Kyle said.

"I was trying to be secretive about it," Tom whispered. "I figured you'd know what I meant."

"Dude," Kyle said, "like anyone is going to know what Krrgmmmpppmmmp means."

Tom considered saying. *If I was the Chosen One I would be more careful than you're being.*

Instead he said, "Whatever. Are we going?"

After falling backward and leaving their Earthly bodies at the hidden gravel spot behind the auditorium, Tom and Kyle appeared in the same crater where they'd first been spotted by the Elgg pack.

"Why do our clothes and everything come through?" Tom said. "Like, is that a reflection of our souls, too? Do our clothes have souls?"

Tom realized Kyle wasn't listening. He was staring at the far wall of the crater, where a perfectly rectangular patch of sand started vibrating and emitting a low hiss. Then, without any sound at all, each grain of sand blew outward. Tom braced himself for stinging eyes and skin, but nothing hit him. It was like the sand knew how to miss them. When it was over, they were in a bubble of sand, like a 3-D map of the stars in the night sky as rendered with floating grains of dirt, and in the center, in the side of the crater, was a rectangular doorway. Kyle walked through. Tom followed him, and as soon as he had stepped over the threshold, the small sand universe contracted, filling in the doorway, and they were left in darkness.

"One sec," said Kyle. With no sound of ignition, a tiny purple flame began to grow in the darkness in front of Tom. As it grew, he realized it was emanating from Kyle's hand, and he also realized they were in a small spherical chamber whose dimensions he could only now see thanks to Kyle's hand-fire.

"The Tame Flame," Tom said. "Gark said it wasn't his peoples' magic."

"It isn't," Kyle said. "Not ancestrally."

"Did he show you that one spell they have, the fart one where—"

"And neither . . ." Kyle continued dramatically, not really listening to Tom, "is *this*." He threw the liquid flame side-arm and it splashed outward on the wall of the chamber, creating a bright, flaming stain.

Tom started looking around the chamber. The walls were lined with pictographs, stick-figure depictions of anonymous people doing fantastic things, like caveman drawings if cavemen had had enough imagination to draw guys shooting fire out of their eyeballs and converting their legs into tank treads.

"You'll recognize this one," Kyle said. He pointed at the wall. One of the pictographs lit up, like the lines in the drawing had been filled in with shiny liquid gold. Kyle twitched his finger ever so slightly and the stick-figure man danced up off the wall at them, finding a home in the dead center of the room, above their heads. A word appeared, orbiting the three-dimensional image like a news ticker that had come to life and then immediately gone insane. SOUL-SWAP, it read. It swirled around the man. The man fell backward, then collided with a man who was standing directly underneath him like a reflected image in a pond, then swung all the way around until he was standing again. An afterimage of the man remained lying at a ninety-degree angle. The reflected man fell upward into this afterimage version of the original man, and then the two that had now become one got up and walked away.

"What is this place?" Tom said.

"The laboratory of J, the greatest citizen in the history of the kingdom of Prrrkggrkrkkk," Kyle said.

"I thought Gark's dad was their greatest citizen."

"When I say 'great' I mean, like, actually great, not just great at being miserable. He designed spells that no one had ever thought of before. Like, for instance, he created the Wall. And he was going to vanquish the Ghelm and free the people of Ffrrgggggggghh from the threat of being destroyed, but he disappeared before he could get it together."

"And they actually liked him? They actually wanted this?"

"They weren't always like they are now. It's pretty recent for them to be so depressed and stuff. I think when he went away, the king figured, eh, screw it, nothing's worth anything."

"So if you're the Chosen One, and it says that the Chosen One will bring down the Wall, isn't that bad since it's the only thing protecting them from the Ghelm?"

"I think it means, once I'm done, they won't need the Wall, because nothing will be threatening them."

Kyle just said it so confidently. It was the same way he'd entered the cave, the way he'd shown everything off. Tom wanted to hit him, or be him, or something.

The animation of the soul-swap had cycled through five or six times. On the seventh, it was accompanied by a voice that seemed to come from everywhere:

"Right, so, the soul-swap's quite simple, actually, for something that's meant to incorporate two separate worlds, and then a third, too, if the intermediary—"

"*Off*," Kyle said.

"What was that?"

"J's recorded instructions," Kyle said.

J had not sounded how Tom would expect a great citizen to sound. He sounded a lot younger, for one. When the ancients spoke, you expected it to be in ancient-sounding tones, like their lungs were filled with the dust of centuries and they had so much wisdom that they could barely lift their heads, but J had sounded around Tom's age. On the other hand, he had sounded British, which more than made up for the wisdom points he'd lost by not sounding old.

"Is the soul-swap something you can learn?"

"Well, yeah, I guess . . . I mean, I learned it."

"Oh."

"But I think it's something where you have to have like, some kind of base of like, magical understanding."

"Which you have."

"Yeah."

"How did you find this place?"

"The king showed me."

"Because you had that magical understanding?"

"No," Kyle said, "I don't know. He just likes me for some reason. But I'm not just passively learning. I'm building stuff, too. You know how I said you can't teleport through the dome of the Wall?"

"Sure."

"Well, yesterday, after you left, I think I figured out how to do it. I think . . . I can turn us into air."

"Wait, what?"

"Okay, the Wall has to allow air in, right? Otherwise everyone would suffocate. So I make us air for a second. Combine that with teleportation, and we're through."

"And this works?"

"Well . . ." Kyle said.

Then: Tom was dead. Or at the very least, he was nowhere. He wasn't even in the between-world void; he was just a consciousness surrounded by nothing. It was kind of how he felt on the inside just about every second of every day—awkward, stuck between things, uncertain even of his uncertainty, especially when talking to girls—made into a physical state of being. Or was it a nonphysical state of being? He wasn't sure.

He hovered in eternal nothingness for three seconds. Could it be eternal if it only lasted three seconds? He wasn't sure.

Then he was alive, in a body, his body. He was in the throne room. He was facing a wall when he reappeared. He was very close to it, in fact, but he knew it was the throne room because he spun around and saw that the king and Gark were there. And he immediately had these thoughts:

1. *How did Kyle know how to do that?* It's one thing to be taught how to do magic and stuff, another thing entirely to *write* magic. Or maybe it was easy to do that? Maybe it was just another thing you could learn, like the spells on the walls of J's cave? Maybe J's magic was like a video game that let you design your own levels. Maybe it was that simple. It probably was, if Kyle could do it.

2. *That was TERRIFYING.* Maybe that was the tell-tale sign of Kyle having created it himself. Last time Kyle teleported them, the world had changed around them instantaneously. This time, they'd hung in not-even-space for three seconds, with Tom unsure of what was happening, unsure if they'd ever come back. And it had spat them out here, dangerously close to the wooden wall.

3. *Aw, crap.*

The "aw, crap" was not inspired by the teleportation, but by the king looking at Tom and yelling, "What is *he* doing here?"

"Hey, King!" Kyle said. "Did you see this? I cracked the thing that J could never figure out . . . how to teleport into—"

"Of course you did, Kyle," the king said, "but that does not change my question."

"I was just showing him J's laboratory."

"*What?*" the king yelled. "What did he see?"

"You know, the cave, and the whole thing. What's the problem?"

"The problem, my dear Kyle, is that was never, and I mean *never*, intended to be seen by anyone but the eyes of a *Chosen One*! And that does *not* mean a *former, disgraced* Chosen One! That means a *current* Chosen One whose place was dictated by prophecy!"

"It's okay," Kyle said. "Tom's cool."

"It is not a matter of whether or not Tom is *cool*," the king said. "Our kingdom is J's secrets. They are the only thing separating us from utter destruction. All you have done for our kingdom, all you have yet to do, could all disappear in a moment, if those secrets were overheard by the wrong pair of ears."

"But Tom's not—"

"Do not finish that sentence unless you intended to say 'Tom's not worth risking the fate of our entire society.' And as for *you*," the king went on, turning to Tom. "You should be ashamed of tempting our Chosen One into showing you J's cave."

"I didn't tempt him into anything! I didn't even know it existed! He brought me there!"

"I failed to make it adequately clear to him that J's laboratory was off-limits to anyone but him. I only showed it to him after grave consideration, once he demonstrated particular strength of character, but I forgot to make clear to him the parameters. He did not know any better."

"I didn't know any better," Tom said. He was being impulsive. He didn't know if it was the right time or not. He didn't care. "I didn't know any better when I said I didn't want to be the Chosen One! I didn't know that there would be all this magic stuff, all these secrets!"

"Of course you didn't," the king said. "They were secrets!"

"But you told Kyle!"

"After he gained my trust."

"You never gave me a chance to gain your trust. You just decided I sucked right off the bat!"

"You never had a chance to gain my trust because *you left*," the king said. "And I thank you for leaving, because if you hadn't, we might never have received an updated prophecy. We would not have our Kyle. And now that you have left, I wish you would stay gone."

"Come on," Kyle said, "I'm sure we can find a place for him."

"I don't believe you understand," the king said. "I was not idly wishing that he be gone forever. Wasn't it you, Tom, who wanted me to decree more things? Well, I am decreeing something now. You ... are ... banned."

"Fine!" Tom yelled, though he didn't actually think it was fine.

"Hey," Kyle said, "if this is about me bringing him to the cave, I'm sorry, and I won't—"

"You have nothing to apologize for, Kyle. Now," the king said to Tom, "begone."

Kyle turned to Tom.

"I'm sorry, man."

Tom shrugged. Kyle raised his arms.

"Can't I push myself?" Tom asked.

Kyle shook his head.

"Okay," Tom said. "Go ahead."

If someone could shove someone else sadly, that's the way Kyle shoved Tom.

Tom expected to land on Earth with his body in a standing position, as he had onstage the other day.

Instead, he landed lying down.

Lindsy Kopec was lying on top of him.

"Whoa there," Lindsy said. "You okay?"

"What?" Tom said. "Yeah. Yeah."

Tom tried to remember if they had any kissing scenes in the play. They didn't. And they definitely didn't have any scenes that took place in a modern-day teenage girl's bedroom, on the girl's bed.

"Oh," Lindsy said. "You kind of, like, twitched."

"Totally involuntary, I swear," Tom said. "Never happen again."

"Cool," Lindsy said, and smiled, and tucked a long strand of black hair back behind her ear. Then she leaned back down and kissed him and they kept making out. Tom didn't know how long they'd been making out, but he knew how long he wanted it to last.

WHAT WAS GOING ON?

It was the second time today Tom had had a feeling like this, of being totally confused, with no point of reference, nothing he could build a sense of the world around. The first time was in the netherworld between J's cave and the throne room. But in that place, or lack-of-place, there was nothing. Here, now, on Lindsy's bed, there was everything. There was Lindsy, there was Tom, there was Lindsy's backpack wedged carelessly between him and the wall, and the wall covered in posters, some of which were doubles of ones in the drama room, and Lindsy's bed underneath him with its sky-blue covers, and there was sixty or sixty-five cents in change that had fallen out of the pocket of his jeans dancing on the surface of those covers. Did his breath smell okay? It probably didn't. Yet all this was happening in spite of it. In spite of him being him, all this great stuff was happening.

He was kissing Lindsy Kopec. Like, in the face. Was he good at it? He didn't know. He'd barely made out with anyone before. Especially if this was actually what making out was. This was intense. Lindsy was kissing him really hard. He was kissing back really hard. It was phenomenal.

What had taken place between now and the end of school? He wished his body had retained some sort of residual memory. Now Lindsy was kissing his neck, and while this miraculous rite was being performed, Tom glanced at the clock on Lindsy's nightstand. It was 4:45. School ended at 3:15. At 4:45 in the afternoon on a school day, he was in Lindsy Kopec's bedroom and Lindsy herself was kissing his neck.

Let's say, just in the normal course of events, he'd gotten to see Lindsy's bedroom. That in and of itself would have been an achievement, something he could be hugely proud of even if that was as far as it ever went. Every straight male he knew wanted to be in Lindsy's bedroom. Even if it was just as part of a study group, it would represent a threshold crossed on the way to making out with Lindsy. And let's say

Tom had crossed that threshold one time, on an afternoon such as this. He would have then estimated that it would take him another year to actually make out with her. Yet here, in a single afternoon, he had blazed through the bedroom threshold, and fallen onto the bed and into her arms.

Who was he when he wasn't him? He wanted to shake that man's hand. And he would shake that man's hand, as soon as someone removed his right hand, his good shaking hand, from Lindsy's butt. He expected it to happen any second now. A couple of seconds passed. It wasn't getting removed! It was just staying there! It practically lived there! If his hand could live there, where else could it go? Should he find out? Better not. He'd just been given the world. Best not to ask for more right away. Should he be thinking right now? He should probably not be thinking. He tried to stop thinking.

Lindsy finished kissing his neck, so Tom started kissing Lindsy's neck. He immediately started thinking again: Was he doing it right? He tried to do it like she'd done it to him. Would that be weird, though, since he was a guy and she was a girl? Should he try to do it manlier than she'd done it? How did you kiss someone's neck manfully? Then he started to worry that there would have been a noticeable difference in his conduct, bedroom and otherwise, between when he was actually in his body and when his soul-swapped who-ever, that glorious genius void-dweller to whom he owed so much, had been inhabiting him. That person, if he could be called a person, would probably do things differently from how Tom would do them. He decided he'd better start kissing differently from how he would kiss. He tried to imagine how plain old Tom would neck-kiss somebody and then tried to do it differently from that.

It was pointless. He gave up and decided to just enjoy it. And, for the first time in a long history of trying to turn his head off and just enjoy something, he actually did.

"Tom," Lindsy said. Lindsy said your name a lot when you talked to her. Not a lot of people actually did this in real life, but Lindsy did it, to everybody. Yet you still felt special when she did it to you. Tom felt special, lying there, looking at Lindsy's face, one of her eyes invisible, buried in a pillow, random strands of her black hair creating a nest for the other eye. You know what, he thought, he was special. He was here. They'd just made out a ton. They might make out more, he thought. Stick around.

"Tom," Lindsy said, "that was incredible."

Tom wasn't sure what she meant. "Do you mean just now?"

Her one visible eye squinched up and it, too, disappeared into the pillow as she laughed. "Whoa! Cocky!"

"What?" Tom said. "It was, right?!"

Lindsy laughed more into her pillow. The blinds on the window above her bed were mostly closed but yellow late afternoon light was still slanting in. She let one eye show again, and the light got caught up in her eyelashes.

"Verrrry cocky," she said. "But then again, that's what I liked about it."

"About what?"

"The meeting this afternoon!" she said. "What else could I be talking about?"

Tom shrugged, but it was hard to shrug effectively when you were lying on your side in a bed. "Tell me about it," he said.

"I *know*," Lindsy said.

"No, I don't mean, like, 'Tell me about it,' I mean . . . actually tell me about it."

"As in what happened?"

"Yeah," Tom said, "like I'm someone else. Like I wasn't

there." He smiled so in case she thought he was joking he could just smile wider and she could be sure he was joking.

She opened her mouth wide, fake astonished, or maybe real astonished. "You *are* cocky! Tom Parking, have you no shame?"

"Clearly not," he said, and smiled more. He didn't know what he meant, but it sounded like the right thing to say. She laughed. *Okay, good,* Tom thought, *it was the right thing to say.* "Seriously, it'll be an interesting exercise in perspective, like, were you in class when we watched *Rashomon?*"

They had watched the Kurosawa movie *Rashomon* in Tobe's Intermediate Drama class. They were supposed to watch *Throne of Blood,* because it was based on *Macbeth* and they were doing a Shakespeare unit, but Tobe said he hadn't returned his Netflix movies in time so he didn't have the DVD and the school library had *Rashomon,* which was still a Kurosawa movie and still had samurai.

"No, I was in LA for an audition."

"Okay, right, well. Well, it's about perspective, and different people seeing different things. Like, that was your perspective. Not being there, being in LA."

"What's your point, Parking?"

"My point is, tell me what happened this afternoon, from your perspective."

"No!" she said. "That would be weird."

"Okay, fine then," Tom said. "Let's act it out."

"What?"

Tom was being very unlike himself, but he didn't think he'd gotten here by being like himself and if he wanted to be back here he needed to know exactly how unlike himself he'd been, so he pressed on.

"Yeah, come on. It'll be fun. You can play me."

"Now *that*," Lindsy said, lifting herself up on one elbow, "is the first interesting thing I've heard all afternoon."

"The first interesting thing?" Tom said. "But you're about to say all the interesting stuff I said."

"Oh, it wasn't that interesting, you're giving yourself way too much credit," Lindsy said. Was this flirting? Tom was pretty sure this was flirting.

"Well, go ahead," Tom said, "do your me impression. I hear you're an excellent impressionist. I heard your Taylor Swift impression, for instance—"

"Who told you about that? That was just for a dumb English class skit! I never claimed to be able to do a Taylor Swift impression!"

"And I don't claim to be able to do a you impression, but here it goes anyway."

"Wait, you're going to be me?"

"Of course."

"Okay, well, be extremely good at acting while playing me."

"I will."

"Capture everything about me."

"I will! Okay, so I'm Lindsy, and it's earlier today, and I'm . . . where?"

"Out in the courtyard by the Performing Arts wing," Lindsy said. "I was going to ask Tobe if we had to memorize pages ten through twenty for tomorrow."

"You couldn't just text him back?"

"I don't know, this might sound weird, but I like going to see him when I can. Is that . . . ? I don't know."

"I do exactly the same thing," Tom said.

"Seriously? Don't be mean."

"No, I'm serious. I did that exact same thing today. But enough about me, this is about you, and I'm you, and I'm walking through the courtyard."

"That's how I walk?"

"It's hard to demonstrate how you walk when I'm lying down."

"Okay, this is silly. You want to know my perspective? Here it is: I'm walking in the courtyard . . . *not* like that . . .

and you walk up and you say 'come with me' and you grab my hand. You say 'Tobe needs our help.' Any disagreement so far?"

"That's pretty much what I remember," Tom said.

"And I kept trying to ask you what was going on, and you were just being so serious, there was no hesitation. We were headed toward the office. And the principal's secretary was sitting outside, and we just rushed past her, right through the principal's door, and you flung me inside—"

"I *flung* you?" Tom said. Then he corrected himself. "I mean, you thought of that as a fling?"

"It was pretty much a fling, Tom, you flung me. Not that I—I mean, if I'd had a problem with it, I would have said something, I was just completely—caught up, I guess, would be the right way to put it. And you go, 'Principal Scott, Mr. Lowsky, my name is Thomas Parking and this is my associate Lindsy Kopec.'"

It was Tom's turn to laugh into Lindsy's pillow.

"Don't laugh! You said it! You actually said 'associate' with a straight face, so you can't all of a sudden laugh now! I didn't laugh and if I don't get to then you don't get to."

"I'm amazing," Tom said.

"You're something, definitely," Lindsy said, then continued: "And the principal and Tobe were upset at you being there, but you were like—and you *don't* need to hear this because your head's definitely big enough already—but, Tom: you were *commanding*."

"Really?"

"Ugh, this is exactly what you wanted, isn't it? Not enough that I basically tear your face off, I actually have to *say* how great I think you are."

"So what did I say?"

"You were there! You know what you said!"

"I mean, I got kind of caught up in the moment, like you were saying."

"I just remember thinking, did he write this? But I can't remember exactly...."

"Right, it wasn't so much what I said as how I said it."

"No, it was what you said and how you said it. You said that we'd both worked really hard on productions in the past, and how I had all these things going on with academics and also my acting and modeling outside of school, but how I was electing—I remember you used that word, *electing*—to be here because I believed in the project and what it meant and, to sacrifice that, stood in opposition—there's another phrase you definitely used—to the spirit, or something, of the play. And there were all these things that you said, but if there was going to be a thesis statement in all of this, this would have been it, something about how everything Arthur Miller stood for, all his lessons of tolerance and dignity, that could just go away at any time, and it wouldn't have to be in a big court case, it could happen very slowly, just from people being too afraid in situations they assumed really didn't matter because they were so small, like a school play. Small decisions, small moments, they matter. That there are small victories to be had everywhere, in our own lives, not just in the Supreme Court and stuff. Does that sound about right?"

"Yeah," Tom said. "It's all coming back to me now. That part of it, anyway, because the other part—"

"What other part?" Lindsy said. "Oh, you mean the part where, after the principal said he'd have to give some serious consideration to it, but you'd made a lot of excellent points, and then thanked *me* for my sacrifice in light of my many endeavors, we were outside and you said how we still had the whole afternoon free and I asked you if you'd like to come back here, and you said . . . Oh, *god*, I can't even say it . . ."

"Say it!"

"*Ugh*. Fine. You said, and *this* I can quote: 'Only if it's not just to run lines.'"

"I . . . am . . . *amazing*."

Lindsy thwacked Tom so hard he almost fell off the bed.

"And then you said something about telling you all about everything from this afternoon that you said was about getting a 'different perspective' but was really about inflating your already overinflated ego."

"Wait! You skipped a part."

"What part?"

Tom looked at her. She remembered. Then they re-enacted that part, each of them playing themselves this time.

17

THERE WAS A fact so great that it made Tom suspect
that the life he was living wasn't his own, and it was this:

Lindsy Kopec was his girlfriend.

There was an additional fact that once again assured
him that yes, this was Tom's life, the life he'd always lead,
and it was this:

It wasn't going very well.

It hadn't gone poorly immediately. There was the afternoon where they made out, and they even got to make out a
little bit when Tom was actually present in his body, which
was great. Then they heard the garage door open.

"Don't worry," Lindsy said, "they trust me."

Tom and Lindsy got up from her bed and straightened
up their clothes.

"Tom!" Lindsy said, gesturing dramatically to her bed-spread. "Your fortune!"

Tom gathered up the sixty or sixty-five cents that had fallen out of his pockets onto her bed, trying to do it in a manner that indicated he didn't care about sixty or sixty-five cents, that the money was meaningless to him but she was going to have to sleep there sometime, and she didn't want change flying everywhere, now did she?

Going downstairs, Tom had to pretend like he'd seen her house before even though he actually hadn't. It was big and elegant, the kind of house people who buy each other Lexuses for Christmas in commercials have. Lindsy's father was in the kitchen, actually wearing a suit, actually setting down a briefcase. He was opening a bottle of wine when they walked through.

He shook Tom's hand and invited him to stay for dinner but Tom declined, citing some awkward, poorly thought out combination of homework and a family obligation. If he'd been able to express the real reason, it would've been something like: I think your daughter will let me make out with her now whenever I want to so I need to leave now before I ruin it.

She kissed him by the big wooden front door. There

were carvings in the door of ancient people doing ancient stuff.

She said, "You're an egomaniac," and then she said, "Can I have your phone number?"

"Uh," he said, "my phone's kinda . . . broken."

"Really?" she said. "What happened?"

"Fell in a pool," he said.

"Do you still have it?"

"Not on me, but yeah."

"Wait here."

She bounded up the stairs. Tom marveled at his surroundings. This place was more of a castle than the one in Crap Kingdom. And when he tried to kiss this princess, she kissed back instead of laughing at him. Well, she did laugh at him. It's just that the laughing didn't result from the kissing. And really, what more could you want?

She bounded back down the stairs. She was holding something behind her back with one hand. She reached him and held it up: a cell phone.

"My old phone. Take it."

"No, I can't do that."

"Sure you can. Just put your SIM card in it. Boom: Tom's phone."

"Will that work?"

She gave him a look and slapped the phone into his palm. He told her his phone number, and she programmed it into her newer phone. They kissed and he left and the enormous door shut behind him.

It was only when he was six steps down her long, long driveway that he realized what the look she gave him when she handed him the phone meant. It meant, "This is a free phone and I'm a pretty girl, you idiot."

As soon as he got home, he put his old SIM card in Lindsy's old phone. He turned it on. Ten minutes later, she texted him:

this is lindsy. it worked, didn't it?

An hour later, after he and his mom had eaten dinner, Lindsy called him. It was great for exactly twenty minutes. Tom was thinking, *She's calling me just to talk about whatever*, which was an absolute joy until he realized he didn't have anything to talk about. Wasn't he supposed to be smart? Yet after twenty minutes he found himself shockingly bereft of topics. At one point, he actually opened up CNN's website and started talking about events of the day. Lindsy had to admit she didn't know anything about health care reform, which was a relief, because Tom didn't either. There was a good chance that if Tom had been able to pop over to Crap Kingdom and let his other self take over, that guy could've given Lindsy an earful about health care reform in a way that would make her say "I'll be right over" and come tear Tom's face off, as she'd put it. But he couldn't pop over, so he didn't, so he sputtered on until they both said their good-byes and hung up.

The next day, Tobe texted all the kids in the play to tell them rehearsal was on for that afternoon, which meant that whatever Tom had done in the principal's office, it had worked. Immediately after he got Tobe's text, he received another one from Lindsy that said YOU'RE MY HERO. He spent the rest of the day looking back and forth from that text message to his lines for pages one through ten, which he still hadn't memorized.

He deserved to be called a hero, right? When he wasn't looking at his lines or at Lindsy's text, he was wondering about that. It had been him barging into the principal's office to make a big important speech, as far as anyone else was concerned. And it was certainly something he would've wanted to do, if he'd thought of it. And as for the stuff he'd supposedly said in the office, well, it wasn't stuff he'd ever thought of before, but he definitely would have thought of it, right? It was all about the play and Lindsy and Tobe, topics that were in his brain, it just took this other person inhabiting him when he was off in another world to actually put it together and say it. So it was pretty much like he'd thought of it himself and said it himself, right? And since the other person was in limbo and could not be here to share in the spoils of heroism, he might as well enjoy all of it. He was sure this noble, well-spoken soul would understand, and would even want it that way. He'd been in Tom's body. He knew what it was like.

Being Lindsy's hero carried him through the weekend. It got him back to Lindsy's house after rehearsal on Friday. It got him on her living room couch, a long white leather thing that was fancy because it didn't really have a back or arms. They were watching a movie. Lindsy's parents were out. Tom knew he was supposed to kiss her at some point, but he didn't know how exactly. He'd only ever kissed her after he'd already been kissing her. He didn't know how to initiate kissing. Thankfully Lindsy mauled him at a certain point and he just went along with it.

When Lindsy canceled the plans they'd made to see a movie on Saturday night because she needed to prepare for an audition she had to tape and send to her agent in LA, Tom was secretly glad. He needed to be the guy she thought he was, but that guy was in a void somewhere, floating bodiless, and Tom couldn't get him to make an appearance unless he got Kyle to take him somewhere he was forbidden to go.

"Are you okay?" Lindsy asked.

They were at Lindsy's again on Monday night. They were doing homework.

Homework: this he understood how to do. So he just happened to have a homework companion who probably wanted him to put his tongue down her throat. He didn't know how to do that, so he'd just focus on homework. They were on her bed. She was lying lengthwise in front of him, kicking her legs in the air, flipping through a French workbook.

"What? Yeah, of course," he said. On instinct his right hand jumped out to touch her, but then he got self-conscious about it and he let it fell limply between them like a weak, target-less karate chop.

"In rehearsal today, you seemed distracted."

"I did?" Tom didn't know how that could be. He'd spent all his non-Lindsy time that weekend learning his lines to the point where he felt like he'd never known anything so forward and backward in his life, and that afternoon he'd worked really hard to recapture the magic that made him worthy of being called "brilliant," even though he still didn't have any idea what exactly it was that he'd done. But he tried. Tried and tried and tried. Now his voice was ripped up and his legs hurt from pacing. He felt like he had out-narrated every narrator in history in one afternoon. "I didn't feel distracted."

"Oh," Lindsy said. "Okay." She flipped a page of her book, then said, "Is this distracting you?"

"Your book? No."

"No, Tom, this. Us. There was that one day last week where everyone was just blown away by you—and with good reason, you were fantastic—but ever since we've started dating, you haven't seemed . . ."

Last week she had hesitated because she didn't want to give him a bigger head. Now it seemed like she was hesitating for exactly the opposite reason.

". . . the same, I guess. You seem different."

"Not as good?"

"No! Not at all! You were always great. Remember what I told you on opening night of the last show?"

"Vaguely."

Her arm lashed out and thwacked him. She could just fly off the handle to playfully hit him without thinking about it. Why did every instinct he had to touch her require fifteen different meetings in his brain?

"Well, you were always very good but there was just something special about that day last week, but ever since we started this, you just haven't seemed the same, and I would hate to be anything but good for you, so I'm thinking maybe we should . . . put a hold on things."

"What? Lindsy, that's . . ." He tried to say her name the way she said his, but it didn't feel natural. Why didn't anything feel natural to him except lame things like eating peanut butter sandwiches alone in front of the TV? "That's crazy. I mean, not that you're crazy, you're not crazy, but I mean, thanks for being concerned about me and stuff, but no, this, this is awesome. This is great. Seriously."

"You're sure?"

"Of course!"

"Okay," she said. "Just so long as you're sure."

Just so long as you're sure? What other sixteen-year-old

girl in the world said that? God, he liked her so much. *I should just kiss her*, he thought. Instead he looked back down at his homework. Numbers swam on the page. There was no way he could focus on anything else. He needed to act. He needed to be that man of action, that man who grabbed her hand roughly in the courtyard and said "come with me." He had flung her into the principal's office. Flung her. And that was before they'd ever kissed, and now they'd kissed a hundred times, and he couldn't just kiss her again. She was right there! She wanted him, too! She didn't want to be studying French any more than he wanted to be studying Algebra 3-4!

The numbers on the page stopped swimming. They came into focus. There were six more practice problems left. He finished them all. Every so often he would hear Lindsy turn a page in her French workbook.

Flip.

Silence.

Flip.

Silence.

Flip.

A silence longer than all the other silences.

Flip.

"I should probably take off soon," Tom said.

18

TOM CALLED KYLE as soon as he got home. He needed his help. It wasn't ideal, but he'd already had one great thing slip through his grasp, and he didn't want to let another one go. He hadn't known that the first thing was great at the time, but he knew dating Lindsy was great. The only thing making it not great was him being himself.

Kyle picked up on the third ring.

"Hello, this is Kyle."

"Hey man, did I wake you up?"

"I was beginning to sleep, yes."

"Are you ... all right?"

"I'm not sure I know to what you are referring."

This wasn't Kyle, Tom realized. It was his other self. Kyle was in Crap Kingdom.

"Hey, Kyle, call me back when you're *you*, okay?"

"Indeed."

"Can you write that down? Can you write that down for the real Kyle?"

"I am Kyle, if that is your concern."

Tom hung up.

Tom found Kyle at a bench in the courtyard on Tuesday morning before school.

"Are you you?"

"Krrgrgggprrrr..." Kyle said, rolling his eyes back in his head like a zombie. "Nah, kidding, I'm me."

"That's not what you're like when you're not you."

"What am I like?"

"You use way more big words but in this weird awkward way that leads me to believe you're not actually all that smart."

"So like you then."

"Hey, you know what?"

"Dude! I'm kidding. I know he's not that smart. I came back to check my own homework. It's not good. I'm gonna try to fix it in first period and go back after that."

"Cool. I need to go back, too."

Kyle shut his notebook and looked up.

"You can't, man."

"I know, but I have to."

"Why?"

"Lindsy and I are dating now."

"What? Lindsy Kopec? You didn't tell me that!"

"I know, you're always in . . ."

"Krrrgggghhhrr."

"That sounded like your zombie noise."

"Yeah, I guess. But Lindsy, man, that's excellent! When did this happen?"

Tom told Kyle everything. He hadn't heard about the play almost getting canceled, or about Tom waking up in Lindsy's house, or any of it. It was weird. Normally, the second anything happened to either of them, the other one would hear about it. But for the past week of Tom's life, basically the craziest week since he'd found out about Crap Kingdom, his best friend had been several universes away. They used to tell each other everything, but once another world got involved, they'd stopped.

Once Tom finished, Kyle said, "But won't you miss out on the good part?"

"What do you mean?"

"Won't you miss, like, you guys making out and stuff?"

"Hopefully not. Anyway, it's not just about making out, she's great, she's so fun and cool and smart and I think she would like me, the actual me, if I could just be the actual me in front of her. But I don't know how to yet, and I need to learn, and I will learn, but I can't right now. The other me needs to take over for a little bit before she breaks up with me or something."

"The other you sounds awesome. You're lucky. My other me sucks."

"Yeah, he does. So can you do it? The king will never see me. I'll hide or something! I won't get you in trouble. I swear."

"I have to think about it."

Tom texted Kyle in third period:
    ???

Kyle wrote back:
    still thinking

Tom wrote:

dude, if i could soul-swap by myself, i would.

Later, Tom saw Kyle in the lunchroom.

"Man," Kyle said, "school is *boring*."

"Yeah," Tom said, "I know. So are we going?"

"Yes," Kyle said. "But if anybody sees you, I don't know anything about it."

"Don't worry," Tom said. "I have an idea."

Tom met Kyle at the gravel spot behind the auditorium after sixth period like they'd agreed. Kyle burst out laughing.

"Why are you dressed like that?"

"You said not to get spotted, so I figured . . ."

"You look ridiculous!"

"Well, that's fine, right, as long as no one recognizes me?"

"You don't look like someone else, you look like you in a fake mustache and a white wig."

"I look like them! This is how they all dress!" Tom had snuck up to the Drama Department's wardrobe room and now, in addition to the fake mustache and white wig, he was also wearing an oversized checkered blazer over a faded basketball jersey with the number 27 on it. Instead of pants, he was wearing a flowing floral-print skirt. He'd put all of his clothes in his backpack.

"Right, but . . . won't you still be wearing that here in the real world as well?"

"Hopefully my other self will know to immediately change back into my real clothes."

"You should text yourself right before we go."

"Yeah, good thinking." He didn't know if his other self had any grasp of phones, but who wouldn't look at a vibrating, beeping object in their hand?

Tom set his backpack down and took his phone out. He started to write a text and noticed that his text to Kyle, the one about how he would soul-swap if he could, was still sitting there. It hadn't sent. He changed the recipient to his own phone number and sent it to himself as a test. Three seconds later, his phone vibrated. Cool, it would work. He wrote a new text to himself:

> change your clothes immediately! they're in
> your backpack.—tom

He felt lame signing his text the way Tobe did, but he didn't have his own number saved in his phone and he wanted his other self to know where the message came

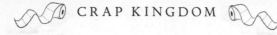

from. He didn't send the text yet. He left the thumb of his right hand on the send button. With his left hand, he grabbed Kyle's hand.

"Ready?"

"Yep."

They fell backward. Tom hit SEND just before they hit the ground.

Realities splashed. They were back in Crap Kingdom, or really, just outside of it.

"Okay," Tom said, peering up over the rim. "Let's go."

"No worries," Kyle said, "I can teleport through the Wall to anywhere inside the kingdom now. I'm getting better every time."

"Does that thing still happen where—"

Before Tom could finish his question, that thing happened where he felt like he was dead for three seconds.

When he came out of it, they were on the very edge of the kingdom, just inside the Wall. Tom was pleased to discover his mustache was still glued on. He was really good at mustache-gluing, at least. The wig was still on, too. His wig and mustache work were teleportation-proof and he was proud.

" All right," Kyle said. "You're gonna find a good hiding spot?"

"Sure," Tom said.

"I'd go with you but if you're with me it will draw atten-tion to you," Kyle said, "plus I got somewhere to be."

"Okay!" Tom said.

"Don't get upset, dude. I'm doing you a favor, remem-ber?"

Kyle walked away fast, leaving Tom alone. Tom felt pretty silly, and it wasn't even because of the wig or the mus-tache or the skirt.

Tom wandered alone in Crap Kingdom. All the things that had been strange to him about the place were old news now. But there were new strange things. For the first time, he could hear laughter in the air, and not cruel laughter, or I-give-up-and-am-crazy-now laughter, but actual warm laughter, from grown-ups and children alike. Had Kyle really taught an entire society to laugh? He couldn't have, right? This wasn't a commercial.

He looked around for hiding places. It was tough to dis-tinguish between what was someone's home and what was just junk. He'd zero in on a big pile of trash bags or a huge concrete tube and be absolutely sure there was no one inside of it and then someone would emerge just as he approached.

It was also tough to find a hiding spot because everything seemed to be in a state of flux. Children were helping their parents move the building blocks of their makeshift homes around. Years of rust and dust drifted up into the air. It was killing Tom's allergies. He was sneezing his head (but thankfully not his mustache) off. Everybody was in motion. Everybody had a purpose. He'd never seen it like this. It felt like the first day of high school when you were a freshman. Everybody else was engaged in all this chaotic activity that seemed crazy to you, like something you'd never get the hang of, but to them it made perfect sense. And you were sure that as soon as you tried to join in, everyone would laugh at you, or chop your head off.

"Excuse me," Tom asked a man dressed exclusively in beer boxes. "What's going on?"

"You didn't hear?" the beer man said. "Kyle said to look at your house today and see if there was any way you could make it better. It doesn't have to be bigger or prettier or anything. Just whatever 'better' means to you."

The man looked down at Tom's skirt.

"That's nice," he said sincerely.

"Thank you," Tom said. He was legitimately flattered.

The beer man turned back to the smashed-in hollowed-out snack-vending machine he'd been attempting to turn right side up. He reached down, dug his fingers underneath it, got it about halfway in the air, then stopped.

"Need some help?" Tom said.

"Why, thank you, that would be . . ." the man said.

Somewhere a loud, flawed bell clanged.

"Never mind!" the beer man said, and dropped the machine. Tom had to jump back to avoid losing his toes. He yelped, and when he opened his mouth to do so, he got a mouthful of the titanic dust cloud the falling machine had kicked up.

As soon as he'd blinked enough dust away, he saw that he was on an empty street, or at the very least, an empty trash-strewn dirt path. The last of its occupants were just disappearing around a corner. A tumbleweed of twisted plastic shopping bags blew by. Where was everyone going?

Tom now had his pick of hiding places. He had been worried he'd have to settle for the first dirt-puddle-at-the-top-of-an-old-shipping-container he came across. Now he could have any dirt puddle on any old shipping container he wanted, but nothing looked promising on this street. Maybe around the—

He bumped into someone much shorter than he was.

"Hey, watch it!"

He looked down. It was Pira. She was dressed in her Viking costume.

"Oh, hey, Tom."

Tom thought quickly. "Wot?" he answered. "'Oo's Tom, then?"

"What's *that* voice supposed to be?"

"'At's how I talk and that!"

"You sound like my dad, Tom."

Tom took this as a compliment, since her dad had sort of a British accent, even though this world did not have an England.

"Yeah, it's me, so what?"

"Why are you dressed like that?"

"Because your dad wants to kill me."

"That's right! He does. So . . . gimme it."

"What?"

"Give me your disguise or I'll tell my dad that you're here."

"Okay," Tom said, and began the excruciating process of removing his mustache without the proper mustache-removal solution.

"Where did . . . *ow* . . . where did everybody go?"

"Kyle's showing off his new invention."

"What is it?"

"Something called music."

"Wait, what? Kyle claims he invented *music?*"

"I don't know why you're getting so worked up about it. It's pretty stupid anyway. I don't see what the big deal is. When he debuted it last week everybody was like, oh, cool, that's so great, that's so *fun.* But who cares? It's just noise, right? I can make noise. I'd make a noise right now if someone weren't following me and I didn't want them to catch me."

"Who's . . . *ow* . . . following you?"

"Gark. My dad sent him after me. He wants me to hear 'music' with the rest of the losers, but if I wanted to hear a noise . . . *man,* do I want to make a noise right now! *That's* fun. That and dressing up as stuff. Why doesn't anyone understand that? No one ever wanted to have fun before and now that Kyle's here and they do, they don't even know how to do it right. Ugh, hurry up!"

"*Ow* . . . Okay! There!" Tom handed her his mustache and wig.

"The rest of it, too. Your clothes."

"What? Why?"

"Because I'm being chased and I need to change disguises!"

"These are the only clothes I have!"

"I bet that rock over there would sound really good against this big hollow metal thing, huh? Then you'd be in serious trouble."

"All right, fine."

"Aren't mustaches the best? There was this guy the other night who I caught sneaking around, and he was wearing this neat fuzzy helmet thing, and when I made him give it to me so I wouldn't tell anybody he was sneaking around, he took it off and he had an actual mustache! If I had a real mustache, I'd never cover it up with anything."

"Yeah," Tom said. "They're pretty great." He finished taking off the blazer and the jersey and the skirt. He had never anticipated being in a situation where someone would order him to take off a skirt and he would be mad about it.

He handed it all to Pira, who skillfully put it all on over her existing costume. When the process was over, in addition to all the other stuff, Pira was wearing a mustache on top of her Viking beard, and a white wig rested precariously between the two horns of her Viking helmet. Tom was wearing white cotton briefs and nothing else. He was embarrassed by them even though he didn't think Pira knew a thing about Earth underwear. Tom knew that at a certain point you were supposed to switch over from tighty-whiteys to some other form of more mature underwear, but he still hadn't made that transition, and it wasn't until someone else saw you in your underwear that you realized you'd failed to make this and other critical transitions, transitions every other kid his age just seemed to know how to make automatically.

"Great. Well, have fun!" Pira scampered off around the corner.

A few seconds later, she scampered back, picked up the rock she'd pointed out earlier and threw it against the piece of metal she'd pointed out earlier. As promised, it made an awful clanging noise. Then she disappeared again. The sound had barely finished echoing when Gark appeared behind Tom.

"Hey, Gark," Tom said.

"Oh, no. Oh no," Gark said. "Tom, you're not supposed to be here."

"I know. I know. I'm sorry. I'm really sorry about everything, okay? Seriously. When I came and saw this place it wasn't what I expected, at all, and the king kind of treated me like crap but you were great, and I should've treated you better, and I guess I should've taken your offer, because Kyle seems to be having a really good time. I just wish somebody had told me—I don't know. The point is, I'm really sorry for the way I treated you and if there's any way at all that you could not tell the king I'm here, I would really appreciate it."

Gark looked pained.

"I always liked you, Tom."

"Thanks," Tom said.

"No," Gark said, "I mean, I always liked *you*. Not . . . gosh, don't tell the king I said this. Not Kyle as much."

"Really?"

"Yeah! When that prophecy first came, I got so excited! I mean, come on, a Chosen One? We used to hear about that kind of stuff a lot when I was a kid, but it seemed like the king and my dad were kind of wanting any Chosen One talk to stop completely. But here was this prophecy through my window, and I brought it to the king, and I expected him to say no and instead he said sure, go ahead."

"It doesn't bother you that he was only letting you do it because he thought you'd mess up?"

"Who cares what he thinks, as long as I get to do it? That's the way I look at it. I imagined it would take such a long time to find you, but you were right there by the portal, and then I had to think of a good way to approach you . . . and I know it didn't turn out to be the best idea . . . but, you were like my project! It was so exciting!"

"You must have been disappointed when I turned out to be a jerk."

"I don't think you're a jerk. You said a lot of things to the king that maybe I couldn't agree with out loud, but they were things I'd always wanted to say. And as soon as I heard *you* say them, I was so excited because I knew I wasn't crazy. And Kyle's great! But there wasn't anything to do, really, to get him here. It wasn't a project. I already knew where he was, because he was friends with you. And the king liked him and took him to J's cave and suddenly he was the king's project. And everybody liked Kyle. And that's great. But it was kind of fun when it was just my thing. You were my favorite, Tom. Yeah. I liked you a lot."

"Is there still something we can do? Because I have to be here."

"Why?"

"It's tough to explain. But I have to be on this side of our two worlds."

"Well then," Gark said, "you should leave Kkkktttnpth. You should be beyond the Wall. I don't see the king chang-

ing his mind, especially if he finds out you snuck in here today."

"Is there anything you can do?"

Gark shook his head. "He's got his Chosen One."

"But I can't go too far," Tom said, "'cause I can't go back to my world without Kyle."

"Then at least hide," Gark said. "You're pretty obvious the way you're, y'know, dressed."

"I know! I was looking for a hiding spot, and I didn't mean to be not wearing clothes. . . . Anyway, if you see Kyle, and there's any way to tell him this without the king finding out, just tell him I'm hiding underneath . . . underneath . . ." Tom looked around. "I don't know, maybe that old canoe?"

"I wouldn't worry about it. Just pick the best hiding spot you can, and I'm sure Kyle will find you with a person-finding spell."

"Oh," Tom said. "All right."

"Did Pira come this way?"

Tom pointed directly behind him, toward the piece of metal and the rock and the corner she'd disappeared around minutes before.

"Thanks." Gark started to walk away, then turned back to Tom and started taking his shirt off.

"Gark!" Tom said.

"You're going to be cold," Gark said.

"Maybe, but I'll figure it out. What's the king gonna say when he sees you without a shirt?"

Gark seemed to really think about this. "I don't know."

Tom laughed. "It was a rhetorical question. Go, I'll be fine."

"All right," Gark said. "Good-bye, Tom."

Gark went out of sight behind a tent flap that was actually an old beach towel. It was blowing around in a wind that was just now kicking up. The sun was just starting to set. The temperature was dropping rapidly, even without the wind's help. Tom was freezing. He sincerely hoped that, back on Earth, his soul-other was using his body to win a fencing competition or something equally cool, to make it worthwhile that the real Tom was here, freezing in his underwear in a world where nobody wanted him.

At least Gark liked him. At least he was Gark's favorite. Then Tom remembered that Gark was not the smartest guy, and was the kingdom's least respected citizen. If the dumbest person liked you and no one else did, did that mean you were a bad person? If the smartest person here, which the king seemed to be, hated Tom, then that meant he was the worst, right? But Tom didn't like the king. The king was mean and judgmental. A smart mean person hated him, and a dumb nice person liked him. Whose approval was he supposed to want?

It was finally time to pick a place to hide. As usual, he had started out with every intention of making a really good decision, but as usual, the options had overwhelmed him, and he was tired and cold, so he gave up and climbed into what he thought was called a wardrobe. It did not take him to a second fantasy world, though. What had seemed appealing about it was that it had doors, and he could just open it, climb in, and not even have to crouch down because it was a little taller than he was, and he could close the doors and be out of the wind. What was unappealing about it were the things piled up at the bottom. He saw them as he stepped in. They appeared solid enough, but they crunched underneath his feet as he turned around to shut the doors. He looked down. They were like smooth, gray circular rocks, and they all had holes in the middle. But why were they crushed so easily if they were rocks? Because they weren't rocks, he realized. They were doughnuts. Extremely old doughnuts. The sprinkles were the dead giveaway. The bread and frosting had molded over, but the sprinkles, the cockroaches of the confectionary world, had maintained their color and shape. *Ewww,* Tom thought.

He considered kicking them out into the road, but he figured once he shut the doors, a pile of doughnuts outside would be a dead giveaway to whoever had placed them in here. This was what he could've done as Chosen One. This was how he could've been a leader. He could've said, "Hey, you know what? GET RID OF THE DOUGHNUTS!"

He winced, shut the door, and tried to be thankful that Pira hadn't asked for his shoes. No one here seemed to recognize the value of shoes. Kyle was teaching them music? Kyle needed to be teaching them shoes.

In the periods when the wind died down, Tom could hear Kyle's show, or gathering, or whatever it was. There was loud recorded music playing. It sounded like The Beatles. Maybe Kyle had found a boom box and some D batteries underneath a different pile of rotting doughnuts. Would Kyle do a whole lot to dissuade the people from thinking he'd invented music and not just brought it over from another world? Probably not. Tom didn't know why he assumed that, but he did. He was no longer sure whom he was mad at, exactly, but if he kept being mad at people it would keep him from being mad at himself.

After what seemed like forever, Tom heard applause

and shouting. The music died away. Seconds later, there was a thudding sound in front of the wardrobe doors. They swung open.

Kyle said, "Ready to go?"

Tom returned to his own body to find that body lying on a bed. His bed. There was no one with him this time. He was lying on top of his sheets. His other self had made the bed, and had done a way better job than Tom ever did when his mom made him do it. Tom was wearing his street clothes. That meant his other self had followed the instructions to change clothes, too. He really loved this guy.

Tom was holding something. His new phone. He looked at it. It seemed his other self had figured out how to send texts. Or really, he had figured out how to send one text message. A really, really long one. To Lindsy.

Tom sat up. He scrolled down and down, reading the message, his horror growing.

It was the dirtiest thing he'd ever read.

The time stamp said it had been sent twelve minutes ago. There was no undo button, no grabbing the text back from her inbox. The damage was done.

The text was something Tom would never, ever say.

Would he think it? Definitely. All the time. Alone. But he would never say it. He would certainly never put it in written form and send it to a girl's phone, because she would definitely respond by deleting the message and deleting his number from her phone and not speaking to him again, ever. It would not be unreasonable for Lindsy's father to come after Tom with a shotgun. Two shotguns, even. Tom had shaken Lindsy's father's sizable hand. He could definitely handle the weapons. Two shotguns, each of them double barreled. Four barrels of paternal teenage-boy-killing fury headed up the stairs of Tom's apartment building. Not unreasonable. Not at all. Tom had earned it.

What he hadn't earned was Lindsy. Not really. And it was over now, and that made sense, because he'd never earned it in the first place. He'd had some stranger's soul pinch-hit his entire brief relationship with a girl he would never have gotten just by being himself.

Tom laid his head back down on his pillow. He was back where he'd started, staring at the ceiling the way he had one night a couple of months ago when he was certain no fantasy creature would ever burst through it telling him he was the Chosen One in some other world. He decided it was way worse to get something like a Chosen One—hood or the love of Lindsy Kopec and then have it taken away from you than it was to never know those things were options at all.

His phone vibrated in his hand. He brought it up slowly to his face. He could barely look, but he did. It was a text from Lindsy. Her response was long. Really long. He scrolled down and down and down. He sat up in bed again.

She was into it.

She was really into it.

Lindsy's text was now the dirtiest thing he'd ever read.

This happened a lot. Not hot girls sending him sexually charged texts— that never happened. But there were always times when Tom's head was on the chopping block and he would learn all kinds of lessons in that moment of need, gaining the wisdom of a man whose death was imminent. And then, at the last second, his head would somehow be saved from the chopping block and he'd completely forget all the things he'd learned when it was there.

He'd had a final in Tobe's Beginning Drama class last year. He'd really wanted to do a good job on it to impress Tobe and he'd told himself he wouldn't do what he normally would've done, which is wait until the absolute last second to do everything. A good two weeks before the project (a diorama of a stage design for a reimagining of *Julius Caesar*) was due, he sketched out the diorama he planned to build. He was so proud of himself for doing this, for behaving so unlike his normal self, that he didn't work on it the next afternoon, or the next. He would think about it occasionally and think, *I'm ahead of the game. I worked really hard that one afternoon and I could do it again anytime.*

He came into class a few weeks later and everyone was sitting on the carpeted amphitheater steps of the drama room with shoe-box dioramas on their laps. He had been so ahead of the game that he'd forgotten when the due date was, presuming that since he was so far ahead of the game and the due date was so far in the future, no matter how many days actually passed, his ahead-ness and the due date's far-away-ness would always stay the same.

Tom sat down on the carpeted steps. He was doomed. He watched the door, waiting for Tobe to come in. But Tobe never came in. A substitute came instead. She asked for everyone's dioramas shortly after taking attendance. All the other kids placed their dioramas on a table by Tobe's desk at the front of the room.

That night, Tom worked like a demon building his diorama. Instead of the cocky feeling he'd had that first day a few weeks ago, he was now filled with a grave resolve, an adultness, an I've-learned feeling. He would hand it in the next day. He would not offer any explanation or excuse, only an apology. This wasn't middle school anymore. His life, as his mom had told him many times, was now happening in the present tense. He would accept the consequences and learn and do better next time and never ever do anything like this again.

Tobe was back the next day. Tom was the first student in the room. Tobe's back was turned and all the dioramas were still on the table where they'd been the day before. Tom realized it would be simple just to set his diorama with the rest of them. But no: that would be the cowardly, childish way out. He waited until Tobe turned around. He began to offer his no-explanation, no-excuse apology, when Tobe waved him off.

"Just set it there. Thanks, Tom."

Tom never got to deliver his noble I'm-sorry-and-if-you-fail-me-I-understand speech. He would go on to receive a B-plus on the project and an A-minus in the class. He would also continue to do things at the very last minute.

Now the same thing was happening with Lindsy. Why

would he ever stop entrusting his romantic life to his other self, who was so dynamite at saying exactly what Lindsy wanted to hear and doing exactly what Lindsy wanted done?

But he couldn't get back over there without Kyle, and once he was back over there, he couldn't be within the borders of Crap Kingdom. That part sucked.

His phone made a beep indicating he had a message from earlier that he hadn't read yet. He looked again. This text was from himself to himself. He opened it. It was longer than his dirty text to Lindsy and her dirty text back to him combined.

The first few lines read:

the soul-swap's easy enough. what follows are simplified instructions.

MAGIC ISN'T DOING something extraordinary in your world, it's doing something ordinary in the tiny world you've created inside your own world. in the tiny temporary world you've created, such things are possible. normal even.

magic's not the hard part. magic's probably not even a good name for it, because as i said, it's all very normal. the hard part is the creation of tiny worlds inside whatever world you're in currently.

Tom leapt up from his bed. He started clearing dirty clothes off the floor, throwing them in piles on either side of the room. He would need room to fall into the other world, he figured. He didn't know how to do any of this yet but he was too excited not to do something immediately. It was the same as when he'd gotten really into chess in seventh grade: he'd checked out a *Chess for Dummies* book from the library and got home and read half a chapter and got so excited about the strategies he was supposedly learning and chess in general that he ran to his computer and fired up the chess program and played a bunch of games and always lost and never applied what he'd learned.

Focus. He had to focus. He picked up his phone again. He read:

> these temporary worlds that allow for otherwise impossible things to take place are what you might more simply refer to as "spells." to internalize a spell and be able to employ it just by thinking is to modify it, to create a tiny new world every time. this requires a great deal of time and skill and training. lucky for you there exist borrowed worlds you can employ, without having to call them into being from scratch. you

will be able to invoke a simple soul-swap by using some basic magic words. the difference between a spell invoked with magic words and a spell invoked from within one's own self is the difference between checking a book out from the library and purchasing it from a bookshop, or perhaps more accurately, writing an entire book yourself. but if i am reading the above correctly, you are only wishing to be able to do the basic swap, not become a level-5 gandalf or any such thing.

Tom was confused in a couple of ways. He scrolled up. The texts from himself, to himself, before this one read:

dude, if i could soul-swap by myself, i would.

And then:

change your clothes immediately! they're in your backpack.—tom

So his other self had received the second text immediately after the swap and, upon opening it, seen the first one, about Tom wanting to be able to soul-swap. His other self had then provided Tom a long and properly punctuated reply. When that was done, his other self had sent Lindsy the *Iliad* of dirty texts, which she'd loved. This other self apparently knew about bookstores, and about Gandalf. Had this other self had the time to be a brilliant actor, a romantic dynamo, and a scholar of magic, *and* read the entire most influential fantasy saga ever? Tom himself had only ever gotten halfway through *The Fellowship of the Ring*. How great could one guy be? Tom wanted to buy this guy a soda, or maybe a body of his own.

> this is a newer version of the spell, slightly improved from the one i take it you've been using. every time i take residence in your body, that body is flat on its back, completely out of breath, and in a great deal of pain. this spell will simplify both your life and mine by eliminating the need for any sort of fall. i never had a chance to finalize it, but it should be stable enough for our purposes.

Oh. So Tom hadn't needed to clear that space on the floor. Well, anyway, now his room looked cleaner. Maybe his other self would take the hint and clean his whole room. This was kind of like having a robot butler that lived inside your body.

the trigger words are "crabsaw griddlefriend." just think of doing the spell and say the words, and, as they say, "presto." the word "presto," interestingly enough, is not used in any spells that i am aware of. i would try to work it into one but the words must be very carefully selected, for reasons too arcane and very likely too dull to go into here.

wish to return from the other world? say the words again. simple.

i hope this proves useful. i will continue managing your affairs on this side in the manner i have been. i presume you are content with said management, since i've been asked back into your life several times.

This was great! Tom could come and go from the nameless kingdom, or more important, the world around the nameless kingdom, without Kyle's help. Tom was in control. He knew *magic*.

Tom stood in the center of the room. He held his phone up to look at the "trigger words." Before he could say them, his phone buzzed. It was a text from Lindsy. It read:

GET OVER HERE. NOW. ;)

That other world would still be there. He was going to do whatever Lindsy said. He was going to go over there, now, as himself.

He'd earned it.

20

TOM RODE HIS bike over. Lindsy's mom let him into their house. Tom mumbled something about him and Lindsy needing to run their lines for the show. She told him that Lindsy was upstairs in her bedroom. For some reason it was the word "bedroom" that did it. He went from very excited to very scared.

He had no training, basically no experience with any other girls. In fact, he had basically no experience with Lindsy. He'd barely been able to kiss her without help from his personal void-soul assistant. He was going to screw this up. He was in no way prepared. He had not even known what some of the terms she used in her text were. That should have never been the case. He was a teenage boy who had the Internet.

He was almost to the top of the stairs. He'd ridden his bike over, so it wasn't insane for him to be out of breath already, was it?

He tripped on the very top stair. He didn't fall flat on his face. He caught himself. It was almost more embarrassing to catch yourself than it was to just plain old fall, and even worse when no one saw you trip. You still knew what had happened. You still knew you were a total goober.

Why was he like this? Why did it take getting the things he really wanted to bring out the worst emotions he was capable of feeling? Weren't those feelings only supposed to surface when really bad stuff happened to you? Why did they show up when good stuff happened? If that was always going to be the case, why ever want anything good to happen at all? He was beginning to think the king had been right. Why get excited for anything? You're just going to screw it up. But you can't screw up something you don't want. Well, you can, but you won't care when you do. His hand was on her doorknob.

He paused. He raised his fist to the door. Five full seconds later, he knocked.

"Tom?" Lindsy said from inside.

"Yup," he said. *Yup?* he thought. *YUP? That's sexy?* Is that what he thought sexy was?

"Come in," she said.

He put his hand on the doorknob.

Open it, he thought. *She already knows you're out here. You're being weird, and you're being a coward. Other You would just barge right in. Other You would just* do *and not think.*

He turned the doorknob. He could hear soft music playing inside Lindsy's room. Female vocalist. He stepped inside. He closed the door. He looked at the door as he closed it for some reason, probably because he could not trust his body to perform simple actions such as closing a door and felt he had to supervise with his actual eyeballs.

"Hi," Lindsy said.

Tom looked up.

Lindsy was lying across her bed, on top of the covers, like Tom had been on his bed earlier that afternoon.

Except unlike Tom, Lindsy was beautiful.

And also unlike Tom, Lindsy was naked.

Tom had a very quick panic attack. Then his panic attack had a panic attack.

"Hey," he burped.

The old Tom was dead. All that was left was a being made entirely of terror. Naked terror. Ha, that was funny. He had thought of a joke. How could he think of a joke at a moment like this? The fact that he would think of a joke at a moment like this said everything about why he would never be the kind of person that could actually *do* this.

"I have to go to the bathroom," he said.

"What?" Lindsy said. "Really? Okay ..."

He put his hand on the doorknob again.

"Heyyyy," Lindsy said, playfully, "dummy!" She pointed to another door in her bedroom. Right. She had a bathroom of her own in here. Tom knew that. He'd used it many times. He'd probably even used it at times he didn't know about. He crossed to the bathroom. This brought him closer to her than he'd been yet tonight.

"But at least kiss me first?" she said. Still playful. Maybe everything wasn't totally screwed up. He turned. She was smiling in a sexy way. How could girls smile in a sexy way? Smiles were inherently goofy. Lindsy was pulling it off, though.

All he had to do was walk over and kiss her. The rest would take care of itself. It wasn't about what he did and didn't do. It was just about doing something. That was the difference between him and his text-messaging magic-knowing otherwordly cohort: that guy did stuff. Tom thought about doing stuff until the chance to do anything had passed. *Do something.*

"I'll be right back," Tom said, and ducked into the bathroom.

He shut the door and leaned against it. He pulled out his phone and looked through his text messages.

"Are you okay?" Lindsy called to him.

"Crabsaw griddlefriend," Tom said.

"What?" Lindsy yelled.

Crap, it didn't work. And she'd heard him. Maybe he was supposed to say it louder. But when he said it louder, would she be even more weirded out? What if his other self just barged back out of the bathroom without flushing the toilet, and she thought all Tom had done in here was yell nonsense words to himself? Should he pee now, and flush, and wash his hands? The flush would cover the sound of him speaking the trigger words, right? It would help, at least.

He started trying to pee standing up. His hands were shaking. He couldn't pee. Nothing in his body was working right. What would she think about his hands shaking? He hoped his other self had a hand-steadying spell. *Just flush the toilet*, Tom thought.

But wait, what if his other self didn't know to wash his hands and Lindsy thought Tom didn't wash his hands?

Just go, he told himself. *Just let the other guy handle it.*

Tom reached out and smacked the handle. Water spun in the toilet. There was the *whoosh* of water in the pipes. Now was the time. What were the words again? He looked at his phone.

"CRABSAW GRIDDLEFRIEND!"

21

IT WAS NIGHT just outside Crap Kingdom, and it was cold in the crater.

Tom looked down. Of course it was cold: he was naked. Not even just as naked as he'd been when Pira took his Crap-Kingdom-resident costume. This time he was *naked naked*, the way he probably should've been within twenty-five seconds of entering Lindsy's room. He was naked in the entirely wrong dimension.

He'd always wondered how, when characters in movies and TV teleported, the teleportation technology or magic spell knew to bring their clothes along and not just their naked forms. Turns out they didn't know to bring their clothes along. Not automatically.

That's okay, Tom thought. *I'll just pop back over.* Surely by

now his other self had had a few seconds to do whatever suave Casanova-like thing needed to be done. At the very least, he and Lindsy were kissing by now. He just needed to go back. Simple! *Now, to say the trigger words.*

What were the trigger words?

No. No. No.

In addition to the physical sensation of cold caused by wind whipping into the crater, Tom had the acute mental sensation of something slipping away, something he'd known for just a second, but never firmly enough for it to actually be permanently in his brain, like when someone would leave his mom a voice mail where they gave her a number to call back and she didn't have a pen so she'd remember the area code and the first three digits, and she'd shout to Tom in the living room, "Honey, remember these last four numbers." If she asked him right away, Tom could tell her those last four numbers, as long as it was the only thing he was focusing on, but if she took too long and he had time to turn his attention back to the TV, they'd be gone for good and she'd have to listen to the voice mail again and would probably just go get a pen this time.

He'd read the words off the screen of his phone. His phone was in his pants back on Earth. How could he not remember them? Why wasn't memorizing them the first

thing he did? They were magic words, in his actual possession, known only to him on Earth, and he hadn't just learned
them straight off. Why? He'd learned reams and reams of
text for *View*. This was just four simple words combined into
two nonsense words.

He looked in his brain. He saw the space where the
words had been. But with every tooth-chattering second in
the crater spent trying to recover them, they slipped further away. It was hopeless. He was a naked boy in a ditch in
the middle of the night in a universe not his own. He was
the very definition of hopelessness.

He could freeze to death out here. No one was going
to come along except for an Elgg, and running from one
or more of those things would keep him very warm for a
minute before he was captured and eaten alive. Kyle might
appear here randomly, but that presumed Kyle ever came
back to Earth anymore, which Tom doubted very much.

He peered up over the opposite rim of the crater. The
dome of the Wall shone faintly in the distance. There were
no Elggs between here and there that he could see. Maybe
they slept at night. If he was going to go, he should run for it.

He lifted himself up over the rim, got to his feet, and
started running. He wondered if he should tread carefully,
watching for threats to his bare feet, or just break into a

dead run and let pure velocity take care of any problems. Then he wondered why he would ever use the phrase "pure velocity" to refer to anything he might do. The only time the phrase "pure velocity" could be used to describe Tom was when he headed for the refrigerator on Saturday mornings where when there was guaranteed to be leftover pizza.

Tom started running to the best of his ability anyway. He stuck to the path he and Kyle had taken when they made this sprint, over an open plain and through a mini canyon. He could see the tracks of the Elggs that had pursued them that day, the occasional Elgg-shaped dent in the ground where they'd been tripped up by Kyle's energy vines. The ground was dry, which he guessed was a plus, until his feet started to sting again and he longed for a nice cooling mud puddle or two.

Every few seconds he would remember he was running naked and feel newly shocked and embarrassed. But the Greeks had run around like this all the time, right? The way he understood it, they'd flapped their way through the entire first Olympics, and they just thought it was normal.

His breathing became rhythmic, and his lungs actually seemed to be getting and distributing enough air to meet his body's demands. There was a certain point immediately after Tom had just been forced to do strenuous physical activity when he could actually understand why people like Kyle's middle-school self might have gotten up on a Saturday morning for reasons besides cold pizza, might have actually strapped on cleats and taken the field to engage in a sport Tom usually thought of as way too exhausting, pointless, and shin-endangering. That was kind of fun, he'd think, in the postexercise endorphin rush. He should do that more often. Then the brain chemicals would wear off and he would realize there was nothing he wanted to do less. He could only want to do it once he had already done it.

His stride found, he blasted out of the canyon. This was him, Tom felt, in his purest form. He was not just a floating brain being carried around by an indifferent body. He was *man*. He was a man in the physical world. Two worlds, even. He was glorious in his speed, in his form, in his nakedness.

The sheen of the dome dissipated as he approached, until it became truly invisible. Three hundred yards to Crap Kingdom. Why three hundred yards? He wasn't sure. He didn't know the distance, exactly, but it was pretty far, and three hundred yards seemed a manly distance, a manly distance to be manfully traversed by him, a man. He was close. Then he was closer. Then he was there. Then he tripped.

He fell forward, bonking his head on the invisible barrier. He hadn't even hit his head on it. Hitting your head was for real men. When Tom's head collided with something, it was a bonk.

Tripping on Lindsy's top stair, he'd thought about how it was almost worse to catch yourself before you fell entirely. Now he lay on the ground, sand working its way into his hair as he rolled onto his back, and he realized it was always worse to fall. His head really hurt, but he was thankful for the barrier preventing him from falling flat on his face, as a full belly flop onto the ground would have been a serious threat to his more vulnerable naked parts.

Tom stood up. He thought, *Now, to bring down the Wall.* Simple enough. He just had to say the magic words, the magic words he'd heard both Gark and Kyle say before. He'd heard them twice. How many times did scientists say you needed to hear something to remember it? He couldn't remember. Where the words ought to be, there was yet another empty space in his brain.

Both times he'd heard the words, he'd been running for his life, so he hadn't been paying attention to who was saying what. It was yet another thing that if someone had just told him it would be important, he would have found it to be important, but no one had told him. He remembered the word to get it to close. It was *Close*. So there was that.

He stood up and peered into Crap Kingdom. He couldn't see anyone out and about. There was music playing in the distance. The Rolling Stones. At least Kyle was exposing them to both sides of that debate, even if he was probably passing them both off as his own super band. Kyle and the Kyles, maybe. Colored lights appeared sporadically above the kingdom, their reflections shimmering at the top of the dome. There were echoes of loud noises and applause. Had Kyle found an old stash of fireworks and was now saying they were his own creation?

It probably wasn't fireworks, Tom realized. It was probably just Kyle showing off his fantastic and effortless magic.

Then Tom saw it. Hanging in the glassless window of a structure made of old wooden boards right on the other side of the Wall: underwear. Several pairs of it. All different kinds, too: the tighty-whiteys he presently favored, along with enough other varieties that he could have settled this whole what-underwear-should-I-wear-as-a-fully-grown-adult thing for good by sampling all of them at once. He needed them. And they were right there, taunting him, so close that if there wasn't an invisible energy field blocking him he could have reached right out and grabbed them all. Tom could have been wearing all four pairs at once! He could've been King of Underwear Mountain!

If he had been wearing them, though, he would've taken them for granted. But since his underwear had been taken away, and since these pairs were so close yet were denied to him, he wanted them more than anything. Those people who hung them in their window, they had no idea what they had. Tom knew what it was worth. But it was too late. It would never be his.

He gave up. He leaned face forward against the barrier, thinking maybe its magical energy would give off at least a little bit of heat. No luck. It was as cold as everything else.

Tom decided he would not cry. With his luck, the tears would freeze, and he refused to die with frozen eyeballs. He would despair without expelling any extra moisture doing it. But, boy, would he despair.

There was a growl behind him. Tom peeled his face off the freezing invisible wall and turned around, slow. He was tearless-eyeball to eyeball with the biggest Elgg he'd seen in any of his visits to Crap Kingdom.

Now it was really time to despair.

22

TOM FIGURED HE should go ahead and prepare for death. But there was nothing to do, it turned out. You just died. *Here it comes,* he thought.

The Elgg came closer. Standing on all four legs, its eyes were level with Tom's. The scariest thing about it was that it didn't look angry or hungry or murderous. It just looked in Tom's eyes, totally placid, with its own baseball-sized eyes, orbs of ridiculous beauty, that probably would have been considered priceless museum pieces in any universe if they hadn't been in the skull of a giant, vicious pack beast. Tom forgot to be scared. It was like the thought you had just before slipping into a dream. A second later, he was in it.

He was high above the clouds again. A crystal spire was

breaking the clouds the way a boat's prow breaks the surface of the ocean. A hand came into view, an enormous human hand, like God's in a Renaissance painting, and it brushed all the clouds away with two or three swipes, laying bare the crystalline kingdom nestled in the jagged rocks of a mountain, surrounded by warring armies. Tom's view zoomed out and he saw that all these armies, all these clouds, this entire kingdom, were all on a tabletop, and the hand belonged to a man sitting at that table, watching the action intently. He was wearing crystal armor of almost impossible intricacy, its every interlocking piece holding in raging clouds of crimson smoke, like someone had fashioned it out of Jupiter's atmosphere, and he was sitting in a grand chamber made of the same material as the armor, all of it pulsating with the same angry vapors.

The man looked up at Tom. Tom realized he was actually in the room. The man raised his eyebrows, and indicated the table's surface with another broad sweep of his hand. Tom raised his own hand and decisively pointed to three points on the table. Glowing red markers appeared at each of these three points. Armies changed direction at once and began sweeping toward the markers. The man smiled and nodded. He clapped a hand on Tom's shoulder.

Tom didn't feel it: he looked down and realized he was wearing a smaller version of the man's armor. It swirled with the same red smoke. Then the smoke filled his field of vision. It blew in every direction, and then shapes appeared in it, stock-still and uniform, like those Chinese terra-cotta soldiers, and the smoke curled around them until a wind snatched the final traces of it away, and Tom saw that he was on a parade ground, a thousand or more men stretched out before him. The man in the crimson armor was standing before them, his back to Tom. The man was addressing the assembled soldiers, all of whom were wearing armor like the man's, though much less intricate. Tom was seated among a row of men in chairs, most of whom looked to be four or five times Tom's age. They all nodded as the man spoke, and they began to applaud, and Tom looked up and saw that the man in the crimson armor was pointing to him. The man waved him up, and as Tom stood, the man sat down. Tom did not hesitate; his feet drew him up to the edge of the stage. The wind was blowing harder than ever now, so Tom could not hear a single word he was saying, but he paced back and forth and gestured firmly, and he could feel his voice-box humming confidently, and the looks on the soldier's faces and on the faces of the seated elderly men and, most important, on the face of the man in the crimson armor indicated that Tom was saying something very important and very righteous indeed, and saying it much better than anyone else could say it.

The sound of the wind in Tom's ears grew louder, and the wind grew so strong that it blew all the soldiers and in fact the entire parade ground away and it blew the old men's chairs in around Tom, and a long crystal table appeared in the center of all of them, and they were all at a banquet and Tom was still standing, still speaking, and when he finished all the men laughed, and Tom saw that the man in the crimson armor was there, laughing hardest of all, and Tom felt great. The man in the crimson armor reached out and grabbed his glass, because there was now a feast on the table in the center of everything, and he raised it, and toasted Tom, and the elderly men did likewise, and when the glasses came down and people started drinking, Tom saw that one of the faces behind one of the glasses had not been a man at all but in fact a beautiful girl, not even a girl but a woman, and she wore no armor but the clouds simply clung to her like a gown made out of an overcast day, and she smiled, and the wind got louder than ever, and then they were alone.

It was just the two of them face-to-face at the center

of a whirlwind. He did not hesitate even for a second. He pulled her close and kissed her.

His eyes closed and the wind died down and when he opened them he was once again naked and staring into the oceanic eyes of the biggest-ever dragon-dog.

He was now able to break the Elgg's gaze. He looked up over its head and for the first time ever he noticed, on the horizon, a glow competing with the glow from the dome of the Wall and Kyle's magical fireworks. It was faint. It was red.

The Elgg shifted. Tom was startled. But it wasn't lunging forward. It was bowing. Somewhere, in the space vacated by a few sets of magic words, Tom knew absolutely for certain that the thing wanted him to climb on its back.

It was definitely better than being eaten. It would also beat freezing to death, naked and alone. But if he did it, it would not just be for reasons of survival. That vision that the Elgg filled his mind with, Tom thought, what if it was a prophecy? Presentation-wise, it sure beat the hell out of a piece of printer paper with a couple of lines of Times New Roman on it. What if the Ghelm weren't so bad?

He was naked, so there was no non-awkward way to climb onto the thing. He hoped the Elgg did not have any concept of "awkward," any concept of "ew, gross." He came around and turned to face Crap Kingdom. There were still fireworks and music. He swung one leg up over the beast's back.

As soon as he was on, the Elgg once again stood up to full height. It wheeled around, facing away from the Wall. Tom wrapped his arms around its neck. He was prepared for it to break into a dead run across the plains.

He was not prepared for it to grow wings and fly.

23

THE ELGG GALLOPED three or four times before it leapt up and never came down. Its dragon-like wings started beating and they left the plain behind. Like any takeoff Tom had ever experienced, it was as thrilling as it was terrifying.

Tom's ears filled with wind as they soared into the night sky. For a moment he had forgotten that he was naked and freezing, but now he remembered, and he knew the cold was only going to get worse as they got higher into the atmosphere. The skin of the Elgg, smooth and scaly and vaguely translucent, looked like it would have been cold to the touch, but it was growing warmer by the second, perhaps because of the physical effort of flight. Or, Tom thought, perhaps it sensed that he was cold. *How consider-ate*, he thought. A comforting green glow was even starting to spread underneath its translucent scales. Tom hugged it even tighter.

He turned his head. The dome of the Wall was reced-ing in the distance, shining brightly now that they were so far away. Was this a bad idea? Gark had said the Ghelm wanted to destroy Crap Kingdom. Well, Russia had wanted to destroy the United States at one point, but they didn't anymore, and now there were at least three Russian kids in Tom's high school class. Nations could be enemies. It didn't necessarily mean the people in them were bad.

Who said that he and Kyle couldn't each have their own kingdom? It seemed pretty ideal actually. And while Kyle's kingdom was mostly made of junk from Earth, Tom's kingdom, if the visions were any guide, had a look that let you know that you were somewhere fantastic. Tom figured he was stuck in this world anyway since he didn't know the magic words to get home. He could either spend his time here dying or spend it flying. He was pleased that this thought had rhymed. It went a long way toward making it seem true.

He hugged his Elgg more tightly—was it too soon to

start thinking of it as *his* Elgg? It was keeping him warm and airborne and alive. It had probably saved his life.

Tom stared up at the blue and craterless moon. *Just a boy and his dragon-dog,* he thought, *soaring through the night sky.*

Before long, they seemed to be descending. Something dead ahead and cloud level glinted in the blue moonlight, and Tom realized he was looking at an after-dark version of the vision he'd seen twice, the spire breaking the clouds. The spire's tip winked with the faintest red light, like the top of a skyscraper and the little red light that tells planes not to crash into it. Even in darkness he could see the dark strip of land made visible by the wedge where the clouds broke, then re-congealed a mile or so away from the spire. Tom didn't know when he'd become such a decider of how far things were away from other things. But it looked like about a mile.

He waited for the clouds to dissipate as they'd done in the vision, but they stayed solid as his Elgg plunged toward the spire. It looked bigger and bigger as they descended, the Elgg seemingly on a collision course with it, and as it went from big to huge in Tom's field of view he could see that the spire was actually filled with incandescent gas, like a neon sign, except unlike with neon, you could see the gas itself swirling up to the top if you looked closely. Soon Tom didn't have to look closely because it was fifty feet in front of them, then twenty-five, then ten, and they were definitely going to crash, then at the last second, *whoosh*, his Elgg rolled to one side and slipped just to the right, into where the cloud layer broke, and they were underneath, swirling around the spire, heading straight down, all the way to the spire's origin, a blinding round shape pulsating with a thousand different dancing colors that lit up the surrounding black rocks of the jagged mountain. This structure, this thing, was at the summit of the mountain, emanating from the rock, the spire leading down to a huge bulge like the prow of a boat, covered in a network of bubbles and tubes and crystal tunnels, some of them empty, some of them swarming with people, some of them filled with incandescent gases of different colors. A multitude of crystalline structures cascaded from the center tower down one side of the mountain, a multicolored glass-and-neon cityscape of seemingly infinite complexity. Tom was a little bit nauseated but a whole lot in awe.

They seemed about to dash themselves on the rocks when the Elgg swooped under a glass tunnel filled with purple neon vapor that created a sort of bridge between two jagged cliff faces and suddenly they were dodging diamond- and orb-shaped chambers and their interconnecting tubes in a perfectly executed series of maneuvers taking them down the mountain. Tom wondered if all the acrobatics were necessary or if they were strictly for his benefit, not that he was complaining either way. Tom had been breathless from biking over to Lindsy's house to humiliate himself, and then he had been breathless next to Crap Kingdom sprinting naked from one disappointment to another, but now he was breathless from catapulting through a wonderland of crystal towers full of mysterious people and harnessed, pulsating clouds of indescribable brilliance. There was no question which one he liked best. They had entered a tunnel that seemed barely wider than the Elgg's wingspan. Every so often a walkway or balcony would jut out from the tunnel walls and the Elgg would be forced to duck one way or the other, but it seemed instinctively aware of the size of the rider on its back, somehow always managing to leave Tom just enough room to duck and not get his head sheared off. It trusted him to duck, Tom thought. It believed in him.

Then the sky was open above them again, and the tunnel's bottom spread out to become a landing strip. The beast slowly brought its wings in and touched the ground. It galloped to the edge of the landing strip. There was nothing but darkness beyond. Then it turned, and Tom could see they were at the foot of the mountain, staring up at the crystal-enclosed brilliance that climbed up and up, all the way to the tower that tapered off until it became that tiny spire blinking red up there in the unharnessed clouds. Tom sat up. He cracked his back. He remembered he was naked, but he didn't care. He enjoyed hanging out naked in his room at home. Maybe he could convince them that being naked was part of his culture.

Men Tom hadn't noticed before appeared out of dark corners of the landing strip. They looked like soldiers. They had the armor Tom had seen in his visions and brandished long crystal pikes that were almost twice as tall as the men themselves and had jets of dancing red smoke coming from their tips. They surrounded Tom and lowered the smoking ends of their weapons at him without a word.

"Easy, gentlemen! Easy!"

Hearing this, the soldiers lifted their weapons and looked up. On a platform high above the landing strip, a slim-faced older man had appeared. He turned and ran down a flight of steps to reach them. Instead of armor, he wore a sort of tight-fitting translucent material that had been made into a jumpsuit and was filled with yellow smoke. "We've got one at last! We've got—"

He stopped on the last step and actually took Tom in, in all of his nakedness.

"Oh my. It's like the old days. Step down, son."

As if it understood what the man had said, the Elgg bowed, and Tom did as he was told. The man in the yellow jumpsuit chose that moment to start looking up and around the room and basically anywhere except for directly at Tom. One of the soldiers laughed and elbowed a coworker.

"Let's have it quiet now!" the man in the jumpsuit shouted. "Errr... let's see what we can do here...." He looked around. "You," he said, indicating the soldier who had just been snickering at Tom. "The hose."

Reluctantly the soldier disappeared into the shadows, then reappeared, holding the end of what looked like a fire hose except its length was completely see-through. He handed the nozzle of the hose to the man in the yellow jumpsuit.

"Hold still, son," the man said. He pointed the thing at Tom and twisted a lever on the nozzle. A jet of white steam shot out the end. Tom braced himself instinctively, because, as many misadventures pulling lids off boiling pots of macaroni had taught him, steam was very, very hot, and would burn you. It turned out he didn't need to worry. This steam didn't burn at all. He tried to move his arms from where they sat wrapped around his body after he'd tried to protect himself from the steam, but they wouldn't move. His legs were stuck together, too. The steam had formed a solid cloud around him that didn't dissipate and acted like a straitjacket.

"I told you to hold still, I think," the man said. "Right, just try to hold your arms at your sides." The man grabbed the giggling soldier's pike. "And let's please really hold still this time?" With no hesitation, he plunged the smoking end of the pike toward Tom, who didn't even have time to prepare for death. The man made three cuts, two at his sides and one at his legs, then lifted the pike back up. Tom was still alive. He tried lifting his arms and found that he could. The steam still clung to him, except now, instead of a straitjacket, it acted as a shirt and pants, encircling his arms and legs, completely opaque and, he found, quite warm, but without the sensation of wearing anything at all. It was the freedom of nudity combined with the warmth and protection of clothing. Well, this was just the best. Tom wanted to ask if he could maybe get one of these steam-suits for around the house.

"Thanks!" Tom said.

"No thanks necessary," said the man, handing the pike back to the soldier. "It benefits all of us. Now, there is little time for pleasantries, as I am sure the king will want to see you immediately, but I am Glubwhoa Tchoobrayitch. If you wish, you may call me by the abbreviation 'Tchoobrayitch.'"

Tom's first thought was that the abbreviation wasn't much shorter than the name. His second was that he didn't think he'd ever get tired of hearing that a king wanted to see him immediately.

"Nice to meet you," Tom said, "I'm Tom."

"Hello, Tom." He got Tom's name right on the first try. Tom liked everything about this kingdom better so far.

"Bring me another Elgg," Tchoobrayitch said to his men, and they fell all over themselves to run off the landing strip and into the shadows. They came back with an Elgg that was smaller than Tom's. It didn't have to be led by a leash—it simply walked alongside the soldiers up to Tchoo-brayitch, who hopped on.

"If you'll retake your Elgg, Tom," Tchoobrayitch said, smiling, "hopefully you'll be more comfortable this time."

Tom's Elgg bowed once again in front of him, and once Tom got on, it rose to its full height.

"The king may be sleeping," Tchoobrayitch said, "but we shall wake him. He will want to be made aware of you right away."

After a few minutes of dodging through a tangle of interconnected tubes and tunnels, Tom and Tchoobrayitch emerged into an enormous chamber. It was easily four times bigger than any stadium Tom had ever seen on Earth. The whole swirling-gas theme of the Ghelm kingdom kept making Tom think of Jupiter, but what they found embedded in one wall of this chamber looked almost exactly like it. It was an orb whose surface was all tumultuous, miniature super-storms. Tom had seen it in his visions. Opposite the orb, the visible stone workings of the mountain ringed a circular chasm, deep and dark and black with a steady, howling wind blowing out of it that seemed to be coming straight from hell. All around the orb's station in the wall were portholes, presumably for ventilation for the impossible wind. Tom looked down. The wind was tearing his mist-clothing apart but luckily, it was being regenerated at exactly the same rate. Tchoobrayitch turned left, starting up a path carved into the cliff face of the chamber. They were headed away from the chasm, toward the orb.

Tom clung hard to his Elgg, which was struggling not to be blown up against the chamber wall. He wondered if he would get to keep it during his stay here. He sure hoped so. He could name it. He'd never had a pet bigger than a goldfish. It would be neat to have any pet at all, let alone a pet he could ride around as it flew.

Finally they reached the orb. Tchoobrayitch reached out a bare hand and placed it on the orb's surface, then took it away, leaving a red handprint. The handprint lingered there for a second and then fluttered away into the orb's interior storm, like a paper cutout blown down the sidewalk on a windy day. A second later, the entire orb began to float out and down toward the center of the chamber. It left a huge vacant hole in the wall, and on the other side of the wall was night, and bare country.

The orb stopped moving and hovered in mid-air several feet away from the edge of the path . Tchoobrayitch's Elgg leapt off the edge, into the wind, landing on the top of the orb. It skittered to the dead center and, as soon as it had found its footing, Tom's Elgg did the same. Tom clung harder than ever to the back of his faithful but as-yet-nameless Elgg, worried that he would be blown off its back and dashed against the cliff wall or sucked out of the giant space left by the missing orb.

Instead, his Elgg nobly achieved the summit of the orb. It positioned its feet in a very specific way, and then, synchronized, both Elggs deployed their impressive wings, and none too soon, because the second they did so, the top of the orb opened and they plummeted down into it. The Elggs' wings acted as parachutes, and Tom and Tchoobray-itch floated straight down into a throne room. There was no mistaking it, Tom thought. For one thing, it actually had a throne.

Sitting on the throne was the man in the crimson armor from Tom's vision: the Ghelm King.

He was young for a king, maybe in his mid-forties, though Tom was notoriously bad at judging the ages of people over eighteen, and for all he knew, the Ghelm aged at a different rate from Earth people. He had a beard, but it was brown and manicured, in stark contrast to the Crap King's tangled white monstrosity. He didn't look mean or evil or even mad. He looked at his subject and then at Tom. Tchoobrayitch dismounted and his Elgg trotted to the back of the room. Tom's Elgg lowered its head and Tom dismounted. Instead of heading for the back of the expansive throne room, his Elgg padded up toward the king. It came around to his right side and hopped up, landing with its front paws on one arm of the throne and its back legs still on the ground. The king nested his chin on his right fist and leaned in, toward the Elgg. It began whispering in the king's ear, its mouth displaying the full range of articulation that a human's mouth had, its tongue flicking in and out as it told the king something.

It was disturbing to see a creature Tom had assumed did not have the power of speech suddenly betray the fact that it could talk, and especially to see it do it so conspiratorially. What was it saying? More disturbing: Tom had been naked on that thing. He'd presumed it wouldn't mind, because it was an animal and therefore didn't draw any distinction between clothed and not clothed. But it could talk, and talking meant culture, and culture probably meant a general dislike of having naked kids climb all over you. There was a very real possibility that right now it was saying to the Ghelm King, *This kid was naked when I found him, and then he just climbed on me like that, like it wasn't a big deal. I know! Eww, right? What a gross kid!* Tom just couldn't catch a break when it came to kings.

The Ghelm King nodded. The Elgg took its legs off the throne and joined its friend at the back of the room. The king smiled. He looked at Tom.

"Hello, son! What is your name?"

"Tom," Tom said.

"Tom!" the king said. "I am King Doondredge Anyet-teese-Krx. You may shorten it to Doondredge if you like, when addressing me." The Ghelm kingdom, Tom thought, was definitely big on having long names that didn't get much shorter even when you shortened them. "This is one of my Out-of-Orb Lieutenants, Tchoobrayitch, though I presume you've met. And those," Doondredge gestured to the back of the room, "are the Elgg. They are hearty creatures and also have the gift of being remarkably perceptive. Excellent judges of character. The one that brought you here after finding you on a routine patrol tells me, having looked you in the eye and employing its innate biological ability to tell a great deal about a person by doing so, that you would be an excellent candidate."

"A candidate for what?" Tom asked.

"I'm surprised you hadn't guessed," Doondredge said. He raised an eyebrow. "For Chosen One."

24

"YOU NEED A Chosen One?"

"Yes, of course! Nearly all cultures have a story that
speaks of an unlikely outsider who will come to their aid in
a time of great need. Our culture is something of a curator
of other cultures, and across worlds, we have seen that this
is the case."

The Ghelm were Crap Kingdom's enemies, Gark had
said so. The first time Tom had fled the clutches of an Elgg,
it had chased him down and shown him a vision where the
Ghelm were burning Crap Kingdom and enslaving its people. Maybe that vision wasn't a threat, though. Maybe it was
a warning. Maybe it was really his destiny to save the people
of the nameless kingdom by being the Ghelm's Chosen One,

and somehow brokering peace. It seemed complicated, but who said prophecies were clear-cut? The only clear-cut prophecies came on pieces of printer paper, and those were the kind of prophecies that put Kyle in charge.

"What do you need me to do?"

"Recall, if you will, the visions you saw when our Elgg made contact with you this evening. Realize that they can be, and shall be, very real, should you do the very simple thing I ask of you.

"We are an adventurous people, Tom. Unlike some races, we are not content to merely pine for a lost and glorious age, stewing in our own filth. We venture forth. We view the Vortex on which our city rests as our birthright, and we have built our society around exploring the worlds it grants us access to."

As he spoke, the floor, which had seemed solid a second before, revealed itself to be translucent, and the dark, stationary clouds that had given the glass floor the appearance of being made of stone or marble began to part. Through the orb's bottom, the gaping mouth of the Vortex came into view.

"This is no piddling portal, blowing open and closed at odd times, offering us passage to merely one world. We believe it to be the main inter-world artery, and we believe a controlling cosmic entity entrusted such a magnificent prize to a race strong enough and smart enough to defend it, to exploit it, to use it for a great and glorious end: nothing less than a total takeover of the All-Worlds.

"We have, for countless generations, been assembling a force of warriors bred from every race, of every sentient species the Vortex has cycled us into contact with. The time is drawing near when that force will have reached a state of readiness, of toughness forged in permanent war, to stage this attack. This time will draw near faster if I have a skilled protégé by my side. The attack will go more smoothly, will be less costly in terms of lives, will leave more intact societies for us, the conquerors, to manage. And that management, the new cross-world order, leagues stronger than the loose cooperative that is in place now, will only be possible if it is done in partnership with someone with the qualities described to me just now by our Elgg friend there. I need someone like that, Tom. Someone I can entrust with many, many, many worlds."

Tom thought: *This is amazing.*

Then he thought: *This is evil.*

Still, he wanted to know: *What are the All-Worlds?* There

were more universes than just this one and Earth's? Why did it have to be this guy telling him all of this? It was all exactly what Tom would have wanted to hear a month and a half ago staring up at his ceiling, but he had to hear it from a guy who was very probably evil. And this evil guy was promising Tom a part in all of it. A huge part. Leader not just of a bunch of people in what was essentially a junkyard in the middle of a barren plain, but of many, many, many worlds.

Could he maybe just look at the worlds? Did he have to do all the evil stuff, too?

"All you need to do to take part in our glorious destiny is this: Tell me the words to bring down the Wall."

Okay. Now there was no doubt about the evilness.

Doondredge didn't want Tom to be the Chosen One at all. He only cared about Tom because he thought he was from Crap Kingdom and therefore knew the words to make the Wall disappear. But how had he known to say the "Chosen One"? How had he known what Tom wanted to hear? Then he realized: *the Elgg*. It hadn't been reading Tom for qualities of strength and bravery; it had been scanning his weaknesses, and then showing him an instantly generated 3-D movie based on those weaknesses.

It was that easy. Any fantastic creature could look him

in the eyes and tell how much he hated that Kyle had what he had, because it had once been Tom's but Tom hadn't known how to appreciate it. And it took Kyle getting it, and loving it, and earning it, to make Tom see what he'd done wrong, and the more he burned with envy, the further away he got from ever getting anything like it again.

Now that Tom knew Doondredge was certain he would betray his friend, he was determined not to. Tom wondered, though: Would he have sold Kyle out if it wasn't just a trick Doondredge was playing, if it was all real? He didn't know, and now he would never know, but the fact that there was even any possibility that he might have done it, under the right circumstances, made him feel like the jet-black Vortex he could still see through the unclouded glass floor was actually inside his chest, and always would be.

"I don't know the words."

"I find that hard to believe. Every denizen of that wretched kingdom knows them; it's the one thing you people care about."

"I'm not even from there!"

"Really? Where are you from?"

It was asked so innocently that Tom was almost about to respond, but then he thought about the Ghelm marching through and enslaving everyone in his suburb and how pissed at him everybody would be if that happened. He stayed quiet.

"Wherever you claim to be from," the king said, "I know you've heard the words, because I've seen . . . this." The king waved. The Elgg Tom had thought of as his stepped in between him and Doondredge. The tiny lightning storms underneath its skin began to crackle and congeal until a clear image appeared. On this Elgg-mounted biological screen, Tom could see bushes and grass and scrub rushing by. It was like someone had made a first-person shooter level out of Crap Kingdom's outskirts. He noticed bounding feet at the bottom of the image: it was an Elgg's point of view. And then Crap Kingdom appeared, and so did two figures on its border: Gark and Tom, forever ago. They got huge in the frame quickly as the Elgg pursued them. Then Gark and Tom were on the other side of the Wall, and the Elgg's eye camera smashed into the invisible barrier. It bobbled there momentarily, watching Gark holding onto Tom, making sure his freshly discovered Chosen One was all right. Then the image dissipated, the lightning dancing off in a thousand different directions beneath the thing's skin.

"Yeah, so, I've heard it. I can't remember it, though.

Honestly." It was the truth. He was pretty much born without a memory for anything but the name of obscure planets in the Star Wars universe and lines in plays. If a piece of information was actually of any real-world value, it would not stick to his brain.

"You've heard it before," Doondredge said, "but you can't remember it."

"That's right," Tom said.

"Just as long as you've heard it, we can make you remember."

"Look, you can torture me all you want, I'm not gonna know what it is!" It was the bravest thing Tom had ever said, but it was only brave by accident.

"Oh no no! It's nothing so sinister as torture. It's simply that we have the ability to allow you to recall things you don't know you know."

"Uhm, no, that's okay actually. I don't think I want to tell you what it is."

"You can want to tell me or not want to tell me. It has little bearing on whether you actually will. Tchoobrayitch?"

"Yes?"

"Awaken the Retriever."

✳ ✳ ✳

The Retriever was not, as Tom had hoped, a friendly golden retriever who would lick Tom's face until he said, "Yep, you know what? I remember!" But it also wasn't a giant spiderlike creature who emerged from a pit and shoved its proboscis through Tom's brain, so that was good. The Retriever was a short, tired-looking man in his sixties, though again, Tom was not a good judge of adult age. When the crystal doors of the man's work chamber flew apart to admit Doondredge, Tom, and Tchoobrayitch, he was yawning.

Doondredge indicated that Tom should have a seat in a chair that was as plain-looking as a chair could be in a kingdom where pretty much everything was made of smoke-filled glass. He wished that the words to trigger the soul-swap and return to his body on Earth would just pop back into his head, but he knew that now that he really needed them, they'd be further away than ever. Maybe he could ask the Retriever to retrieve them for him while he was rooting around in his memory.

With a combination of great care and extreme boredom, the Retriever produced a glass face mask with tubes emanating from it. The tubes trailed back into a case that looked not entirely unlike the Igloo cooler that served as the king's throne back in Crap Kingdom, except it was made of glass and filled with white steam. The Retriever placed the mask on his own lap and looked up at Doondredge.

"The words to bring down the Wall," Doondredge said.

The Retriever nodded.

"We are extremely proud of this little bit of technology. We've only just perfected it," Doondredge said to Tom. "The principle is simple: a bit of memory is enhanced into clarity by making all other memories in the brain slightly less clear. Since this obscuring process is spread over the whole of memory, typically the subject cannot tell anything has happened at all, and the rest of their memories are more or less intact. Now, if we give you this light treatment, will you still be inclined to tell us the information we've made clear for you? Or will only a Tom who has been made to forget everything he's ever known except for that one bit of knowledge be open to sharing it with us?"

If he agreed to tell them what they wanted to know in order to save his memory, but then ended up refusing to tell them once it was over, they might torture him, or kill him. But if he said he wouldn't tell them, they'd turn his brain into mush. He should say no, he would never tell them. Of the two bad choices, that choice was the brave one.

The Retriever did not seem to care either way. He

placed the mask on Tom's face. Tom wondered how it would stay on, and then he found out. It attached itself right to his eyeballs. It hurt a ton. He tried to say, "I'll never tell you." His own hot breath shot up into his forced-open eyes and he was not sure if anyone out there could hear him. If you were brave but no one could hear it and it didn't matter anyway, did it still count?

Gas filled the mask. It was not easy or pleasant to breathe. His eyes burned. But for some reason he didn't focus on the pain. Suddenly he could only think of Gark and the Elgg and the Wall. Maybe it was because whenever you tried not to think of something, you of course ended up thinking about it. So he tried not to think about not thinking about it. He actually tried to focus on his pain and his discomfort and his fear. He found he couldn't stay panicked or pained, he could only think about Gark and the Elgg and the Wall. He could see it all clearer and clearer. He could see it and hear it and smell it and even taste the metallic taste he got sometimes in his mouth when he ran faster and breathed harder than he was used to. It was all so clear. Then it was too clear. It was clearer than it had been when he'd been there. He felt superhuman. He could hear Gark's heart beating, the Elgg's many lungs breathing fast at different intervals. He could hear his own blood in his own veins. He knew the number of hairs on Gark's head. Then he knew the number of hairs on the head but could not identify the person whose head they were on. Then he could not tell the difference between the thing chasing him and the thing saving him from the thing chasing him—they were all just things. And then everything he saw became a blur of things, none of which was distinct from any other. Then he forgot the word *things*. Then he forgot himself.

And then finally, his mind was a fog, endless and complete, and standing in the center of that infinite fog, the only clear thing, clearer than anything he'd ever known or heard or remembered, were the words SLOWWAVE TRUEPANTS, towering in the fog, lit up for all to see.

part three

25

IT WAS ASLEEP and then it wasn't anymore. It could still walk, but if you asked it what it was doing when it was walking, it couldn't tell you because it didn't know what what it was doing was called and also, it couldn't speak. except for two words. And it would not have thought of that as speaking. It would have thought of that as its entire reason for being, what it was made of, what it lived for. So when the man, whom it could not have identified as a man, asked it a question, which it could not understand or identify as a question, the words poured out of its mouth automatically:

"SLOWWAVE TRUEPANTS!"

The man smiled and took the other standing man to one corner of the room and whispered about it and ges-

tured to it. It had no idea what was going on, but it had just fulfilled its purpose, so it was deeply happy. Though it could not have identified the emotion as happiness, it noticed the difference from the way it had felt a moment before. To feel this way was better than to not feel this way.

The first man, the man who had initiated the fulfillment of its purpose, was gone now, and there was just the other man standing there across the room. It was sad the first man had gone, as it associated the first man with the happy feeling, though it could not have identified the emotion as sadness any more than it could have identified the first thing it felt as happiness. The other man waved for it. It did not know what this gesture meant. The other man was still for a second. Then the other man came across the room fast, and grabbed its arm, and pulled it up, and it was walking now, and the other man was holding its arm, pulling it along.

They went out of the room. As far as it had been concerned, that one room was the entire world. They were leaving the world as it knew it. The hallway they were walking down was a new world, and it greeted the new world with the wonder befitting such a discovery. They went through a door into a different room, so now there was a third world. The other man flung it onto a horizontal surface, and then the other man left, and it was alone, and then it could not

see anything anymore. A minute or two later it fell asleep, though it had not been trying to fall asleep because it did not know what the act of sleeping was. In dreams its mind set to work creating fantastical worlds beyond the ones it knew, as dreaming minds will do. It dreamed of fourth and fifth and even sixth rooms. It dreamed of words besides the only two words in existence.

When it was awake again, in the third world, it could see that the other man was standing over it. He smiled, though it could not have identified the expression as a smile. The other man grabbed its arm again and pulled it out and down the hall and into yet another room (a fourth world, nothing like the one in its dreams!) and the other man left and again it was alone and then the room began to fill with a mist, and it could not have told you what mist was until the mist touched its skin and then it could, it could tell you what mist was and what skin was and that it was the mist being absorbed through its skin that was teaching it these things. Things it already knew but had forgotten.

He knew he was a man. And more important, he knew what man he was.

He was a soldier in the King's Army, Right-Blooded

Ghelm Division. He served at the pleasure of King Doon-dredge Anyettis-Krx and he would do so until he died the most noble death he could hope for, on the battlefield in the service of his king, and he wanted this death more than anything. He was Ghelm, he knew as the mist reached his nostrils, and he could picture the ceaseless work of the Ghelm as they approached their ultimate goal.

He could picture the Vapornauts, in their specially designed suits of armor, floating into the Vortex, fighting its mighty wind, and returning with an entire enslaved population from whatever world the Vortex, in its furious wisdom, had been a gateway to that day. From there the population would be led down to the Fields of Permanent War, where it would be driven up against older battle-hardened slave races, and this perpetual churning war game would eventually produce the unbeatable army that would conquer the All-Worlds. He could picture the king, watching from a clear spot in the base of the Executive Orb, where he lived with his trusted advisors and other royalty. The king was watching the new race being led, dazed and wind wrecked, out of the Vortex and down the hill toward the Fields without a stop for food or water or whatever nourishment these far-flung beings required. Now the Orb was floating, as the king had brilliantly designed it to do, over the War Fields,

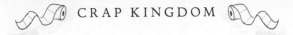

observing the perpetual bloodshed that would forge the force that would bring all known existence under the king's command.

His next opportunity to achieve the glorious death he wanted more than anything would be right now, this morning, when the glorious Ghelm war wind bore down on the unsuspecting cretins of the nameless kingdom.

He was happier than he could ever remember being, though he had only eight hours of memories. He had been fitted for armor, and once it was given to him, he knew exactly how to put it on. Its crystalline chambers filled with nourishing mist, and his body was stronger, his reflexes were quicker, he was smarter and angrier and more eager to kill.

The thing that made him happiest of all was that he would be at the king's side during the entire battle. He did not understand exactly why this was the case, but it was thrilling nonetheless, and he would hurl himself toward death harder because of it. If he did not die today, he would die in one of the numerous glorious battles that would follow this one as the king established his grip on the All-Worlds. He was sure of it. He couldn't wait.

The king climbed on his Elgg. He climbed on an Elgg

of his own. Men twice his age and with much more experience were riding in transports, and he was part of the Elgg cavalry next to the king himself. He had come a very long way since last night when he thought there were only two words in the world.

It was a war tide greatly to be feared, cresting the cloud layer, taking to the sky: seven Elgg-mounted squadrons, four hundred men in Vapornaut armor, foot soldiers in a dozen diamond troop transports, with three additional transports left empty to accept a slave population after the Ghelm's inevitable triumph. The transports gleamed in the sun as they left the rocky surface of Ghelmghaad behind and reached open sky.

The cloud layer trailed away. At this distance the Wall was fully visible, a glow that faded in and out almost imperceptibly but never blinked out entirely. Soon it would. He knew that somehow he was instrumental in bringing down the Wall, and he was extremely proud. The king trusted him, and the king was the wisest and strongest man among the Ghelm and therefore the wisest and strongest man in the All-Worlds. The king's Elgg dived first, and his Elgg followed suit without him having to tell it to. They nose-dived toward the top of the Wall's dome, and even with the wind in his ears he heard the king yell the two words that still seemed, for some reason, like the center of his soul.

It was hard to tell, at this distance, if it had worked, but then the king's Elgg dived without stopping and soon it breached the point where it would have collided with the Wall. It was done. The Wall was down.

Pitiful men and women and children, dirty and dressed in motley rags, looked up in awe. The smarter ones scrambled into their hovels and huts and lean-tos. Soon they would all be quite orderly indeed, packed into diamond transports, or, if they resisted—

Then they were gone. Just the way the Wall had blinked out of existence, all the people he could see running around were suddenly gone. The king pulled up hard on his Elgg and looked at him, at first in confusion and then in anger. Then the king returned his attention to the ground and directed his Elgg toward a large wooden structure in the center of town, a completely ramshackle thing, but certainly the only thing in the kingdom worthy of being called a building. It had some child's idea of a castle mounted on the front of it.

The legions of Elgg-mounted men and the Vapornaut squadrons followed the king while the diamond transports landed all around the castle building, crushing crude structures that were now depopulated, presumably by treacherous magic.

He and the king closed in on the castle, the king's rage somehow now transmuted into the speed and fury of his Elgg's flight. It was flying at top speed when a blue ball of energy appeared around the castle building, deflecting the king and his Elgg. The Elgg was splattered, and the king went skipping across the top of the solid energy ball.

The man whose privilege it was to ride beside the king pulled up sharply and jumped down onto the surface of the ball. He ran along the top of it and dived. He grabbed his dazed majesty before the king could slide off the surface and fall the probably fatal distance to the ground. He looked up. The Vapornauts and Elgg calvary were circling, confused. What next? He looked down. His hand held the king by the wrist. The king was slowly regaining consciousness. His nose was bloody.

Looking out across the kingdom from this artificial perch on top of the castle's new protective Wall, he could see the crow's nests of three of the now-landed diamond transports, their spires miniature imitations of the one at the top of the Ghelm kingdom. The farthest one began to topple. Then the next one followed suit, then the closest

one, as though they were being knocked over by a powerful beast. From the beast's apparent path grew blue energy
tendrils that shot up into the air and started grabbing Elgg-
mounted men and Vapornauts out of the sky. The men who
were merely ensnared and not immediately tossed miles
away by the tendrils' impressive power tried to fight back
with maces and swords, but there was nothing to be done,
as these tendrils were not biological: there was nothing to
injure or cut or kill.

Seconds later, the enemy could at last be seen, running
up the side of the energy sphere surrounding the castle
building toward him and the king. The energy tendrils
grew from his footsteps, each one springing immediately
to glowing life and whipping up into the sky to fell another
Elgg rider or Vapornaut. When the enemy crested the rim
of the sphere, the warrior saw that he was little more than
a boy, wearing no armor, holding no weapon. The short-
sleeved garment covering his torso had letters across the
front, reading:

ARROWVIEW HIGH SCHOOL THEATER DEPT

The words resonated with the Ghelm warrior on a deep
and preconscious level. It was like these words had existed

long before the two words his soul was built around.

He looked into the face of the boy enemy. The boy enemy stopped running and looked at him, puzzled. He would have pounced were he not puzzled himself, by the words on the enemy's chest and by the look on his face.

The king sprang up, produced a diamond blade from the right wrist of his armor, and grabbed the Ghelm warrior, his own soldier, his right-hand man, who had come into being just this morning. The king put the blade to his throat. He faced the boy enemy.

"*Shut it off!*" the king yelled.

The boy enemy nodded, putting one hand up in the air in surrender and reaching down with the other hand. The enemy touched the surface of the blue energy sphere. The blade's edge came off of his throat and flew toward the boy enemy's raised hand. He turned around just in time to see his king fall through the surface of the still-intact sphere and hang there in a cocoon of blue energy. A second later, the sphere spat him out toward the sun. He flew past the troops who were being strangled by tendrils, and he and the boy enemy both watched as the king became a dot in the sky. An equally small dot, an Elgg that had escaped the tendril defense, flew perpendicular to the king, scooping him up and flying back in the direction of the Ghelm homeland.

The warrior looked at the boy enemy.

The boy enemy looked at him.

He charged at the boy enemy.

He managed to knock him off the sphere. They fell toward the ground. He had his armored hands on the boy enemy's sides, intending to drive him into the soil, but the boy enemy clambered over him in midair, and it was he who landed with his back in the dirt. The boy enemy landed on top of him. Since he had his crystal armor, he was still fully conscious, in no pain, just dazed. Regaining his faculties, he got a hand on the boy enemy's throat. A drop fell onto his face. Then another. He reached up with his fingertip to wipe these drops away. He looked at them. They were not blood. They'd come from the boy enemy's eyes. They were tears. He paused for a second.

In this one-second window of distraction, the boy enemy raised a bare fist and brought it down onto his face.

Everything went foggy once again.

26

TOM HAD NEVER drunk, so he'd never had a hang-over. But when he woke up, he felt the way he'd heard a hangover felt. It was Kyle who'd told him, actually. Tom had felt oddly betrayed at the time. All that stuff scared him, so he liked to think of himself as better than it. It was supposed to be years before that stuff invaded their lives, wasn't it? But he now felt the way Kyle had described feeling the morning after that party he'd gone to at some senior's house: nause-ated and headachy and oh God what was this taste in his mouth? The whole top half of his body was cold and wet. What was happening?

"One last bottle should bring him around fully," he heard someone yell. Well, they weren't yelling, but it sounded to Tom like they were.

He sat up. His head felt like it weighed about as much as a small van. He blinked. There was Gark. There was another man, who looked like a grizzled old prospector. The prospector was holding a sun-bleached plastic bottle.

"Ready to take down another bottle?" the prospector said. "For someone who's never drunk this stuff before you're doing an awfully good job."

"What stuff?"

"Thinkdrink, of course!" the prospector said, smiling.

"Did you get it out of the toilets?" Tom said.

"Of course! Don't worry, it's the good stuff," the prospector said. "I know I ain't supposed to be talking to you, but I'm just happy someone wants to drink what we make. Folks ain't so interested in thinkdrink since Kyle came around. Young folks especially."

It was the drink that came out of port-o-potties that made you remember stuff instead of forgetting it, and he was in Crap Kingdom, and he remembered everything all at once. Everything.

"Gark, what's going on? Is everything okay with—"

As soon as he said Gark's name, Gark turned away and pulled the thinkdrink man by the arm out of the small dark room. Gark slammed the door behind them and Tom heard a heavy lock click into place.

He remembered everything that had happened, the way you would remember something stupid you thought when you were a kid. It was like remembering the logical leaps you used to have to make to still believe in Santa even after you were probably too old, if those logical leaps had resulted in you endangering the lives of an entire society, if they resulted in attacking your best friend after he saved you from the man who was threatening to kill you, a man you thought, for some reason, was your friend.

A few minutes later, he heard the sound of the door unlocking. Two large men came in and grabbed him, one on each shoulder. They pulled him down a dark hallway. He remembered what the king had said about having an army whose job it was to stay home and do nothing. He imagined these men had been called into active duty now that there had been an assault on Crap Kingdom. Or it was possible they had already been called up under the new Kyle regime, but he doubted it. Kyle's regime had mostly seemed to be about fireworks and underwear art projects and Beatles music. It was totally harmless. Why had Tom disliked it so much? Just because it wasn't his?

They walked up some stairs and around a corner and

they were in the throne room. Tom was almost relieved to see the little Igloo cooler full of towels that served as a throne. He was almost relieved to see the king sitting on it. He was definitely relieved to see Kyle standing next to him. He was happy to see Kyle was alive, though he had a very clear recollection of Kyle knocking him out, and not the other way around. He was even relieved to see Gark standing off to the side. None of them seemed very happy to see him.

"*Traitor!*" the king yelled.

Tom just stood there.

"You will *not* just stand there. You *will* tell us everything!"

He didn't know where to start, but he figured he'd better start anyway.

"Just, I just have to say . . . I am so, so sorry. I can't even tell you how sorry I—"

The king held up his hand. "What. Happened."

Tom paused for a second, realizing that there would be no apology that would suddenly make it all better, and that the only reason he was, or should be, allowed to speak would be to confess. And he was not being asked to confess so that he or anyone else could feel better. The confession was only useful if it contained information that could protect them from future attacks.

So he opened his mouth to speak, then closed it again, realizing that large parts of the story implicated Gark and Pira and Kyle. He knew that only honesty could help at this point, but he knew that certain kinds of honesty could hurt, and he had no desire to hurt any of them. What sickened him more than anything was that he knew at some point, under Ghelm brainwash, he had had a desire to do just that.

He would implicate only the person at fault: Tom.

He started with the texts.

"... and my other self," he said, halfway through his story, "had sent me this text message with instructions on how to soul-swap. He said it was a better spell than the one we'd been using. One that he said he hadn't really had time to complete, which it later turned out was really true, because I got here and I was completely—"

"Stop," the king said. "Say that part again."

Tom said that part again.

After he had finished, the king looked at Kyle. Kyle looked at the king. Tom was relieved when Kyle did this, as the way Kyle had been looking at Tom, with a mixture of disappointment and sadness and love and hate and worst of all, fear, had been destroying Tom more completely than any spell could ever hope to.

"His other self is J!" the king said, suddenly sitting straight up, in contrast to his normal question-mark-shaped posture.

"Are you sure?" Kyle said.

"Quite sure," the king said. "J had been working on a new soul-swap spell immediately before he . . ."

"Wow," Kyle said.

Was it true? The man who was better at being Tom than Tom could ever be was J, the only man who was ever worth anything in Crap Kingdom? A great man had chosen his body to live through. Did this mean Tom was worth something after all?

"It follows, actually," the king said. "The soul of a great man would need a character that was completely vacant to inhabit. Your former friend is barely a human being and thus he would allow lots of space for J, the greatest man I or anyone who remembers him has ever known," the king said, and Tom could swear he watched all the lines fade from his face. "This is most miraculous news! We must discuss."

Something about seeing a man so generally depressed and so definitely old suddenly become so young-seeming fooled Tom into thinking, for a second, that he would be part of that discussion.

"Gark, take this man away. We may need him later but not at the moment."

Gark, flanked by the two presumed army men, led Tom back to his cell.

"Thank you for not mentioning that I saw you in the kingdom," Gark said as Tom reentered his tiny windowless cell.

Tom turned, still having so much apology to make and so much story to tell.

"Please don't speak to me," Gark said.

The door slammed and the lock clicked.

A tiny Tame Flame had been stuck to the ceiling of the cell. Tom wished it would go out. He did not feel deserving of light or heat.

He thought about the king and Kyle and their conference. For a moment he let himself feel a little left out. Then he remembered what had happened the last time he felt left out. What he had done. *The reason you feel left out a lot,* Tom thought, *is because people leave you out a lot, because you deserve* to be left out. If they left you in, you'd destroy everything. You'd make them regret it sooner or later.

He sat in what he wished was darkness for a long time thinking that exact thought, or thoughts very much like it. There was no way of telling how much time had passed before the two men appeared at his door again and dragged him back to the throne room.

"I am," the king said, "maybe for the first time, happy you came here. Through no conscious effort on your part, in fact, entirely due to Kyle's ingenuity, you may have brought the greatest citizen this kingdom has ever known back into our midst, and for that, I thank you. I thank you for having a slim enough soul. Despite your treacherous attempts to destroy this kingdom, you may have given us the opportunity to do the very opposite: to vanquish the Ghelm tyrants once and for all.

"Shortly before he was killed, J was working on a plan to do just that, a plan that we once again have the ability to put into action. Your part in this plan is simple, and you will submit to it willingly, if there is any residual bit of honor in your treacherous soul."

"I'll do it. Whatever it takes."

"Good. Tomorrow morning, you will be sent into the void, which is J's current resting place. When our mission is over, you will go back to your world, never to return, and J will return to the void, where I am happy to learn his soul resides, for at least it is not absolute oblivion."

"All right."

"Now. It's late. We need our rest. And you, I suppose, need yours. I do not know how strenuous it is floating in limbo. I suggest you pass the time thinking about all the wrong you've done."

Half an hour later, Tom was trying to focus on his part of the plan and how he could void-float in the most helpful way possible when he heard the lock turn and his cell door opened.

Kyle was standing outside.

"Just tell me they kidnapped you or something, man," Kyle said. "Even if it's a lie."

Tom told him everything, not worrying about not implicating Gark or Pira. He was more honest than he had ever been with himself.

". . . and I was just standing there thinking, he said he invented *music*?"

"I never said I invented music. I told them where it was from and everything. If she says I invented it, that's just her being . . . Pira."

"I know. But I was just so mad, and you weren't around to ask about any of this stuff. You were always here and . . . do you know what it's like when you want to talk to somebody, and the person is there, their body is, but you know it's not really them inside?"

"How do you think Lindsy feels?"

"Yeah, you're right . . . but she likes that other me. I mean, she doesn't know it's not me, but she likes that guy, not me. She likes me for not-me."

Kyle laughed, then said, "I don't know, man, she was pretty into you before all that."

"You think?"

Kyle nodded. "Hey, I'm sorry I wasn't around more," he said. "But you didn't have to join the enemy."

"I didn't know I was joining the enemy. I was cold and I thought I was gonna die so I just . . . got on the thing's back."

And he realized he had started building another alternate lie-world. Because for a minute, cold but fully conscious and fully himself, he had known what he was doing and tried to make himself either think they weren't the enemy or that it was somehow okay.

"I think, for a minute, I knew what I was doing. But then there was part of me that thought, maybe I could be their Chosen One. I mean, you turned this place around. I thought, sure, these guys might be evil, but maybe I can turn them around somehow. Or maybe I could like, work from the inside, to bring them down."

"Well, now you're kind of doing that, so congratulations."

"What's gonna happen tomorrow?"

Kyle looked at Tom for a long, long time.

"I shouldn't tell you what's happening tomorrow. Because, like, for all I know, as soon as I tell you you're gonna grow wings and burst through the wall and go flying back there."

"Dude, like I said, they brainwashed me, please believe me, I—Kyle?"

Kyle's eyes were closed and his head was down. "Please be quiet," Kyle said. "I'm reading your intentions."

Tom sat still.

"Wow," Kyle said, his eyes still closed. "You really hated me."

"I hated all you guys, that's just how they programmed me to—"

"I mean before that. Before you were programmed."

"...I didn't *hate* you."

Kyle's eyes sprang open. "Now it looks like you want to help us."

"I do." Tom realized he was in no way a part of the "us" anymore. He could have been at one point. But he just wouldn't accept a gig at the Rat-Snottery.

"So I'm going to tell you what's going to happen," Kyle said, "and you're going to tell me if any part of it contradicts what you know about the Ghelm and their kingdom and how it works, okay?"

"Okay," Tom said.

"There's this thing, double soul-swap. The goal is for J to come here and inhabit your body, or the copy of your body, in this world. When that happens, your soul, or whatever you want to call it, your experience of you, goes to the void where J lives."

"And who's in my body on Earth?"

"A placeholder soul. Randomly pulled out of the void."

"Okay."

"And once J's in your body he gets to complete the maneuver he was going to do before he died. There's a Vortex portal at the center of the Ghelm kingdom, correct?"

"Yeah."

"He's going to get in there and use a spell called Reverse Worldflow. It's not a spell he can just cast, though, because spell-casting is about creating a world and you can't, by definition, create a world between worlds. So he designed this thing called a Reverse Worldflow grenade. He tosses that into the Vortex portal, and instead of the world-wind blowing out, it starts sucking in, like an ultrapowerful vacuum. It pulls the entire Ghelm kingdom down and into the portal."

"Why does J have to be here for that to happen? Why haven't they done it already?"

"He didn't leave instructions for designing the grenade. He has to build it, and he has to be the one to deliver it because he's the only one who's ever been inside their kingdom and come back alive. Their king asked him to come, pretending it was diplomatic, pretending they'd stop attacking if J would just come and listen to them. Then, when he was there, the king tried to recruit him to their side. J said no. He escaped. And based on what he saw there, he came up with this plan."

"And he died before he could do it."

"No," Kyle said, "he died trying to do it."

* * *

"Hey, uhm, Your Majesty?" Kyle said. "Wake up!"

The king stirred in his bed, or more accurately, "on" his bed. It was tough to be "in" a bed that was just a mattress on the floor with no sheets or covers on it, in one corner of an empty room.

"What?" the king said without opening his eyes.

"Tom raised a really good point about the plan."

"Was his point, 'I'm a traitor in your midst still in league with the Ghelm, so don't go through with it and leave them alone'?"

"No. It was that we can't let the entire kingdom go down the Vortex. Just the Executive Orb."

"What? Why? That sounds like a something a traitor would say."

"I've been there," Tom said, not able to keep silent anymore. "There are a lot of people there. I don't know if they're innocent, exactly, but they're civilians, they're not soldiers, they're not actively planning to take over all the worlds."

"The *All-Worlds*," the king corrected him.

"Right," Tom said, "and more important, there are all these slaves, races from everywhere, from all the worlds the Ghelm are planning to conquer, that they're training as an army."

"Surely you're not suggesting we leave our enemy with a standing army."

"They're a standing army of slaves," Tom said. "They don't want to be there."

"And the men who assisted in the assault on this kingdom? They were slaves as well?"

"Not all of them, but . . . the point is, if you try to get rid of the entire kingdom and everybody who may have a single ill intention against *your* kingdom, that Vortex is going to turn that whole structure into this whirling hurricane of glass or diamond or whatever it's made of, and it's not just going to suck everyone into another dimension harmlessly. They're all going to be killed." Tom always thought he was good at speaking, because he read a lot and he had a big vocabulary, but he felt like this was the first thing he'd ever said that he'd actually said as well as he'd meant to say it.

The king rolled his eyes.

"And isn't there a chance," Kyle said, "that, if we leave it open, it will suck in our kingdom, too?"

The king sighed and flopped his head back on the mattress.

"All right, what do you suggest?"

"Let me resize the Wall," Kyle said, "bring it to the

mouth of the Vortex, and use it to plug the hole. It'll stop the wind and lock our enemies inside all at once."

"No! No! Absolutely not. It is one thing to leave a remaining Ghelm population of questionable intent alive in this world, but it is quite another thing to remove our only proven line of defense and send it to another land!"

"It's not your only line of defense anymore," Kyle said, sounding hurt. "You have me."

"I know, Kyle, but . . . things one relies on . . . if one relies on them too heavily, they have a way of . . . disappearing."

"I'm not going to . . ." Kyle said, "Look, if it'll make you feel better, that barrier I put up around the castle after I teleported everyone inside during the attack? I'll put up a bigger one of those before I leave for the Ghelm mountain, okay?"

The king lay silent for a moment, staring up at the ceiling. Finally he said: "Optimism does not come easy to me, Kyle."

"I know," Kyle said.

"Trust does not come easily to me."

"I know."

The king sighed. "The plan is altered."

"Thanks, Your Majesty."

"But *not* the part that will send *him*," the king said, pointing to Tom without looking at him, "to a mysterious void. That part remains the same."

"I understand," Tom said.

"I've read him," Kyle said. "He doesn't want to hurt us."

"I suggest you think back to what I said a moment ago," the king said. "About trust."

He turned over on the mattress, facing the wall. He was snoring before Tom and Kyle were all the way out of the room.

They walked through the throne room. Tom turned to go back to his cell.

"There's an extra mattress in my room," Kyle said.

"You sure?" Tom said.

Kyle nodded.

TOM AND KYLE were standing in the crater at first light.

"Normally you fall backward," Kyle said. "This one, you fall forward."

"That's it?"

"That's it. I mean," Kyle said, "there's other magic stuff going on that I have to do, but as far as what you have to do that's different, that's it."

"No problem," Tom said. He was tremendously scared. He had no idea what was going to happen, what the void would be like, but he didn't want to let Kyle in on any of this fear. He wanted to bear it silently. Heroically, even. He wanted to bear it like someone who, standing in this very crater, had cursed his friend and his friend's kingdom and ended up trying to destroy them, and now wanted so, so badly to make up for it.

"Let me know when it's done!" the king shouted from over the ridge. "I'm ready to greet my old friend!" The king wanted to be there when J took residency in Tom's body, but he didn't want to see Tom off.

"Is there anything else? I mean, anything else you need to know about the Ghelm, or their kingdom, or—" Tom said.

"No," Kyle said. "I mean, maybe. But either way, we have to start now. This thing's going to take J the whole day to build, and we want to attack in the dead of night, when they're sleeping."

"Okay," Tom said. "Tell him to take care of me, okay? I need this body."

Kyle didn't laugh or acknowledge the joke. He just frowned, looked down, and started sweeping the sand Tom would land on in a very specific pattern. "You're not your body," Kyle said. "Your body's on Earth. What you are right now, what J's going to inhabit, is a copy of you."

"So, let's say J dies here . . ."

"You shut up!" the king shouted from over the hill.

"The you that's you lives on in the void forever. Your body on Earth continues on with that temporary soul inside of it."

"Okay," Tom said. He wished he hadn't heard that. The thought of his body going about its business on Earth, filled with an impostor living out the rest of his life, was far scarier to him than the prospect of actually dying.

"Don't worry," Kyle said. "He's not going to fail. You ready?"

"Yes," Tom said, and he realized he had just created another alternate lie-world, one in which he was ready.

Kyle stood behind Tom.

"Three ... two ... one ..."

Kyle's hands hit Tom's back. Tom flew forward into the sand, then through the sand, into the world between worlds that was not a world at all.

28

WHEN A MEAN kid in second grade had told Tom that there was no heaven, Tom had spent that entire night in his bed with Pokémon sheets trying to think of what else there could be after you died. Did you just float in nothing? he thought. And if you were supposed to spend eternity in heaven, did that mean you instead spent eternity in that nothing? He had closed his eyes and tried to imagine that, that blackness, forever. And then at a certain point he stopped even thinking about the nothingness and got stuck thinking about forever. Forever. The craziest thing about forever is that it went on forever. Thinking about forever there in bed in second grade, Tom felt like he might break his brain. And floating in the void after the double soul-swap, he felt like he had taken up residence in that scary broken-brained place he had imagined was "forever" when he was very small.

A long time passed before anything happened. It wasn't forever, because it ended. Something happened. The void stopped being just unlimited black. There was the vaguest red tint appearing somewhere. That meant he could see, even if he didn't have actual physical eyeballs.

Then the redness started to drift to one side of Tom's eyeless vision and then to the other. Something came into focus. A light. The light got bigger and brighter. Something like a jellyfish made of light floated up to Tom. Tom was relieved because something floating up to him meant that there was, in fact, a him. And he could begin to see, within the light-jellyfish, faces. Human ones. Not physical or real: just flashes, images in the pulsating mass of light. They darted around inside the thing like a string of Christmas lights wrapped in a ball and set to "chase" mode. On the third or fourth rotation, Tom realized it was the same face. And then, coming from everywhere, an echo that slowly became a voice.

"Youyouyouyouyouyououoouuooou're not Jason."

Tom didn't know how to answer without a mouth or a body.

"No," he answered. Oh, so that was how. His voice didn't have the strange reverse echo, and it didn't come from everywhere. It just came from him.

"Youyouyouyouyouyouyouyoooooou're in Jason's spot."

"You guys have spots?" Tom said. "Even in a void?"

"Susususususuuuuuuuuure," the thing said. "And this is a good one."

"Oh," Tom said.

"IIIIIIIIIIIIIIIIIIIII was joking."

"Oh, sorry," Tom said. "Ha."

"Yoyouoouououououououou don't have as good of a sense of humor as Jason," said the thing. "Where is he?"

"Who's Jason?" Tom asked.

"Hihihihihihihihihis soul is usually here," said the thing, "except recently sometimes it's not. He's been getting to go to his home world, a place called Earth, and act as this boy."

"Did he say the boy's name?"

"Tttttttttttttttttim."

"Tom?"

"Tttttthhhat's it. Tom."

"You mean J," Tom said. "You're talking about a man named J, like the letter."

"Iiiiiiiii'm talking about a man called Jason, whose spot this is. I've been here for as long as I've been here, and one day, he appeared. And I come by when I come by, and we share stories from being alive. He's had lots of new stories since getting to go back to this Earth. It's nice to hear about life in a world. We don't even talk about what he does sometimes. We just talk about how nice it is to feel like you have a body, or to feel how an object is heavy, or very light, or how nice it is to feel time pass. I miss him when he goes, but I'm glad he gets to go and bring the stories back. I was getting pretty tired of the old one."

"What was the old one?" Tom asked.

"Sssssssssssssssso he came from this place called Earth, and when he was a boy, he stumbled upon a portal to another world. We know about these things in my world, and in many other worlds, but Earth doesn't know they have them. He says he found it playing in a 'rubbish heap.' And on the other side was this kingdom without a name, and they were very poor and very scared, because they spent all of their time fighting off attacks from a much stronger kingdom. Their existence was defined only by survival. The king of this kingdom without a name had a son, and this son befriended the newcomer, Jason, and convinced his father to let him stay. He taught Jason what little ancestral magic he knew, and Jason took to it very quickly, and had soon broken those spells down into their component parts to figure out the very fabric of magic, and was able to build grand spells of his own design. So that the kingdom might for once worry about something besides its own destruction, he created an invisible barrier around it, which their enemies could not penetrate. Contained within this sphere was a lake, and contained within that lake was the portal that took him back and forth between Earth and his new home. By night, he and teams of divers would bring 'rubbish' from Earth and make glorious things out of it, much the way he had taken the native magic of the nameless kingdom and made it into something better. Safe from harm, the kingdom experienced a golden age of peace and prosperity.

"The king of the rival kingdom extended a message of peace to the kingdom without a name. Jason went abroad as the rival king requested. Once there, he told Jason of a master plan to conquer the All-Worlds, if only Jason would share with him the magic he'd developed. Jason refused. He fled. But while there . . ."

"He developed a plan to destroy the other kingdom once and for all."

"Yyeeeesssssssss," the thing said. "How did you know?"

"What's your name?" Tom said.

"IIIIIIIIIIIIII've forgotten," the thing said. "What's yours?"

"I'm Tom," Tom said.

"Ththththththe famous Tom," it said. "Jason has said, from what he has seen of your life, being inside of it, that you are very much like him. He is reminded of himself by you."

"Really?" Tom said. Tom let himself feel proud of the comparison for just a second.

"Ssssssso then, you know the rest of the story?"

"He was killed trying to pull off his plan," said Tom.

"Nnnnnnnot just killed," the thing that had forgotten its name said. "Captured and tortured and then killed once he still would not give up his secrets. And he says he knew he was dead, and then he was pulled up. Pulled up, he says. Pulled up to here. And the first time he said that, I was glad to hear it, because it means I am not truly dead. I am just between places. Now, I am not so sure I am still glad. I grow weary."

"You might get pulled out into a world," Tom said. "Like Jason."

"The idea is appealing. I would also settle for my friend Jason returning here. It's good to have friends."

"It is," Tom said.

And then, he was no longer in between places. He was pulled up and up and up, out of the void, and into life.

He was flat on his back. His head was wet, like when he'd awoken in the nameless kingdom soaked in think-drink. But it wasn't a cold wet this time. It was a warm wet.

He reached up with one hand and touched the wet spot. He looked at his hand with the eyes he now had back, the way he'd done when he was brainwashed and fighting Kyle and he'd thought there was blood on his face but it was actually tears.

This time, it was blood. Lots of it.

29

SOMETHING HAD GONE very, very wrong.

Tom was staring at the ceiling. He seemed to do a lot of that everywhere he went. It was kind of his superpower. But this ceiling was glass, with multicolored gas swimming behind it. He was back in his body in the Ghelm kingdom and he knew that something had gone wrong.

He looked to his left. There were bloody animal foot-prints leading across the glass surface of the floor and out of the arched doorway. He had run afoul of an Elgg, it seemed. Maybe he'd played dead. And he was bleeding, and soon he might really be dead.

He was wearing the frayed clothing they had placed on him before he'd awoken in Crap Kingdom, jeans and an old black T-shirt, not entirely unlike what he might have worn on Earth. In place of a belt, a crude rope made of tied-together plastic shopping bags was strung through his belt loops. On his right hip, hanging off the rope, was another plastic shopping bag with something inside of it. It was small but extremely heavy. He reached inside and pulled out an old water bottle with its cap taped shut thoroughly with duct tape. Inside of the water bottle was what looked like a tiny self-contained galaxy. Its center burned brightly, throwing off little whorls of blinding light. *This must be the grenade J needed to build,* Tom thought. The Reverse World-flow, the spell you couldn't just cast, but actually had to hurl into the Vortex. If it was here in a plastic bag tied to his jeans, it meant the mission had gone only as far as J breaking into the Ghelm kingdom before he got Tom's body mauled by an Elgg.

There was a significant chunk taken out of Tom's shoulder and distinct claw marks in the black fabric of his shirt. The Elgg must have figured him for incapacitated and gone off to alert his master, which meant there wasn't much time. And his shoulder didn't hurt that much. Tom didn't know if that was good or the worst thing imaginable. No, it couldn't be the worst thing imaginable, the worst thing imaginable was that he was here, in his own body, and the mission had gone awry. He was the last person in any universe who should be doing this. The very last person.

Tom cleared blood from his eyes and looked around. He was in some sort of armament room. Suits of Vapornaut armor lined the walls. So this was where it would end, and some soul, be it J or some other anonymous placeholder soul thrilled to be freed from its luminous jellyfish form and given a place in a body in a world, would rattle on in Tom's body for the rest of that body's life. Him, the being that really was Tom Parking, would end here, on the floor, staring up at the ceiling, which was pretty much all he ever did.

Something thundered up from inside of his soul or his mind or his heart and spoke to him. And it didn't tell him to be brave. He wasn't suddenly clever or magical. He was still himself. He was not supposed to be in his body right now, but, by accident, he was himself, and now something was speaking from inside of him.

It said: *get up.*

Be stupid, be weak, be confused, be scared, but GET UP.

He breathed in and exhaled. There was blood in his nose, too. That was fine. He'd had bloody noses all the time as a kid. This part, the bloody-nose part, life had prepared him for.

He tried to sit up. That part was hard, but only because he was out of shape. It would have been hard for him to do a sit-up even if he wasn't bleeding to death. In his physical prime, halfway through freshman PE, he'd been able to do thirty sit-ups in a row with minimal complaint. He could squeeze out just one right now, couldn't he? He did it.

As soon as he was upright, he started to feel the shoulder. The pain was impossible. He hissed and whimpered the way he'd seen an actor playing a Civil War soldier do in a movie they'd watched in history class. The soldier was about to get his leg amputated above the knee. That guy had had a belt to bite on. Tom didn't. He only had a rope made of shopping bags, and he probably needed it to hold his pants up. He'd spent too much time in this world without pants already. Also, he needed it to hold the grenade. There wasn't time to bite down on anything. It was time to stand up.

He had shoes on. That was exciting. They didn't match, but they were both sneakers, and the one on his left foot was a left shoe and the one on the right foot was a right shoe. It was remarkable, really. It was a golden age of correct clothing in Crap Kingdom. He got his correctly-shoed feet underneath him.

Now that he was standing, the pain had gone beyond impossible to somewhere in the neighborhood of super impossible. He could actually hear blood coming from the wound. He was sure that wasn't good. Right now, finally on his feet, Tom's right hand was numb. His whole arm, in fact. It didn't matter. He didn't need his arm to walk. He walked through pools of his own vital fluids to the nearest suit of Vapornaut armor.

This part would be easy, he thought, because he remembered putting on armor back when he thought he was Doondredge's right-hand man. This kind was a little more complicated, because it was designed for flight, but it was mostly the same concept. He kicked off his shoes and stepped into the spiked diamond boots. They locked on automatically once they sensed there were feet inside of them. The legs came next. He untied the plastic bag containing the grenade from his jeans and placed it gently on the floor, upright so it wouldn't roll away, or get all bloody, or worse. The leg pieces also clicked on automatically once he had them in the general area of his legs. The codpiece—it was it a codpiece, wasn't it?—went the same way, and Tom realized

it was the most supported he'd ever felt in that area. Maybe codpieces were the real long-term solution to his underwear dilemma.

Then he put on the breastplate. It was cool to be able to do something like putting on magical armor so easily, like a blindfolded soldier assembling a rifle. He wished he had not had to join up with a brainwashing evil empire in order to gain the knowledge. Apparently he had to learn things the very, very hard way. The breastplate hugged his wound, and pain leveled him. If he hadn't been propped up by the armor he would have fallen over. His brain wanted to pass out to save him from the hurt. He ordered it not to. He was very commanding. He rewarded his brain for not passing out by encasing it in a very cool-looking helmet he grabbed off the wall. His face was now the only exposed part of his body, and all the bits of armor seemed to realize they were in place and they emitted many more clicks and whirs and then there was the hiss of gas filling the cavity between his skin and the armor.

All at once, his shoulder didn't hurt anymore. He felt universally great. He wondered if there were nanomachines in the gas, stitching up his wounds. He should have asked Doondredge, during his evil period.

* * *

Tom's most common dream involved flying. In the dream, he was going about his business and suddenly, he remembered that he knew how to fly. He wondered why he'd forgotten and why he didn't remember more often as he relaxed into himself and then lifted off the ground into effortless, thought-propelled flight, which would usually take him to the roof of some girl from school's house, though not in a pervy way.

It was like that with the Vapornaut armor. He just relaxed and a hundred different points on the armor became tiny jet engines emitting little cones of fire.

He rose.

He willed the suit to take him forward through the arch, following the trail of bloody Elgg footprints into a large, empty hallway. It was night, and everyone was asleep, just the way Kyle and the king had planned it. The roaring of the Vortex was louder now. Tom followed the prints, and the roar grew and grew. He followed them to a dead end and looked up. There was an opening the size of a manhole cover. He floated up and through the hole, and found himself in the enormous, deafening chamber between the Vortex and the Executive Orb. His feet touched ground again. He looked toward the Orb and saw the Elgg who had nearly killed him.

It was almost all the way up the spiraling path, fighting the world-wind. He could still intercept it and buy himself some time. Tom stepped off the precipice. The fall would have done to him what the Elgg had tried to, if he had not been wearing a suit of auto-flying armor. The jets went into overdrive and Tom began to fly across the chasm between himself and the Elgg. About halfway across, he entered the jet stream blowing straight out of the Vortex, and the jets on his armor became almost unnecessary. He was catapulted toward his target. The Elgg turned its head. An expression crossed its face like it was thinking, *Didn't I just fatally injure you?* They were kind of cute when they were confused, Tom thought.

It started bounding at double speed. Tom landed on the path in time to see it placing its paw up to the surface of the orb. Just like when Tchoobrayitch had done it, the print triggered a mechanism that started the Orb floating out from the wall.

Tom was running toward it. It turned and barked a plume of purple electric fire at him. The Vapornaut armor deflected it, but Tom held up his hands up to block his still-exposed face, and when he brought them down again, he saw that the Elgg had skittered up to the top of the Orb.

Tom took a jet-assisted leap, and just as he was closing in on the beast, it spread its wings and dropped down, disappearing, leaving only the glassy, unbroken Orb top for Tom to land on.

On the one hand, this was very bad. It meant Tom had a limited amount of time before the Elgg roused the king and whoever else, and the plan was completely ruined.

On the other hand, he had seen a new expression in the Elgg's eyes: fear. No one had ever been afraid of him before. Not even animals. He'd walk by squirrels on the way to school that wouldn't dart out of his path the way they did when other people walked by, even if those other people were four years old. There wasn't time to enjoy how cool and intimidating he felt, though. He had to go do the job.

He leapt into the wind and found that flying toward the Vortex was much, much harder than flying in the opposite direction. He held his hand up again to keep his eyelids from being blown off. All he had to do was fly far enough into the giant rock-encircled hole and drop the grenade.

Where was the grenade?

It was in his left hand. He'd picked it up without even thinking about it. He just assumed he would have forgotten it. It seemed like a Tom thing to do. But he'd grabbed it without anybody reminding him to, without even reminding himself. It was like there was a more competent person inhabiting him, but he also got to stay inside of his body and see everything through his own eyes.

The straps of the plastic bag containing the grenade began to stretch as the wind blew it backward. Tom was afraid they'd break and he'd end up reversing the Worldflow of the chasm floor instead of the Vortex like he was supposed to, so he unwrapped it as he flew. There was nowhere to put the empty bag. His armor didn't have pockets. He let it go. It flew right up into his face, temporarily blinding and suffocating him, held there by the wind. He ripped it away. He held the bag out as far as he could and let it flutter away. It flew back toward the Orb opening on the far side. He felt bad about littering in a world that wasn't his own, but then again, he was in a particularly evil part of that world. They probably littered all the time. This was a just and righteous littering.

The rim of the Vortex drew close. He couldn't tell if the armor had somehow enhanced his hearing or if the howling wind was truly the loudest noise he'd ever heard. He entered the cave. He didn't know how deep you had to go before you reached the point where one world became another one. It was even darker than it had been in the void.

He wanted to just throw the grenade, but he was pretty certain that if he did, the wind would blow it backward, and he would be like a klutzy character in an old silent movie throwing a baseball and having it land behind him. But he also didn't want to be over the line that separated worlds when the thing went off. He wondered if it would actually "go off," if it would explode, or what. He hoped he could observe it without getting pulverized by the cross-world super-wind.

He held the bottle out in front of him and crawled forward, through the air. The jets on his armor were working so hard he looked like the grand finale of a fireworks show that never ended. The ultra-dark got darker somehow.

Then the bottle wasn't in his hand anymore. But he hadn't dropped it. It had been pulled away. He could suddenly feel the incredible wind on the fingers of the hand that had been holding it. He held the hand up to his face. In the light of his armor's jet flames, he could see that the fingertips of the armor had been snatched off along with the bottle, by the portal. He was lucky: he still had his actual fingertips.

He was wasting precious milliseconds being concerned about his fingers. He turned himself around. The wind buffeted him forward toward the Vortex's mouth, and then it didn't anymore. The wind died. Compared to the unreal sound of the wind, the hundreds of jets on his armor sounded like the lightest spring breeze.

Then it started up again, twice as hard, in the opposite direction. On the one hand, that was good: it meant the grenade had worked. On the other hand, it was bad, because the jets immediately kicked in full blast to compensate, yet Tom was still barely crawling forward against the Vortex's suction. He crested the mouth. Something was flying at him. It hit him in the face, spreading and sticking and flapping. It covered his face. He reached up and pulled it away: it was that stupid bag. His littering had come back to haunt him. He let it go and looked up just in time to see something much bigger coming at him full-speed: the Orb.

He rolled away to the left and watched the Executive Orb go shooting by, exiting perfectly through the rocky mouth of the Vortex. It worked! It actually worked! He had *done* something!

As the Orb went by, Tom saw a shattered spot on its surface, an outline, like when a cartoon character runs fast through a wall, leaving a brick silhouette of their tortured form. He looked back toward the big circular hole in the wall where the Orb once nested and saw a figure in Vapor-naut armor framed by the night sky, all jets blazing on full: King Doondredge.

It was dark in here now that the light given off by the Orb was burning in some other world. Tom couldn't see if Doondredge was coming after him or trying to fly in the other direction and escape. Either option was unacceptable. He willed his suit to fly at his enemy. It became very clear a moment later that the king was headed right at him, thrusters on full, aided by the Vortex's suction. He was coming at Tom fast.

Tom went to roll left again. Doondredge missed him, but wheeled around, leaving a sparking arc in his wake, and punched Tom in the side of the head. Tom was thankful for the helmet for one half second, until his head hit the inside of the helmet. Why didn't they pad these things? Then he was grateful for the helmet again two seconds later when automatic healing mist made the side of his head feel better.

Doondredge was fighting his way back to Tom through midair. All Tom could think was, *He's not supposed to be in here. The Vortex: he's supposed to be in there.*

Tom held up the gauntlet of his left hand to block another punch. He could punch back, right? He was wearing strength-equalizing super-armor, after all. He swung at Doondredge's head. It ended up being more of an open-handed slap that bounced harmlessly off his enemy's helmet. Doondredge looked at him now with more confusion than anger. They were in a midair battle to the death. Why was his enemy slapping him?

With his opponent shocked by his lame tactics, Tom took the opportunity to do something even lamer. He reached out with the glove that no longer had fingertips and poked Doondredge in the eye. Hard. He left his fingers there. Doondredge swatted his hand away. Tom could see him scream in pain but he couldn't hear it over the wind. He saw blood droplets get sucked away into the abyss. Had he just gouged an eye? Was that how that worked? Doondredge gritted his teeth and floated back a foot or two. Then he punched Tom square in his exposed face.

It seemed like absolutely everything that had happened in his life recently plunged Tom into a pit of blackness, but somehow, the punch didn't. He kind of wished it had, though. His nose now was a blood geyser that would have made the elementary school nurse call in an exorcist. The red stuff was leaking away in a straight line, water-droplets-on-the-space-shuttle style, into the Vortex, chasing Doondredge's eye blood. His enemy was nowhere to be seen.

He felt someone pawing at his back. Tom tried to flip around but he couldn't. Doondredge was behind him, holding him, and Tom could feel his hands clanging around on the back of his armor. Not hitting. Just working.

Tom started to feel flecks of something hitting him in the face. He looked toward the hole where the Orb had once been. Its edges were fraying, flying off toward the Vortex, sending little shards of kingdom past Doondredge and Tom and into the next world. Tom had no choice but to watch as this happened; he still couldn't turn around. Then the hole was eclipsed by a white moon that was very bright and very close and actually not a moon at all but the Wall, uncoupled from the nameless kingdom, resized by Kyle, carried by Kyle. Kyle was flying. He wore no armor. Just jeans and sneakers and his Drama Department T-shirt. Tom found that he was not jealous that Kyle could fly. Tom found he was proud.

Kyle was bearing the Wall from underneath, Atlas style. He swung his legs over the edge of the hole as he passed through. He glided out over the chasm, holding the big pearl of a protection spell. Hopefully it had the strength to hold back a Vortex that now wanted everything in this world to come through it, even if it had to tear it all apart.

Kyle would have to place it just so over the Vortex's mouth. It was energy and wouldn't just move there by itself the way the Orb had.

Suddenly Tom could turn around. Doondredge had let him go after seeing Kyle and becoming absolutely hypnotized with hate. Doondredge hovered, his jets burning steadily, and raised his right arm, pointing his fist at Kyle. Things on his fist began to grow and change and whir and spark. His armored hand was taking on a new shape.

Tom had an opening. How should he use it? Doondredge had seemed to be looking for something on the back of Tom's armor. What if Tom looked for the same thing on the back of Doondredge's? Tom flew around behind him. Doondredge looked back and smirked, as if telling Tom he could do his worst, he was in no way afraid of a slapping, eye-gouging patsy. He refocused on Kyle, who was now halfway over the chasm.

Tom had no idea what he was looking for. Some sort of off switch? He should've just punched him square in the face. But what if it had ended up being another slap? No, what he really should have done is just caught the Elgg before it could wake him; then the bastard would already be in the Vortex with the rest of his cronies. He pounded on the back of Doondredge's armor. Nothing. There was no button. No switch, no panel. There was *nothing*. He pounded harder. He reared back. He punched.

The armor cracked at the small of Doondredge's back. He had punched through the diamond or the crystal or whatever it was and gas was leaking out all around his hand. Doondredge's armor's jets sputtered and died. Kyle was almost at the Vortex mouth. Chunks of crystal were flying everywhere. It would tear the kingdom apart if Kyle didn't cap it soon.

Tom ripped his gauntlet out of Doondredge's back. The king started to fall to the chasm bottom, then was caught by the riptide of world-wind and sucked toward the Vortex. Tom saw that Doondredge's armored hand had changed fully. It was no longer a fist. It was sharp. Something ignited on the king's wrist, and the sharp projectile was launched, leaving a bare hand behind.

Doondredge tumbled and disappeared into the Vortex, but the projectile flew away from him in the opposite direction. It was a fist-sized missile, and it was headed straight for Kyle.

Tom's brain commanded the armor to fly as fast as possible. Faster, even. The missile was arcing, fighting the

Vortex wind, and Tom was catching up to it. It was closing on Kyle. *A hundred meters,* Tom thought. Why did he always try to judge distances? He didn't even know how many feet were in a meter.

Could he catch it? Yes, he could. But not with his hands.

Tom didn't think. He just flew up between his friend and the missile that wanted to kill his friend.

The missile's path was a straight line, Tom's path had been a curved one, and the lines intersected right at the chest of Tom's armor.

And then the missile went through the armor.

And then Tom was in a blackness more complete than the one he experienced when Kyle had teleported them into the throne room, more complete than the void, more complete than any blackness he could have imagined when he was in second grade, lying in bed under Pokémon sheets.

And then he wasn't anywhere.

Tom heard a voice he recognized.

"He's alive! Kyle, you're a genius, my son!"

It was a voice he recognized but he'd never heard it use that tone before, so he almost didn't recognize it. It was the king of Crap Kingdom, and when Tom opened his eyes, Kyle's face was close to his, and the king's was farther away, and the king was clapping and smiling and hooting.

"Welcome back," Kyle said to Tom.

"Thanks, Kilroy," Tom said.

"Kilroy," the king said, "who in the blazes is Kilroy?"

"It's what Tom used to call me in like sixth grade," Kyle said.

"Tom? He's *Tom?*" the king said. "No, this was not the agreement. When I authorized you to use the spell, I did not authorize the reviving of *Tom*, I authorized the reviving of J!"

"Jason?" Tom said. He couldn't help himself. "He's gone."

"What do—how do you know about—what do you mean?" the king said.

Tom sat up. They were in the throne room of the castle in Crap Kingdom. Shattered Vapornaut armor lay piled to one side. Tom was still wearing the black T-shirt. It had a rip in the center, but his torso was miraculously unharmed. He was sure that it had been harmed, and then Kyle had made it not that way.

"I was in the void during the mission," Tom said, "and I met this . . . soul, I guess, and he's, like, soul-neighbors with J—with Jason. And he told me all about him. And then all of the sudden I was in the middle of the Ghelm kingdom, and I'd been injured, or my body had, and J was gone and I was there instead."

"Impossible!" the king said. "He's lying. He's merely trying to take credit for J's actions."

"Then how would I know what happened after that? Because I got in some armor and I flew out and—"

"Sorcery! The same way you know these things about J. Ghelm sorcery. And I will not hear any more of it."

"Listen, I don't know why I ended up back in my body," Tom said. "I don't know if it was an accident I ended up there or if J got hurt so he figured he would rather spend the rest of my life on Earth in my body instead of dying there, for real, in the Ghelm kingdom—"

"And that," the king said, "is blasphemy. You came from Earth to betray and sow doubt. Jason came here to teach and heal. Kyle is the same way."

"Wait," Kyle said. "J's from Earth?"

"England, I think, judging from when I heard that voice recording in his laboratory," Tom said. "Is that why you talk that way?" he asked the king.

"We spent every waking moment together," the king said. "Regardless of his origins, for you to besmirch his legacy is a greater crime than anything you have yet done. You will be sent back to Earth at once and you will never show your face here again, on pain of death. Kyle, send him back at once."

"No, he didn't—"

"Kyle, send him back at once, or you may as well go with him and never return."

"You're being unreasonable!"

"I only believed," the king said, "in one person, ever. We were a warlike people, cynical because we had to be that way to survive. A stranger came out of a lake and changed our way of life. We began to soften. And when that stranger was tempted away from us, instead of buckling, he used it as an opportunity to free us from tyranny and fear forever. He was offered the All-Worlds in exchange for betraying us. Instead, he defended us, a pitiful race concerned only with our own day-to-day existence. He gave his life attempting to free us. When the Ghelm king had finished torturing him and killed him because he would not give away the secrets that would have compromised our safety, and the safety of the All-Worlds, he brought J's body back here and dropped it outside the Wall to torment us. I attempted to use a spell

J had only toyed with and never tried. A resurrection spell. We are congenitally limited in our magical abilities, I more than any of us. It was a misfire. It may have redirected the lake portal from which Jason emerged, but it did not bring back my friend."

"It sort of worked," Tom said. "It pulled him up into the void. If you hadn't done that much, he wouldn't have been in there, and he never would have been pulled out and into me on Earth, and you never would have gotten to talk to him again yesterday."

"I would rather we had never met again," the king said. "It only makes me feel worse now that he is gone once again. There is nothing worse than false hope. I have said that all along. I have stretched my limited affections to my boy Kyle, and they go no further, forever. I have learned, and briefly forgotten, and had to relearn the value of low expectations."

"But Tom saved my life!" Kyle said.

"If this is true, he did so as a sort of dumb meat blocking mechanism. While you saved his infinitely more worthless life by stitching together impossible magic. That says everything about how different you are from each other."

Tom looked at Kyle.

"Tom," the king said, "You. Can. Never. Come. Back."

"How can you—" Kyle said.

"Kyle," Tom said. "It's all right."

"Can we at least have a minute?" Kyle asked.

"I will return, and it will just be you," the king said. He got up from his throne and walked out of the room. Gark went to follow him.

"Good-bye, Tim," Gark said.

"Tom," Tom said.

"I know," Gark said. He smiled sadly and left. Kyle and Tom were alone.

"When you came back," Kyle said, "I wanted it to be you."

"Thanks for bringing me back," Tom said. "I'm so sorry about everything."

"I'm sorry he's a dick," Kyle said.

"You know," Tom said, "you have a dad at home on Earth."

Unlike just about everything Tom ever said, this was something that had not rattled around in his head for thirty seconds to a minute before he actually said it. It came out of his mouth the second it came into his head. Of all the things he'd been jealous about, he hadn't even realized he was jealous of the fact that Kyle got to go home every day after school and see both a mom and a dad. But maybe feeling things he wasn't proud of hadn't been all of the problem. Maybe not telling anyone about them had been a part of it, too.

"I know," Kyle said.

"When are you coming back?" Tom said.

"I dunno," Kyle said. "There's going to be a lot of rebuilding with the Ghelm, and seeing if we can live with them peacefully now that their king's gone, so that'll be a lot of work, and we still have a lot to do here."

"Cool," Tom said.

"Let me talk to him," Kyle said. "It'll probably take a while, but I'll talk to him."

"Cool. Thanks, man."

"Are you guys done?" said someone who wasn't Kyle or Tom.

Tom looked over. A pink bunny in a princess costume jumped out from behind a huge pile of old VHS tapes. The bunny reached up and removed its head. It was Pira. She ran over to them.

"Welcome back, Tom! He didn't want me to be in here for the spell, but there was no way I wasn't going to be."

"Yeah, we were just talking about how your dad's kind of a—"

"No, not my dad," Pira said. "*Kyy-uhhhl.*"

"Don't say my name like that," Kyle said.

"I'll say it however I—what is it? Damn well please?"

"Yup," Kyle said, "that's it."

She stood very close to Kyle. Kyle leaned down and kissed her. They kept kissing.

Tom had no idea this had been going on. He'd missed a lot of things in a lot of worlds. He let himself feel jealous for a second. He'd never even wanted to kiss Pira, except for that one day. He knew he only wanted to now because someone else was. He commanded himself to knock it off. It worked.

His eyes drifted down to Pira's big, fuzzy pink bunny mascot head. He recognized it but he wasn't sure from where.

"Jealous?" Pira said. Tom opened his mouth and realized she was talking about him looking at the bunny head.

"How could I not be?" Tom said. "I've always wanted my own bunny head."

"It's not a 'bunny head,'" Pira said. "It's the fuzzy helmet I got off the mustache guy."

"You ready?" Kyle said.

Tom nodded.

"Hey, Tom?" Pira said. "On behalf of the people of Rfhfhhhuptpth . . . thank you."

Tom smiled. "Was that your princess impression?"

"What?" Pira said. "No, I was being . . . I mean, yes, it was! Funny, right? *Ha!*"

"Bye, you guys," Tom said.

Kyle stuck his arms out and Tom unconsciously braced for the push. One second later he was still in Crap Kingdom because Kyle didn't push him, he hugged him.

Kyle broke the hug. "See you later?"

"Yeah," Tom said.

He pushed Tom.

Tom felt himself swinging backward through the void toward Earth, and then he felt a strong push in the other direction. He stopped in mid-swing. He was hanging upside down in the void. He didn't panic. He was used to voids by now.

"Ggggogogogood. It worked," said a reverse-echoing voice with a British accent. "At least I can do something right."

A jellyfish soul with a hundred dancing faces appeared in front of Tom.

"Jason?"

"Thththththat's me, sorry to say. I'll let you pass back

to Earth in a second, I just—How did it go? I'm afraid I made a right mess of things, and—"

"No. It's okay. Kyle and I took care of it. The Ghelm overlords are gone."

"Ohohohohoh good, that's such a relief, you have no idea. So you're coming back from your big celebration, then?"

"Not at all. The king still hates me."

"Whwhwhwhwhwhaat? But you're a hero!"

"Maybe. Not the way he sees it."

"Anananananand that doesn't bother you?"

Tom thought about it and answered honestly. "No. I know what I did."

"Yoyoyoyoyou're still banished?"

"Guess so."

"Thththththththat's so unfair!"

"Maybe."

"Totototototototototo be a hero in a world to which you can never return. I must say, I know quite a bit about that."

"I have the one world," Tom said. "That's enough for right now."

"Sososososososo after all that," Jason said, "You've reached a kind of *Wizard of Oz*, never-further-than-my-own-backyard conclusion?"

"Not exactly," Tom said. "The backyard trains you for the bigger adventures without you even knowing it." Tom found it much easier to say things he was actually proud of when he didn't actually have a mouth.

"Bububububut you're banished! What if you never get a chance to have any bigger adventures?"

"Did you ever think you'd get pulled up out of the void?"

All of Jason's glowing floating heads shook from side to side in unison.

"Well, there you go. And it was nice being in a body while it lasted, right?"

"Susususususususure, until I went and almost got your body *killed*. Right away, too! I had another chance and I fouled it up and now I've just got to float here and think about it, possibly for eternity."

"You're still a mind, correct? In the void, your mind is literally the only thing you can control. So, I don't know . . . maybe try not to think about it as much?"

"Ohohohohohohoh, I see, big adventurer. You know everything now, I suppose."

"I know almost nothing," Tom said. "But that's a whole lot more than nothing."

Then he said, "Can I go home now?"

EPILOGUE

"YOU GOTTA BE more careful," Tobe said.

Tom looked down. He was in the scene shop behind the stage, surrounded by other kids working with power tools. It was loud, but it wasn't as loud as the Vortex. He must be in seventh-period stagecraft. There was blood on his fingers again, but this time the blood was coming from the fingers themselves. There was a small cut on his right index finger that Tobe was in the middle of putting a Band-Aid on.

"Thanks," Tom said. Apparently the placeholder soul that had been in his body wasn't as skilled at operating it as Jason had been. As it turned out, Tom thought, Jason hadn't been that skilled either. This made Tom, who had always been only okay at operating Tom's body, feel a lot less alone.

"A band saw," Tobe said. "A toy. One of these things is not like the other."

Tobe finished with the Band-Aid and looked up at Tom. "Got it?"

"You have sawdust in your mustache," Tom said.

Tobe reached up and wiped his mustache with his hand. "Thanks," he said, and walked away.

The mustache. Tobe's office. Something about his office and the mustache and that day Tom had tripped over the—

—Bunny outfit. What Pira had called the fuzzy helmet she had taken from the mustache guy the night someone slipped Gark an updated prophecy.

Tom walked up to Tobe, who had moved on to overseeing a kid who was using a circular sander.

Tobe shouted over the machine. "Yes?"

Tom leaned very close to Tobe and shouted: "Jason. Gark. Doondredge. Ghelm. Elgg."

Tobe reached up and put one finger to his mustache.

"We can't talk here," he said. He checked his watch. He motioned for Tom to follow him. They went up the stairs to the wardrobe room. Tobe walked to the last row of costumes, dusty from under use, crappy itchy stuff consigned here, to the back, to get eaten by moths. Tobe shoved aside two big lumps of clothes on hangers. The hangers shrieked against the metal pole that held them up. There was a door there, behind the clothes. Tom had never seen it before. Then again, he'd never needed the twenty nun habits that were in front of it.

Tobe took out his big janitor-sized ring of keys. He stuck a strange, two-pronged key in the door's lock. He turned the knob and the door swung in. It was dark in there. Tobe stepped in. Tom followed.

The walls of the passageway on the other side seemed to be not brick, not concrete, but just plain unformed rock. And at the end of the passageway, beyond a bend, there was light.

They reached the light and turned.

They had come out of a cave onto the top of a grassy hill. Below them was a valley of tiered lakes, one flowing into the other, bodies of water stacked on top of each other, somehow defying gravity. Great arches soared into a golden sky. Stalactite palaces hung down from them, with floating gondolas darting between their upside-down towers. Everything seemed to be made of frozen honey that refused to melt in the ultra-brilliant sun.

"Wow," Tom said.

"Yttethlae," Tobe said. "A real gem among the All-Worlds. Not bad, right?"

"Not at all," Tom said.

"This is not exactly the time I would have chosen to explain, but—"

"Um . . . hi guys."

Tom turned around. Lindsy was standing at the mouth of the cave.

Had she followed them? What would she think? How would Tobe explain this? He hoped he told her the truth, whatever the truth was. There had been enough lying all around.

"Tom and I just needed a place to talk," Tobe said. "Mind if we borrow your world for a minute?"

Moments later, they were seated in the grass beneath the rich amber sky, and Tobe began. "Once, a long time ago, I was what's called the World-Finder General. It's one of the top positions in the All-World Federation. The World-Finder is in charge of finding new worlds that have not yet been made aware that there are other worlds out there, and peacefully bringing them into our organization. At least, that's how I did it. There have been other World-Finders who were more, shall we say, aggressive. And I like to think I'd still be doing it, but I made a mistake. I think you can sympathize with that."

"What mistake?" Tom asked.

"I tried to integrate Earth into the All-Worlds, but I went about it all wrong. So wrong I was stripped of my title as World-Finder General, and exiled to a world of my choosing."

"Why did you chose Earth to be exiled to?"

"Well, Earth is not my first-world. I mean, it's not where I'm from originally. Someday, you might have the opportunity to live in some other world and tell someone, 'This is not my first-world. My first-world is a place called Earth.' I would like everyone on Earth to have that opportunity. And you, and Kyle and Lindsy, and hopefully a few others, will be the first, the ones that prove to the All-Worlds at large that humanity ought to have that opportunity. I chose to be exiled to Earth so that I could figure out how to try again. So far, this second attempt has been sloppy, I'll admit. Planting prophecies by night in a bunny suit and everything. And I think I could have been more careful finding the world for you to be a representative of Earth in. I'm not perfect. But I don't think that my not being perfect is enough reason for me to not try and do something I believe is worth doing, as many times as it takes until I get it right."

"So we're representing all of humanity?"

"Apparently so," Lindsy said.

Tom turned and looked at her.

"Lindsy's heard this already," Tobe said, "when I introduced her to Yttethlae last week. Straightforwardness seemed best. When it came to you and Kyle and Thhhptphtphl, some of my tactics—the prophecies, et cetera—may have hurt more than they helped. But Chosen Ones . . . It seemed like the sort of thing you'd be interested in."

Tom said, "Wouldn't it maybe have been better if you'd told me I was representing all of humanity?"

"Wouldn't it maybe be better if you always behaved as though you were representing all of humanity?"

Tom would have to think about this. He had a lot to think about.

"It's okay," Tobe said. "You'll try again just like I'm trying again. And I'm already receiving reports that you may have done something very brave, something that makes you more than worthy of another shot. Maybe back there, maybe some other world. We'll just have to wait and see."

"Tom," Lindsy said. "What happened?"

Tom didn't know where to start. But he knew that not knowing where to start should not prevent him from starting.

"Okay," he said. "Here goes."

ACKNOWLEDGMENTS

THANKS ARE DUE to extraordinary editor Kendra Levin and everyone on her team, to Daniel Greenberg, Dianne McGunigle, Lev Ginsburg, and to Meggie, Dan, and the rest of DERRICK. Thanks and love to Haley, thanks and love to my family, especially grandmas Pat, Jan, and Mary. Peace to the UCB Theaters on both coasts. Thanks to Idler, Rollins, Quinn, and Fineman, and shouts out to every recovering high-school theatre kid. I beg forgiveness from the immortal Tattoo Club, Darryl Seeliger, Jeremy Seeliger, and Jason Artigas. Thanks to Ken Plume and Eliza Skinner. Thanks to Tom Scharpling and Jon Wurster, who make worlds every Tuesday night, and a salute to all FOTs. Thanks to Brian Jacques, chief world-builder of my young reading life. So long and thanks for all the mice.

The bulk of this book was written while listening to the album *Challengers* by The New Pornographers.